PENGUIN

JAPANESE

LAFCADIO HEARN's colourful life (1850–1904) was matched by the range and variety of his output. Born on the Ionian island of Lefkada, he was abandoned by both his parents in succession, and spent his childhood in the guardianship of his great-aunt in Ireland and England. From 1869 he established himself as a journalist in the USA, first in Cincinnati and then in New Orleans, before moving to the French West Indies in 1887. He spent the last fourteen years of his life in Japan, where he excelled as an early interpreter of a culture that both attracted and baffled Westerners. He is now best remembered for his collection and translation of traditional Japanese ghost stories.

PAUL MURRAY is the author of biographies of Lafcadio Hearn and Bram Stoker, and editor of collections of Hearn's work. He is a former Irish diplomat whose posting to Japan in the late 1970s ignited his interest in Hearn.

LAFCADIO HEARN

Japanese Ghost Stories

Edited by
PAUL MURRAY

PENGUIN BOOKS

PENGUIN CLASSICS

UK | USA | Canada | Ireland | Australia
India | New Zealand | South Africa

Penguin Books is part of the Penguin Random House group of companies
whose addresses can be found at global.penguinrandomhouse.com.

This anthology first published in Penguin Classics 2019

015

Hokusai images: Bibliothèque de l'Institut National d'Histoire de l'Art,
Collections Jacques Doucet, 8 Est 172 (1)
Bibliothèque de l'Institut National d'Histoire de l'Art,
Collections Jacques Doucet, 8 Est 172 (2)
Bibliothèque de l'Institut National d'Histoire de l'Art,
Collections Jacques Doucet, 8 Est 172 (3)

Set in 10.25/12.25pt Sabon Next LT Pro
Typeset by Jouve (UK), Milton Keynes
Printed and bound in Great Britain by Clays Ltd, Elcograf S.p.A.

ISBN: 978-0-241-38127-4

www.greenpenguin.co.uk

Contents

Chronology

Ionian Islands, Ireland and England, 1850–69

1850 *27 June*: Patrick Lafcadio Hearn born on Lefkada or Lefkas, then part of the United States of the Ionian Islands. He is the first surviving child of Charles Bush Hearn, an Irish officer-surgeon in the British Army, and Rosa Antonia Cassimati, a native of the Greek island of Kythira.

October: Father is posted to the West Indies; Rosa and Hearn remain on Lefkada.

1852 Hearn arrives in Dublin with mother. Father joins them the following year but the marriage falters.

1854 Mother returns to Kythira. Hearn subsequently raised by a great-aunt, Mrs Sarah Brenane, in Dublin.

1857 Father leaves Ireland for a posting in India, following the annulment of his marriage to Rosa and his remarriage; Hearn never sees him again.

1863–7 Educated at Ushaw College, a Roman Catholic boarding school in County Durham, England. Loss of sight in one eye, following an accident at school, results in a lifelong sense of disfigurement.

1867 Sarah Brenane financially ruined; Hearn is withdrawn from school and lives in reduced circumstances in east London for the next two years.

USA and West Indies, 1869–90

1869 Arrives in Cincinnati; embarks on a career in journalism, initially on a freelance basis, and then with the *Cincinnati Enquirer*. Develops a keen interest in the city's black culture.

1874 Co-founds the short-lived *Ye Giglampz* satirical periodical.
  14 June: Illegal marriage to black ex-slave, Mattie Foley, which
  later fails.

1875 *August*: Employed by the *Cincinnati Commercial*, having
  been fired from the *Cincinnati Enquirer* because of his
  marriage.

1877 Arrives in New Orleans, where he is introduced to Creole
  culture.

1878–81 Editorial assistant on the New Orleans *Daily City Item*
  newspaper; also writes for the *New Orleans Democrat*. Development of 'Fantastics', a form of creative writing.

1881 Taken on by the *Times-Democrat* newspaper.

1882 Publishes *One of Cleopatra's Nights and Other Fantastic
  Romances*, translations of the work of the French writer Théophile Gautier.

1884–6 Publication of *Stray Leaves from Strange Literature* (1884),
  La Cuisine Creole (1885), *Gombo Zhèbes* (1885) and *Some Chinese
  Ghosts* (1887). Becomes interested in the Orient/Japan, and
  falls under the influence of the philosophy of Herbert Spencer
  (1820–1903).

1887–9 Spends two years in the French West Indies following
  encouragement from the American publisher Harper & Brothers
  that he could live by writing. Work by now reaching a national
  audience through publication in *Harper's New Monthly Magazine*.

1889–90 Publishes two short novels, *Chita: A Memory of Last
  Island* (1889) and *Youma: The Story of a West-Indian Slave* (1890),
  as well as *Two Years in the French West Indies* (1890). Returns
  briefly to the USA, where he spends time in Philadelphia and
  New York.

Japan, 1890–1904

1890 Arrives in Yokohama on the basis of a vague understanding that he would provide material to Harper & Brothers but
  soon breaks with the publisher.

1890–91 Takes up teaching post in Matsue, on the west coast of
  Japan. Marries a Japanese woman, Setsuko Koizumi.

1891–4 Moves to Kumamoto, in the south of Japan, to take up another teaching post, which proves to be an unhappy experience.

1893 *November*: Birth of a son, Kazuo; three further children follow.

1894 *October–December*: Moves to Kobe as editorial writer on the *Kobe Chronicle*. Illness forces resignation from journalism and leaves him unemployed for over a year. Publication of *Glimpses of Unfamiliar Japan* in late 1894.

1895 Publication of *'Out of the East': Reveries and Studies in New Japan*.

1896 Adopts Japanese citizenship under the name Koizumi Yakumo. Takes up appointment as a lecturer at Tokyo University.

1896–1904 Eight further books on aspects of Japan completed, including *Kokoro: Hints and Echoes of Japanese Inner Life* (1896), *Gleanings in Buddha-Fields: Studies of Hand and Soul in the Far East* (1897), *Exotics and Retrospectives* (1898), *Shadowings* (1900), *Kwaidan: Stories and Studies of Strange Things* (1904) and *Japan: An Attempt at Interpretation* (1904), his most academic work. Becomes increasingly withdrawn and immersed in his writing. Health failing, he considers leaving Japan.

1904 Post at Tokyo University terminated; replaced by the Japanese novelist Natsume Sōseki. Becomes a lecturer at Waseda University. Supports Japan in Russo-Japanese War (1904–5).
26 September: Dies from heart disease.

Posthumous

1906 Bitter posthumous newspaper controversy in the USA over his character.

1908 George Gould's denunciatory *Concerning Lafcadio Hearn* published.

1912 Publication of Nina Kennard's biography, following her visit to Japan with Hearn's half-sister, Mrs Minnie Atkinson, in 1909.

Introduction

> Whoever pretends not to believe in ghosts of any sort, lies to his
> own heart. Every man is haunted by ghosts . . . though most of
> us (poets excepted) are unwilling to confess the acquaintance.
> Lafcadio Hearn, 'The Eternal Haunter'[1]

Few writers have been as permeated by horror as (Patrick) Lafcadio Hearn. Successful ghost-story writing probably requires a
certain interaction between the writer's subject and his or her
own personality. What makes Hearn particularly interesting is
that not only was his mind dominated by horror from an early
age but that, to a perhaps unparalleled extent, he laid bare the
roots of this phenomenon himself in his later writing. (Freudian
analysis is redundant when the subject is so obliging.) It was in
Japan, where Hearn lived for the last fourteen years of his life,
that this fascination with horror and the ghostly found its fullest
artistic expression. In the ghost stories that Hearn published at
the end of the nineteenth century and the start of the twentieth,
he drew on traditional Japanese folklore, infused with memories
of his own turbulent childhood, to create narratives of striking
and eerie power. These *kwaidan* – or Japanese ghost stories – are
today regarded in Japan as classics in their own right.

Early Life

Hearn's literary interest in horror and the ghostly was intimately
tied up with the strange circumstances of his early life. He was
born on 27 June 1850 on the Ionian island of Lefkada or Lefkas,
off the west coast of Greece, to Charles Bush Hearn, an Irish
officer-surgeon in the British Army, and Rosa Antonia Cassimati,
a native of the remote island of Kythira, where his parents had met
in the late 1840s. Charles was serving as a surgeon with the army

garrison enforcing de facto British control over the nominally independent United States of the Ionian Islands, a protectorate of the United Kingdom from 1815 until their absorption into the Greek state in 1864. Unlike mainland Greece, which had been under Turkish domination for centuries, the Ionian Islands had previously been under Venetian rule and so had felt the influence of Western developments such as the Renaissance and the Reformation more strongly. The upper classes spoke the distinct Venetian language, which Rosa may have spoken, together with Greek.[2] She seems to have been illiterate, notwithstanding her upper-class birth and the fact that the British had established an educational system for both girls and boys on the island.[3]

Rosa and Charles's first son, George Robert, was born in July 1849 but died in August the following year. Patrick Lafcadio was born after his parents had moved to Lefkada (from which his middle name derives), by which time they had married, just before his father transferred with his regiment to the West Indies. He left his wife and infant son behind on Lefkada. Two years later, Rosa arrived in Dublin with her son and stayed with her mother-in-law at 48 Lower Gardiner Street.

In late 1853 Charles returned from the West Indies and stayed for six months in Dublin before departing in March 1854 to participate in the Crimean War. While in Dublin, he rekindled a former romance with a woman who would become his second wife, and Rosa departed, pregnant, to Kythira in mid 1854. She and Charles had agreed to terminate their marriage and Rosa was subsequently paid a considerable sum of money as part of the settlement.[4]

Patrick Lafcadio remained in Dublin under the care of a well-off, widowed great-aunt, Mrs Sarah Brenane. He never saw his mother again. Nor did he see his father after 1857, when Charles Hearn left Ireland for a posting in India with his new wife. Despite having been abandoned by both parents, Patrick Lafcadio grew up in privileged, upper-middle-class circumstances, surrounded by servants and the trappings of wealth. Records going back to the early eighteenth century show the Hearns as having a tradition of land ownership, education at Trinity College Dublin, service to the minority (Protestant) Church of Ireland and to the officer corps of the British Army. They also had significant artistic tendencies, exemplified by Patrick Lafcadio's uncle, Richard Hearn, a painter who passed much of his life in France.

Terrors on Leeson Street

Patrick spent the ages of four to thirteen under Mrs Brenane's care, mostly at her house at 73 Upper Leeson Street in Dublin. These years were crucial to the formation of Lafcadio Hearn the writer. He appears to have been privately educated at home and, most importantly, had untrammelled access to a substantial library of books, which he devoured with precocious ease. From Milton, he acquired a ghostly vocabulary and from Matthew Lewis, author of the scandalous horror novel *The Monk* (1796), concepts of terror unsuited to his tender years. Lewis's *Tales of Wonder* (1801) was a specific influence and the resultant nightmares terrorized his sleep.

Many disturbing shapes vexed young Patrick Lafcadio's dreams. He begins his essay 'Nightmare-Touch' (published in 1900, it is included as an appendix here) by posing the question: 'What *is* the fear of ghosts among those who believe in ghosts?' (p. 207). His answer, 'that the common fear of ghosts is *the fear of being touched by ghosts*' (p. 208), is illustrated by recounting the terrible nightmares he had endured in the 'Child's Room', his bedroom in Mrs Brenane's house in which he was locked without light to cure his fear of the dark, viewed by his guardian and her servants as a mental disorder. This may have been related to the fact that his mother had revealed symptoms of mental illness during her stay in Dublin and would indeed spend the last decade of her life in a mental hospital in Corfu. If so, this ham-fisted attempt at a remedy failed dismally and only made the problem worse.

In later life, Hearn described how religious terror also affected his youthful imagination. In draft autobiographical fragments that he wrote in his Tokyo years but never published, he makes it clear that Mrs Brenane had left him alone on the subject of religion at a time when a rigid Catholic–Protestant divide was a dominant fact of Irish life. Mrs Brenane's own conversion to Roman Catholicism, the religion of her late husband, appears to have been nominal, and Patrick Lafcadio's religious education was minimal. This state of affairs was drastically altered by a visitor to the household, called 'Cousin Jane' by Hearn, a young lady of strongly Roman Catholic views, who reacted with horror when she discovered his profound ignorance of Christianity:

She stooped and lifted me upon her knees; and after looking all about the room, fixed her eyes on mine with such curiousness that I was frightened. Then she asked: –

'My child, is it really possible you do not know who God is?'

I remembered answering

'No'.

– 'God – who made the world, the beautiful sky, the trees, the birds – you do not know this?'

– 'No'.

'Do you not know that God made you and your father and mother and everybody, – and I who am talking to you?'

– 'No'.

'Do you not know about heaven and hell, – and that God made you in order that you should be happy in heaven if you are good?'

– 'No'.

The rest of the conversation has faded out of my mind – all except the words – 'and be sent to hell, to be buried alive in fire for ever and ever – always burning, burning, burning, always – never forgiven, never. Think of the pain of fire – to burn forever and ever.'

This picture of the universe gave me a shock that probably preserved it in memory. I can still see the face of the speaker as she said those words – the horror upon it, – the pain, – and then she burst into tears. I do not know why, we kissed each other; and I remember nothing more of that day.

But somehow or other from that time, I never liked my so-called cousin as before. She was kinder to me than any other being; but I felt an instinctive resentment towards her because of what she had told me. It seemed monstrous, ugly, wicked. She became for me a person who thinks horrible things. My world had been horrible enough before. She made it worse. I did not doubt what she said, and yet I was angry because she had said it. After she went away in [the] spring I hoped she would never come back again.[5]

Traditional Irish folklore provided further tales and images of supernatural horror that terrified and enthralled the young Hearn. Several of these would find later expression in his Japanese stories. The Irish mythological tale of Tír na nÓg (Land of Youth, a name for the Celtic Otherworld), for instance, has an almost exact counterpart in the Japanese legend of Urashima Tarō, in which a mortal man is lured to an enchanted underwater kingdom to be the husband of a beautiful supernatural woman; Hearn uses the Japanese version in both 'The Dream of a Summer Day' (1895) and 'The Story of Chūgorō' (1902).

Hearn grew up in a time when the middle classes in Dublin were discovering the value of the folklore being collected in the Irish countryside, which would form a key component of the Irish Literary Revival of the late nineteenth and early twentieth centuries. Among the most prominent of these collectors were the parents of Oscar Wilde, Sir William and Lady Jane ('Speranza') Wilde; Sir William published *Irish Popular Superstitions* in 1852 and his wife followed with two collections of folklore in 1887 and 1890, based largely on work done by Sir William prior to his death in 1876.

That Hearn was directly affected by this folkloric tradition is evident in a letter that he wrote to the poet William Butler Yeats in 1901, recalling his Irish childhood:

> But forty-five years ago, I was a horrid little boy, 'with never a crack in his heart', who lived in Upper Leeson Street, Dublin; and I had a Connaught nurse who told me fairy-tales and ghost-stories. So I ought to love Irish Things, and do.[6]

It is important to remember that the fairies of the Irish tradition are man-sized, often evil beings, with grim characteristics also found in the Gothic literary tradition. At that time, a belief in fairies and ghosts as living phenomena with a real power to interact with humans was still common in the Irish countryside. As an adult, Hearn would write:

> Anciently woods and streams were peopled for him [the peasant] with invisible beings; angels and demons walked at his side; the

woods had their fairies, the mountains their goblins, the marshes their flitting spirits, and the dead came back to him at times to bear a message or to rebuke a fault. Also the ground that he trod upon, the plants growing in the field, the cloud above him, the lights of heaven all were full of mystery and ghostliness.[7]

Hearn's own belief in the reality of the world of spirits, perhaps an inheritance from his Irish childhood, was not so different and remained constant throughout his life.

England

In 1863, when Hearn was thirteen, Mrs Brenane relocated to England, where she used her fortune to support a young, newly married English businessman, Henry Hearn Molyneux, whose mother was a member of an Irish Roman Catholic branch of the Hearn family. Mrs Brenane seems to have been something of a soft touch as Hearn's father also borrowed heavily from her. Hearn was enrolled in a boarding school run by Roman Catholic priests at Ushaw, near Durham in the north of England. With a regime that married the monastic and the scholastic, it was not a congenial environment for him. Having lost his real mother at the age of four, he now found himself displaced in the affections of his adoptive mother by Molyneux and plunged into a structured life very much the opposite of that which he had enjoyed in Dublin.

Once the shock of immersive religion had worn off, Hearn underwent a profound spiritual transformation, rejecting not just Roman Catholicism but Christianity as a whole, for which he substituted instead the ideals of ancient Greek civilization. This liberated him from monotheism and also provided him with a connection to his mother's heritage. The fear he had experienced in Mrs Brenane's house slowly dissipated and he would later write:

The terror was not yet gone; but I now wanted only reason to disbelieve all that I had feared and hated. In the sunshine, in the green of the fields, in the blue of the sky, I found a gladness before unknown.

Within myself new thoughts, new imaginings, dim longings for I
knew not what were quickening and thrilling. I looked for beauty,
and everywhere found it: in the passing faces – in attitudes and
motions – in the poise of plants and trees – in long white clouds – in
faint-blue lines of far-off hills. At moments the simple pleasure of
life would quicken to a joy so large, so deep, that it frightened me.
But at other times there would come to me a new and strange
sadness – a shadowy and inexplicable pain.[8]

Hearn emerged from his youth having rejected organized religion
but yet profoundly spiritual in outlook, and he would continue to
seek deeper meanings, not only in the classical world but also in
the twin religions of Japan, Buddhism and Shintō, and their associated folklore. The latter, an indigenous animistic belief system,
caught his attention early on in his Japanese sojourn and would be
crucial to his interpretation of Japan, although it would be Buddhism that would infuse much of his horror writing.

A playground accident in Ushaw at the age of sixteen left Hearn
without the sight of his left eye and, he believed, disfigured; he
would be self-conscious about his appearance for the rest of his
life (he always turned the left side of his face away from the cam-
era when photographs were being taken). Fresh disaster struck
a year later when Henry Molyneux failed in business, wiping out
Mrs Brenane's fortune. Hearn had to be withdrawn from Ushaw
and he was sent to live with a former maid of Mrs Brenane in the
East End of London for two years.

While Hearn's depiction of the East End as a place of murder and
mayhem may have been exaggerated, the area was notorious for
its appalling poverty, as depicted in the contemporaneous engrav-
ings of the French artist Gustave Doré, published in his *London:
A Pilgrimage* (1872), and it would be the haunt of Jack the Ripper
two decades later. Even as a youth, Hearn's attention was attracted
by the culture of the common people; in this case it was the cock-
ney balladeers who composed songs on themes suggested by
contemporary events that stirred the popular emotions – suicides,
murders, political developments – and performed them on the
streets. Hearn saw them as a continuation of the 'habits and customs that gave English literature a great deal of its true and noble

verse'.[9] This keen interest in native traditions and local culture would be sustained throughout his later sojourn in Japan, and in his next home – America.

America: 'Dismal Man' and Reinvention

Overall, the main effect of Hearn's stay in London was to leave him with a horror of large, industrialized cities that he would never lose. At the age of nineteen he was given the fare to cross the Atlantic and arrived in New York, another large city with which he would never come to terms, in September 1869. He quickly moved on to Cincinnati, where he was taken on by an English printer, before making a tentative start in journalism by submitting freelance articles to local newspapers, initially for the *Boston Investigator*, a freethought weekly, under the pseudonym 'Fiat Lux' ('Let There be Light'), in 1870 and 1871.

His big break came in November 1874 when news of a sensational crime – the 'Tan-yard Murder' – broke and Hearn was assigned to cover it for the *Cincinnati Enquirer* as the regular staff were not available.[10] He transformed the lurid basics of the story – illicit sex and extreme violence – into a dramatic narrative that reads more like an eye-witness account than the second-hand reconstruction it actually was. The story was picked up by newspapers across America and Hearn was instantly established as a journalist. Assigned to the police beat of the *Enquirer*, he specialized in reporting on the most debased and squalid stories and revelled in his self-styled persona as 'the *Enquirer*'s Dismal Man, whose rueful countenance was flushed with the hope of hearing or seeing something more than the usually horrible'.[11]

In Cincinnati, Hearn dropped his first name, Patrick or Paddy, and adopted his middle name, Lafcadio, by which he would be known from this point on. His change of name signalled a reinvention of his identity. At the time, the Orient was seen as stretching from Eastern Europe to the Far East, taking in North Africa to the south. Hearn, by virtue of his Greek lineage and new name, could claim to be 'Oriental' according to the perceptions of the era.

The police beat brought Hearn into contact with the thriving black culture of the city's 'levee', or docklands, on the banks of the Ohio river. One of his fellow journalists in Cincinnati, Henry Krehbiel, was keenly interested in 'exotic' music and invited Hearn to join him in an opium den to hear Chinese music played on authentic instruments. The pair also collaborated in collecting black music, although a planned book on the subject never materialized. When he later moved to New Orleans, Hearn sought African elements in Louisiana's Creole music, as he would also do in the West Indies.[12] As an early, sympathetic explorer of the music of black America, Hearn was engaging with the roots of what would become jazz, the blues and, ultimately, rock music in the twentieth century. The black population of Cincinnati attracted Hearn's interest, in a way that mainstream white culture – its more sensational manifestations aside – did not.

Hearn's disregard for the racial divisions of the time brought him notoriety when, in June 1874, he married Alethea ('Mattie') Foley, a biracial woman who had been born into slavery. A servant in the boarding house where he was staying, Mattie was a gifted storyteller, of supernatural tales especially. As interracial marriage was then illegal in Ohio, Hearn had broken the law as well as scandalized respectable opinion and, in any event, the marriage soon foundered. When word of the marriage leaked out, he lost his newspaper position, although he did subsequently find another, with the *Cincinnati Commercial*, albeit it at a lower salary.

In 1877, Hearn shook the dust of Cincinnati off his feet and moved south to New Orleans. Cincinnati would prove to be the pivot of his life. He had arrived as Paddy Hearn, a nineteen-year-old with shattered confidence and uncertain prospects. He left as Lafcadio Hearn, a successful journalist, and he would – with just a few short intervals – be a well-paid professional writer and educator for the rest of his life.

With his move to New Orleans in 1877, Hearn changed direction once more. He again established himself as a successful journalist but now, instead of the police beat and its associated horrors, he became a littérateur and editorial writer, much respected and even lionized as a local literary celebrity. Having written for both the New Orleans *Daily City Item* and *New Orleans Democrat* between 1878 and 1881, he settled into a comfortable niche at

the New Orleans *Times-Democrat* from 1881 until his departure
for the West Indies in 1887. He forged lifelong friendships with
the *Times-Democrat* editor, Page Baker, an old-style Southern gentleman, and with a fellow staff member, the able and supportive
Elizabeth Bisland. Bisland published *The Life and Letters of Lafcadio Hearn*, a substantial two-volume biography, two years after
his death.

Much as the substitution of 'Lafcadio' for 'Paddy' helped obscure
the Irish elements of Hearn's childhood – whose upper-class background was in any case atypical of the majority of Irish immigrants
in the USA – so now Hearn suppressed his radical Cincinnati
past, his failed marriage especially. He adopted the coloration of
the antebellum genteel culture of the old South and, although he
explored the local Creole culture with relish, he now adopted the
pose of a superior observer of scientific bent.

Hearn had begun an immersion in French literature while still
in Cincinnati; in New Orleans, where he lived in the French
Quarter in the midst of a dwindling francophone minority, it
flowered into extensive translations in newspapers and then books.
One of Cleopatra's Nights and Other Fantastic Romances (1882), translations of the work of Théophile Gautier, provided him with an
early book; he also translated works by Gustave Flaubert, Émile
Zola, Guy de Maupassant, Pierre Loti, Alphonse Daudet, Charles
Didier and Gérard de Nerval. Translation of risqué contemporary
French writing allowed Hearn to indulge his taste for sensuality
and violence, and placed him intellectually as much outside the
mainstream of Victorian respectability as his gutter journalism
had done in Cincinnati. He was so engrossed in this fictional
French world that it might be argued that he was almost a French
writer writing in English. Hearn's attempt to remodel English on
French lines proved, however, to be a false direction, as the ornate
forms of his French masters simply did not lend themselves to the
English language. His engagement with Creole life was reflected
in *Gombo Zhèbes: Little Dictionary of Creole Proverbs, Selected from
Six Creole Dialects* and *La Cuisine Creole: A Collection of Culinary
Receipts from Leading Chefs and Noted Creole Housewives, Who Have
Made New Orleans Famous for Its Cuisine*, both published in 1885.

At the same time, Hearn was developing in two other directions, towards the south and east. The southern development would lead him to the West Indies, where he lived from 1887 to 1889. *Two Years in the French West Indies* (1890), an idiosyncratic mixture of travelogue, analysis and a ghost story, shows Hearn honing a leaner, more powerful prose style, which would form the template for his later Japanese books.

His eventual, definitive turn eastward to Japan was foreshadowed in a number of developments while he was in New Orleans. Hearn was impressed by the Japanese section of the New Orleans Cotton Centennial Exposition of 1884–5, about which he wrote in *Harper's Weekly* (31 May 1885) under the title 'The East at New Orleans', and he began to muse on the relationship of Japanese to ancient Greek art; parallels between Japan and classical Greece would later be central to his analysis of Japan. His mind had already turned towards the East as he prepared the material for his 1884 book *Stray Leaves from Strange Literature*, which was partly derived from Buddhist sources, among others, while *Some Chinese Ghosts* would follow three years later. Hearn experimented with more personal expression in the 'Fantastics' of his New Orleans years, short flights of fancy that explored the themes of love and death in the southern city and which he published in the *Times-Democrat*. He published two short novels, *Chita: A Memory of Last Island* (1889) and *Youma: The Story of a West-Indian Slave* (1890), but abandoned fiction from this point. After a great deal of literary experimentation in New Orleans, he would henceforth have a single focus, Japan.

Japan

In 1890, approaching forty, Hearn landed in Japan, where he would spend the rest of his life. Shortly after his arrival, he broke with the New York publisher Harper & Brothers, which had been publishing his work in the latter part of the 1880s, his West Indian material especially; simmering tensions over the amount of his material being published and the manner in which it was being edited, as well as the amounts he was being paid, which had existed since his sojourn in the West Indies, now caused a breakdown in relations with Harper. Whatever hopes he might have had of living by his pen were now dashed; he settled down as a teacher and, from 1896, a lecturer at Tokyo University. In Japan he matured both as a person and as a writer, developing a masterly command of simple English. He maintained an impressive literary output of approximately a book a year, mostly published in and for the American market.

Hearn spent his first year in Japan as a secondary-school teacher in Matsue, a small city on the country's west coast, far from cosmopolitan Tokyo to the east. Here he found traditional Japan and loved it. He was introduced to a Japanese woman of the samurai class, Setsuko (Setsu) Koizumi, whom he subsequently married. She provided him with a companionship that had eluded him up to this point in his adult life and they would have four children together. The cold of winter in Matsue was, however, too much for Hearn and he moved south to Kumamoto on the southern island of Kyushu, where he was again employed as a school teacher. This proved to be Hearn's unhappiest experience in Japan – he liked neither the place nor the people – and he left again in 1894 to take up a short-lived editorial job with the *Kobe Chronicle* before eye problems forced him to resign his post and he was unable to work for a year and a half.

In 1896, Hearn was appointed to the prestigious and lucrative post of lecturer at Tokyo Imperial University. The move to Tokyo can be seen as a watershed in both his life and writing. His Japanese books from this point on, with the exception of *Japan: An Attempt at Interpretation* (1904), are unusual and idiosyncratic mixtures of various elements, including descriptive passages, analyses of rapidly changing Meiji Japan and *kwaidan*, or ghost stories. Flashbacks to a horror-haunted childhood in Ireland are mostly contained in his later books, *Exotics and Retrospectives* (1898) and *Shadowings* (1900) especially.

Hearn professed to hate the bustling, modernizing capital city at the forefront of transformation of the Meiji era (1868–1912), even though he understood the brutal necessity of change; without it, Japan would be at the mercy of predatory Western imperial powers. Hearn was sometimes ambiguous about Japan in private correspondence, professing to a sense of disillusionment and even occasionally considering leaving the country, but his commitment to Japanese culture never wavered. He would hold the post at Tokyo University for eight years, during which time he adopted Japanese nationality under the name Koizumi Yakumo (Koizumi being his wife's surname) to safeguard his family's right of inheritance. This had the effect, however, of a parting of the ways with Tokyo University in 1904 when it decided to apply to him the lower salary paid to Japanese nationals. He was replaced at Tokyo University by the distinguished Japanese novelist Natsume Sōseki, whose 1914 novel *Kokoro* would bear the same title as Hearn's 1896 volume. Hearn immediately found alternative employment and had just taken up his new post as lecturer at Waseda University when he died of heart disease on 26 September 1904.

Japanese Ghost Stories

It was in Japan that Hearn's literary output became increasingly dominated by ghost stories. Although written in English and largely for a Western audience, Hearn's stories stand apart from those of his contemporaries in Britain and Ireland. Victorian ghost and horror stories were mostly products of the imaginations of writers such as Joseph Sheridan Le Fanu, Bram Stoker and M. R. James. They may have had roots in folklore but were essentially literary in nature. Hearn is unique in creating a coherent body of ghost stories based entirely on folk originals translated into English from another language and culture.

Folklore in all its forms had always captivated Hearn, from the goblins and fairies of his Irish childhood through to the ballads of east London, the Creole and Cajun cultures of New Orleans, and the tales of zombies in the West Indies. When he reached Japan, he was again enthralled by native folk traditions, this time in the form of ghost stories. He was fortunate that his wife, Setsu, eagerly sought out old books of ghost stories, which she translated and interpreted for him. (Whether others, such as his students, were also involved, is a moot point.) In her 'Reminiscences', Setsu laid bare the combination of Hearn's technical mastery and emotional engagement with the raw material which lay at the heart of his *kwaidan* output:

He loved ghost stories very much and was always saying, 'Books of ghost stories are my treasures.' I hunted for them from one second-hand bookstore to another. On dreary nights, I would tell him ghost stories, having lowered the wick of the lamp on purpose. He listened to my tales with bated breath and with a terrified air, and when he asked me something, he did so in a very low voice. Since he looked as if he were really frightened while listening to me, my narrative increasingly took on a life of its own. On those occasions, my house seemed as if it were haunted, and I sometimes had horrible dreams and came to be afflicted with nightmares. When I mentioned this to him, he would say, 'Well, then, let's take a break for a while.' And we would stop. But when a story that I told him caught his fancy, he was extremely pleased.

If it was an old tale, I always summarized the story first. Then, if he found it interesting, he would write down the plot. Next, he would ask me to tell the story in all its details; he made me repeat the same story several times in succession. If I was going to tell a story by reading it from a book, he would say, 'Don't read from a book when you tell a story. You must tell a story as if it were your own story – in your own words and from your own thoughts.' Consequently, I had to digest and assimilate the story before telling it. That was the reason for my dreams.

Once he took an interest in a story, he always changed and became very serious: he turned pale and a sharp fearful look came into his eyes. The extent of this change was extraordinary. This was the case, for example, with the story of O-Katsu-san in 'The Legend of Yūrei-Daki' which appears in the first part of the book *Kottō*. As I was telling the story, his face became very pale and his eyes fixed. That was not uncommon, but on this particular occasion I myself suddenly became frightened. When I finished telling the story, he took a long breath as if relieved and said, 'It's a very engaging tale.' Then he asked me to say, 'Oh! It is blood!' again and to repeat it over and over. He then asked me, 'How do you think she said it? What was the tone of her voice like? What sound do you imagine her clogs made? What kind of night was it?' He consulted with me about many things that were not written in the original, saying, 'I think it was like this. What do you yourself think?' If anyone had seen us from the outside, we would have appeared like two mad people.[13]

That Hearn drew heavily on old books of Japanese ghost stories is confirmed by the information he himself provides. He acknowledged his debt to *The Classical Poetry of the Japanese* (1880), by the English Japanologist Basil Hall Chamberlain, for the story of Urashima Tarō, contained in 'The Dream of a Summer Day'.[14] He also footnoted sources for his ghost stories in his published work, many of them older anthologies such as Aoki Rosui's *Otogi Hyaku Monogatari* ('One Hundred Tales for Keeping Company') of 1701 or Ueda Akinari's *Ugetsu Monogatari* ('Tales of Moonlight and Rain') of 1776. Some were based on legends or on conversations with rural inhabitants.

His painstaking note-taking is confirmed by Setsu: 'All the things Hearn saw and heard at this time were new to him, so he took a lively pleasure in them, always writing copious notes, which gave him a lot of pleasure.'[15]

Spirits and Spirituality

Why did ghosts become so important to Hearn in Japan? It was partly because his life story, though seemingly linear – a long odyssey that culminated in his maturity as a writer in Japan – also contained circular elements. In Japan, the terrors of his childhood dreams resurfaced and he reverted to an interest in Buddhism which had developed while he was in New Orleans. A bridging element was his earlier loss of faith in Christianity and, by extension, monotheism while he was in England.

Hearn expressed a coherent philosophy of the supernatural in his early years in Japan, one that aligned with the rejection of Western materialism – which he believed had squeezed the spiritual out of people's lives – evident in his interpretative work. In the story 'The Eternal Haunter' (1898), for example, Hearn characterizes a relationship between a tree-spirit and a mortal man as 'the Impossible' and defiantly sets out a non-materialist philosophy at odds with the mainstream values of the nineteenth century:

I hold that the Impossible bears a much closer relation to fact than does most of what we call the real and the commonplace. The

Impossible may not be naked truth; but I think that it is usually truth, – masked and veiled, perhaps, but eternal. (p. 33)

In 1893 he discussed the passing of 'the aspirational' from everyday life in a letter to Chamberlain:

What made the aspirational in life? Ghosts. Some were called Gods, some Demons, some Angels; – they changed the world for man; they gave him courage and purpose and the awe of Nature that slowly changed into love; – they filled all things with a sense and motion of invisible life, – they made both terror and beauty. There are no ghosts, no angels and demons and gods: all are dead. The world of electricity, steam, mathematics, is blank and cold and void. No man can even write about it. Who can find a speck of romance in it?[16]

Much of Hearn's writing for the rest of his life would be concerned with presenting the supernatural elements inherent in the Japanese folk tradition to his largely American audience. He could hardly have anticipated the appetite his Western and, later, Japanese readers, mostly now living in a modern world of electricity, steam and mathematics, would have for this work.

The Victorian era, especially for Anglicanism, was a period of immense religious turmoil as the hammer blows of science put traditional beliefs under strain, in response to which artists and intellectuals began to explore alternative spiritual avenues. Many looked to the East, and to Buddhism in particular, for enlightenment. Madame Helena Blavatsky (1831–91), for example, a Russian occultist who counted the poet W. B. Yeats among her many adherents, developed the Theosophy movement, an esoteric synthesis of science, religion and philosophy. Supposedly reviving an 'Ancient Wisdom' underlying all the world's religions, Theosophy took Buddhism as one of its key elements. Hearn himself would attempt a synthesis of Buddhism with the then fashionable evolutionary philosophy of Herbert Spencer.

Hearn was deeply drawn to the Buddhism of Japan. As Kenneth Roxroth, editor of *The Buddhist Writings of Lafcadio Hearn*, writes, 'There is no interpreter of Japanese Buddhism quite like Hearn . . .

It is the Buddhism of the ordinary Japanese Buddhist of whatever sect.'[17] Early in his stay in Japan, Hearn had also become fascinated by Shintō, the ancient animistic religion with its belief in ubiquitous *kami* or spirits and the essential continuity between the *kami* and the human world. In its ancient form, it envisaged three different worlds or states of being, which included the *yomi-no-kuni*, a land of the dead or world of darkness, similar to the realm of Hades in classical Greek mythology. Hearn believed that Buddhism's status as the official state religion was due to its 'absorption and expansion of the older Shintō worship of many gods, ghosts, and goblins (the gods, Buddhas or Bodhisattvas, the ghosts beings [*sic*] in transit from one incarnation to another, and the goblins, *gakis*, beings suffering in a lower state of existence)'.[18]

Within Buddhist doctrine, souls were thought to live in zones of formlessness until the time of rebirth. They were fed by surviving relatives and, if nobody cared for them, they could haunt living people. If sickness or calamity afflicted a community, it was attributed to inadequate propitiation of ghosts. The *yūrei* of Japanese *kwaidan* folklore, corresponding to the Western idea of ghosts, are the spirits of those whose manner of death precludes them from a peaceful union with their ancestors, and they can return to the human world.

In the late seventeenth century, the *yūrei* began to feature in literature, theatre and art. Maruyama Ōkyo's (1733–95) painting *The Ghost of Oyuki* (1750) reflected the popularity of this ghostly subject matter. Just how powerful the Japanese belief in ghosts remained prior to the modernization of the Meiji era is best illustrated, literally, by the work of the great artist Katsushika Hokusai (1760–1849), creator of the iconic *Great Wave off Kanagawa* print in his famous series *Thirty-Six Views of Mount Fuji* (*c.*1830–32). In the words of the American author and art expert James A. Michener (1907–97), Hokusai 'lived in a demon-riddled world . . . where gods and spirits and men overlapped, where ghosts walked and where a man could quickly allow himself to slip away into fantasy'.[19] Describing Hokusai's ghost-story prints, Michener says:

These drawings deal with the terrifying ghosts that haunt Japan, and in studying Hokusai's depiction of these fiends, the Western observer becomes convinced that for the artist these ghosts were real. Faithful wives whose husbands abused them were known to have the capacity of returning after death to haunt their spouses. Blood cried out from the grave, and victims of injustice gained revenge.[20]

This is also the world of Hearn's Japanese ghost stories. While some Shintō influences can be seen in them, Buddhism is their common denominator. In 'Story of a Tengu' (1899), for example, a pious priest is transported back in time to hear the voice of the Buddha preaching the law as a reward for a good deed. 'The Sympathy of Benten' (1900) features a Buddhist deity acting as a matchmaker for two of her worshippers, while the pilgrim in 'Fragment' (1899) climbs a mountain of skulls that are the product of his billions of former lives. Reincarnation features prominently and can result in serious complications for the social order, as in 'Riki-Baka' (1904), where a dead simpleton is reborn into a rich family, or 'The Story of Itō Norisuké' (also 1904), where fateful meetings have taken place in previous lives. Other stories illustrate the positive power of Buddhist prayer and divine intervention.

Hearn's use of reincarnation as both a motif and plot device gives his stories a particularly Japanese flavour but themes familiar from Western horror also abound, including vampirism, revenge by the dead (especially on the part of women who feel betrayed), shape-shifting, the consequences of impiety or immorality, and intermarriage between ghostly women and mortal men.

Vampirism, which featured in nineteenth-century European literature from John Polidori's *The Vampyre* (1819) through Joseph Sheridan Le Fanu's *Carmilla* (1872) to Bram Stoker's *Dracula* (1897), also recurs throughout Hearn's *kwaidan*. The title character in 'The Story of Chūgorō' has been drained of his blood by a female vampire; 'Jikininki' (1904) tells the story of a debased priest who becomes a devourer of human flesh; and in 'The Story of O-Kamé' (1902), a dead wife leeches the life out of her husband.

Bram Stoker was Hearn's contemporary growing up in middle-class Dublin in the 1850s and 1860s and, although we don't know whether their families knew each other, the parallels between

Hearn's *kwaidan* stories (1890–1904) and Stoker's *Dracula* (1897) are striking. In 'A Passional Karma' (1899), ghosts can enter the house 'like a streaming of vapor' (p. 56), just as Count Dracula does, while the sacred Buddhist *mamori* performs much the same function in combating evil as Roman Catholic religious objects do in *Dracula*. Just as Count Dracula is able to freeze Jonathan Harker while he vampirizes his wife, so, in 'Of a Promise Broken' (1901), a supernatural power is able to render its unfortunate victim frozen and motionless. In 'Rokuro-Kubi' (1904), the power of the goblins is effective only in the hours of darkness, parallel-ing the limitations of Count Dracula. And like Count Dracula, Hearn's ghosts enjoy immunity to mortal weapons. Although Stoker's inspiration was European and Hearn's largely Japanese, the similarities in their writing indicate the common folkloric and fairy-tale elements that underlay much of the output of their generation of fin-de-siècle Gothic writers.

Hearn had always gloried in writing horrifying descriptive prose, from his earliest American journalism to his translations of the erotically charged and sadistically tinged French masters. His Japanese tales, too, often feature elements of the horrifying or grotesque – as when a man in 'The Corpse-Rider' (1900) has to spend the night riding on the back of a reanimated female corpse to exorcise her murderous spirit. However, his prose style, shorn of its previous striving after ornate effect, matured in his Japanese *kwaidan* into a hard-edged simplicity. The opening sentence of 'The Corpse-Rider' illustrates this new-found stylistic restraint: 'The body was cold as ice; the heart had long ceased to beat: yet there were no other signs of death' (p. 76).

In dealing with real-life horror, Hearn was often laconic, know-ing that he could achieve more by letting events speak for themselves rather than piling on literary effects. As a relatively young journalist, in August 1876, he witnessed a judicial execu-tion in Dayton, Ohio. His account is all the more terrible for its restraint, eschewing the linguistic pyrotechnics that had marked his imaginative reconstruction of the 'Tan-yard Murder' less than two years previously.[21] Now, in his Japanese story 'In Cholera-Time', published exactly twenty years after the Dayton execution, he treats the subject of infant mortality among the poor with similarly powerful restraint. One simple sentence encapsulates the horrifying but prosaic reality: 'It costs only forty-four sen to burn a child' (p. 24). In writing about horror – whether real or supernatural – Hearn had become a master of his craft.

Afterlives

Hearn's extraordinary life and remarkably varied output make him a difficult subject to pin down. Although most famous for his writings on Japan, he was powerfully shaped by his Irish background. He was deeply influenced by the folkloric traditions of his homeland, a subject on which he corresponded with W. B. Yeats, who regarded him highly. His predilection for the Gothic connected him with other Irish writers of the period, most notably Bram Stoker. And in the horror stories dealing with his conflicted childhood, Hearn pioneered Irish Catholic auto-biographical writing, later developed by James Joyce, Patrick Kavanagh and John McGahern, among others. At the same time, his achievements far exceeded any parochial bounds. His sympathetic exploration of black culture (especially music) in the United States was remarkable by the standards of the time. He was also an excellent critic of mainstream English and American literature, as evidenced by his lectures at Tokyo University, which were published after his death.[22]

Notwithstanding a bitter posthumous newspaper controversy over his character in America in 1906 – much of it driven by rage at the discovery of his interracial marriage – and the publication of *Concerning Lafcadio Hearn* (1908),[23] a vituperative memoir by George Gould, a former friend, Hearn's reputation remained high in the years following his death. His works became popular in his adopted homeland after their translation into Japanese in the late 1920s, where his role in collecting and preserving folklore was much appreciated.[24] Hearn's writings also played an important role in shaping the views on Japan of the American brigadier general Bonner Fellers, military secretary and head of psychological warfare to General Douglas MacArthur, commander of US forces in the Pacific from 1941. Described as 'the most influential theorist and practitioner on MacArthur's staff',

Fellers was a key player in the formation of American policy towards Japan during the Second World War.[25] After the war, MacArthur accepted the arguments put forward by him that the emperor, Hirohito, should not be prosecuted for war crimes.[26] As a devotee of Hearn's writings, Fellers would have understood the importance of Shintō, the emperor's place within it especially, and the likely catastrophic consequences of putting him on trial. Thus Hearn exercised a profound posthumous influence on post-war Japan through the medium of Fellers. The relationship between MacArthur and Fellers is examined in the 2012 movie *Emperor*, directed by Peter Webber.

Hearn's standing among academics declined after the Second World War and reached its nadir in the 1970s when, according to the leading Japanese authority on Hearn, Professor Sukehiro Hirakawa of Tokyo University, his writings were so discredited among American Japanologists that if a young student quoted Hearn sympathetically, he or she was almost certain to be criticized by academic advisers and considered unfit for serious scholarship.[27] Happily, his reputation has now recovered and his output is the subject of a good deal of ongoing scholarship.

According to Professor Hirakawa, Hearn has always been regarded as pre-eminent among foreign observers of Japan by the Japanese themselves.[28]

He remains enduringly popular in Japan, where his *kwaidan*, translated back into Japanese and included in the school curriculum, have become part of the cultural landscape.

The 1965 film *Kwaidan*, made by the Japanese director Masaki Kobayashi and based on four of Hearn's stories from 1900 to 1904 in this current collection ('The Reconciliation', 'In a Cup of Tea', 'The Story of Mimi-Nashi-Hōïchi' and 'Yuki-Onna'), is considered to be a cinematic masterpiece. 'Yuki-Onna' also inspired director Tokuzō Tanaka's *The Snow Woman* (1968); the 'Lover's Vow' segment of *Tales from the Darkside: The Movie* (1990) and Kiki Sugino's full-length film *Yuki-Onna* (*Snow Woman*, 2016).

Hearn's reputation is now growing internationally. There is a Lafcadio Hearn Memorial Museum in Matsue (the director of which is Bon Koizumi, Hearn's great grandson), where Hearn spent his first year in Japan, as well as Hearn museums at

Kumamoto and Yaizu, a seaside location where his spent summer holidays during his time in Tokyo. The Lafcadio Hearn Japanese Gardens opened in 2015 in Tramore, a seaside town in south-eastern Ireland where Hearn spent childhood holidays with Mrs Brenane; the gardens are laid out to reflect the story of his life. It was on the beach at Tramore, visible from these gardens, where Hearn had a last meeting with his father. In England, where Hearn was educated in the 1860s, the Lafcadio Hearn Cultural Centre now forms part of the University of Durham. A Lafcadio Hearn Historical Centre was opened on Lefkada, Greece, in 2014.

There are many important collections of Hearn material in the United States, including in the cities in which he lived: Cincinnati, at the Public Library of Cincinnati; and Hamilton County, and New Orleans, at the Lafcadio Hearn Collection of the Howard-Tilton Memorial Library, Tulane University.

Hearn's Japanese ghost stories provide a thrilling exploration of an Eastern culture by a peripatetic Western traveller whose life before the age of forty seems, in retrospect, like an unconscious preparation for the great work he accomplished in Meiji Japan. Crucial to his achievement was a respect for the validity of a Far Eastern culture, unusual among contemporaneous Western observers. There are few Victorian writers whose work chimes as comfortably with our own values in this era of globalization and cultural relativism.

NOTES

1. See p. 33 in this volume.
2. Hearn claimed to have spoken both Romaic (modern Greek) and Italian (presumably Venetian) when he was a child. See Lafcadio Hearn, letter to Basil Hall Chamberlain, 7 September 1893, in Elizabeth Bisland (ed.), *The Japanese Letters of Lafcadio Hearn* (Boston and New York: Houghton Mifflin Company, 1910), p. 160.
3. John Davy, *Notes and Observations on the Ionian Islands and Malta* (London: Smith, Elder & Co., 1842), vol. 2, p. 112.
4. Eleni Charou-Koroneou, 'Roza Antoniou Kasimati, Mother of Lafcadio Hearn', *Kithiraika* (May 2006), p. 11. Published in Greek and a copy sent to me by Despoina Mavroudi; kindly translated into

English by the then Cypriot ambassador to Ireland, Dr Michalis Stavrinos, in 2014.

5.   Lafcadio Hearn, 'Draft MSS Autobiography', Lafcadio Hearn Papers, 1849–1952, Albert and Shirley Small Special Collections Library, University of Virginia Library, Charlottesville, Virginia; quoted in Paul Murray, *A Fantastic Journey: The Life and Literature of Lafcadio Hearn* (Folkestone: Japan Library, 1993; reprinted London and New York: Routledge, 2005), pp. 248–9.

6.   Lafcadio Hearn, 'MSS letter to W. B. Yeats', 24 September 1901, Tokyo; photocopy kindly provided by Dr John Kelly, St John's College, Oxford; quoted in Murray, *Fantastic Journey*, p. 35.

7.   Lafcadio Hearn, *On Poetry*, ed. Ryuji Tanabé, Teisaburo Ochiai and Ichirō Nishizaki, 3rd edn (Tokyo: Hokuseido Press, 1941), p. 13.

8.   Elizabeth Bisland (ed.), *The Life and Letters of Lafcadio Hearn*, 2 vols (Cambridge, MA, Boston and New York: Houghton Mifflin Company, Riverside Press, 1906), vol. 1, p. 32; quoted in Murray, *Fantastic Journey*, p. 265.

9.   Hearn, *On Poetry*, pp. 14–15.

10. [Lafcadio Hearn], 'Violent Cremation', *Cincinnati Enquirer*, 9 November 1874; see also 'Killed and Cremated', *Cincinnati Enquirer*, 10 November 1874. The stories were not published under Hearn's byline.

11. [Lafcadio Hearn], 'Golgotha: A Pilgrimage to Potter's Field', *Cincinnati Enquirer*, 29 November 1874; quoted in Murray, *Fantastic Journey*, p. 30.

12. See, for example, the appendix, 'Some Creole Melodies', to Lafcadio Hearn, *Two Years in the French West Indies* (New York and London: Harper & Brothers, 1890), pp. 424–31.

13. Setsu Koizumi, 'Reminiscences', in Yoji Hasegawa (ed.), *A Walk in Kumamoto: The Life and Times of Setsu Koizumi, Lafcadio Hearn's Japanese Wife* (Folkestone: Global Oriental, 1997), pp. 19–21.

14. Lafcadio Hearn, 'The Dream of a Summer Day', in his *'Out of the East': Reveries and Studies in New Japan* (Boston: Houghton, Mifflin and Company, 1895), p. 12. Basil Hall Chamberlain (1850–1935) was one of a trio of great British Japanologists, the others being William George Aston (1841–1911) and Ernest Satow (1843–1929) of the Meiji era. As professor of Japanese at Tokyo Imperial University, he was a friend and benefactor of Hearn's, although they later fell out.

15. Koizumi, 'Reminiscences', p. 3.

16. Lafcadio Hearn, letter to Basil Hall Chamberlain, 14 December 1893, in Bisland (ed.), *Japanese Letters of Lafcadio Hearn*, p. 214.

17. Kenneth Roxroth (ed.), Introduction to *The Buddhist Writings of Lafcadio Hearn* (London: Wildwood House, 1981), n.p.

18. Ibid.

19. James A. Michener, *The Hokusai Sketch-Books: Selections from the Manga* (Vermont and Tokyo: Tuttle, 1958), p. 197.

20. Ibid., p. 196.

21. 'Gibbeted', *Cincinnati Commercial*, 26 August 1876. The text is reproduced in Malcolm Cowley (ed.), *The Selected Writings of Lafcadio Hearn* (New York: Citadel Press, 1949), pp. 203–15.

22. John Erskine (ed.), *Appreciations of Poetry by Lafcadio Hearn* (New York: Dodd, Mead and Company, 1916), *Life and Literature by Lafcadio Hearn* (New York: Dodd, Mead and Company, 1917) and *Books and Habits: From the Lectures of Lafcadio Hearn* (New York: Dodd, Mead and Company, 1922); Ryuji Tanabé, Teisaburo Ochiai and Ichirō Nishizaki (eds), *On Poets* (Tokyo: Hokuseido Press, 1934) and *On Poetry* (Tokyo: Hokuseido Press, 1934).

23. George M. Gould, *Concerning Lafcadio Hearn* (Philadelphia: George W. Jacobs & Company, 1908).

24. Rie Kido Askew, 'The Politics of Nostalgia: Museum Representations of Lafcadio Hearn in Japan', *Museum and Society*, vol. 5, no. 3 (November 2007), p. 132.

25. See Paul Murray, 'Lafcadio Hearn's Interpretation of Japan', *The Japan Society Proceedings*, Autumn 1994, p. 62; see also Patrick Porter, 'Paper Bullets: American Psywar in the Pacific, 1944–45', *War in History*, vol. 17, no. 4 (2010), pp. 479–511.

26. Paul Murray, 'Lafcadio Hearn's Interpretation of Japan', in Sukehiro Hirakawa (ed.), *Rediscovering Lafcadio Hearn* (Folkestone: Global Oriental, 1997), p. 257.

27. Professor Sukehiro Hirakawa, 'Supplementary Comment on the Lafcadio Hearn Paper', paper given at the Woodrow Wilson International Center for Scholars, Smithsonian Institution, Washington, DC, 19 July 1978; published in Louis Allen and Jean Wilson (eds), *Lafcadio Hearn: Japan's Great Interpreter: A New Anthology of His Writings, 1894–1904* (Folkestone: Japan Library, 1992), pp. 302–8.

28. Hirakawa (ed.), *Rediscovering Lafcadio Hearn*, p. 1.

A Note on the Text

In this anthology, the text, spelling, punctuation and romanization generally follow the first editions of Hearn's Japanese books. Hearn used the Hepburn system, developed in the late nineteenth century and based on English and Italian pronunciation, for romanizing Japanese words. Although *Kunrei-shiki*, a rival form of romanization, has been promoted by official Japanese policy for many years, Hepburn romanization remains in widespread use. Diacritics are differently applied in modern romanization, however; 'e' no longer has an acute accent over it, for example, making old-style romanization more like French than Italian in this respect.

Hearn's spelling and punctuation mostly followed American usage and that has been retained. Similarly, where he followed English usage, that, too, has been retained. His punctuation, spelling, italicization and romanization could be idiosyncratic – a product of an attempt to reproduce the *sound* of language on the printed page – and not always consistent. It was an issue on which he felt deeply and over which he had many differences with his publishers. Given his obsessive attention to the detail of language, it has been assumed that the inconsistencies were in general deliberate on Hearn's part and, for this reason, they have usually been retained; however, some italicization has been made more consistent, especially where Hearn has varied its use within the same story. All square-bracketed interpolations in the text are Hearn's, rather than editorial insertions, with the exception of two instances where text has been omitted, as are all the footnotes. Editorial comments and explanations take the form of endnotes.

The order in which Japanese names are presented in Hearn's text adheres to the Japanese style of giving the surname first, followed by the given name. In the editorial matter, the order follows convention rather than consistency. Thus Lafcadio Hearn's Japanese name is generally rendered Koizumi Yakumo, surname followed by his given name, in both Japanese and English, probably because his Japanese name is seldom used in English. His wife's name, by contrast, is generally written as Setsuko or Setsu Koizumi, the surname following the given name in the Western style. The name of the Japanese novelist who replaced Hearn as a lecturer at Tokyo University, would be rendered as Sōseki Natsume in Japanese, but in English, including on the title pages of his books, he is Natsume Sōseki.

The stories are presented in the order of publication of the books containing them, as this represents the best way of showing how they evolved throughout Hearn's Japanese sojourn. Thus Hearn's presence as a narrator is more evident in the earlier stories, while the later ones seem more directly hewn from their folkloric origins.

The images have been selected from the fifteen volumes of *manga* by the famous nineteenth-century artist Hokusai. Published between 1814 and 1878, these collections of woodblock prints were huge bestsellers in Japan and many of the sketches were inspired by the fantastical and sometimes grotesque stories of Japanese legend. Although they didn't appear in Hearn's books at the time, Hokusai's *manga* are close in spirit and sensibility to his ghost stories, and draw on many of the same sources. Among them are famous *yūrei* (ghosts), *tengu* (supernatural beings with both human and bird-like characteristics) and *rokurokubi* (phantoms with impossibly stretching necks, or heads that come off and fly around), all of which appear in various guises in the stories. Hokusai's illustration of a rabble of demons besetting a Buddhist holy man (p. 2), meanwhile, anticipates one of the main themes of Hearn's ghost stories: the interaction of the world of demons and Buddhist piety.

Further Reading

The titles in the first two sections are listed chronologically.

Books by Lafcadio Hearn (1890–1905)

Two Years in the French West Indies (New York: Harper & Brothers, 1890)

Glimpses of Unfamiliar Japan (Boston: Houghton Mifflin Company, 1894)

'Out of the East': Reveries and Studies in New Japan (Boston: Houghton Mifflin Company, 1895)

Kokoro: Hints and Echoes of Japanese Inner Life (Boston: Houghton Mifflin Company, 1896)

Gleanings in Buddha-Fields: Studies of Hand and Soul in the Far East (Boston: Houghton Mifflin Company, 1897)

Exotics and Retrospectives (Boston: Little, Brown and Company, 1898)

In Ghostly Japan (Boston: Little, Brown and Company, 1899)

Shadowings (Boston: Little, Brown and Company, 1900)

A Japanese Miscellany (Boston: Little, Brown and Company, 1901)

Kottō: Being Japanese Curios, With Sundry Cobwebs (New York: Macmillan Company, 1902)

Kwaidan: Stories and Studies of Strange Things (Boston: Houghton Mifflin Company, 1904)

The Romance of the Milky Way (Boston: Houghton Mifflin Company, 1905)

Posthumous Collections of Hearn's Work

The Life and Letters of Lafcadio Hearn, ed. Elizabeth Bisland, 2 vols (Cambridge, MA, Boston and New York: Houghton Mifflin Company, Riverside Press, 1906)

The Japanese Letters of Lafcadio Hearn, ed. Elizabeth Bisland (Cambridge, MA, Boston and New York: Houghton Mifflin Company, Riverside Press, 1910)

The Writings of Lafcadio Hearn, 16 vols (Boston and New York: Houghton Mifflin Company, 1922)

Some New Letters and Writings of Lafcadio Hearn, ed. Sanki Ichikawa (Tokyo: Kenkyusha, 1925)

Japanese Goblin Poetry: Rendered into English by Lafcadio Hearn, and Illustrated by His Own Drawings, ed. Kazuo Koizumi (Tokyo: Oyama, 1934)

The Selected Writings of Lafcadio Hearn, ed. Malcolm Cowley (New York: Citadel Press, 1949)

The Buddhist Writings of Lafcadio Hearn, ed. Kenneth Roxroth (London: Wildwood House, 1981)

Lafcadio Hearn: Writings from Japan, ed. Francis King (London: Penguin, 1984)

Lafcadio Hearn: Japan's Great Interpreter: A New Anthology of His Writings, 1894–1904, ed. Louis Allen and Jean Wilson (Folkestone: Japan Library, 1992)

Lafcadio Hearn's Japan: An Anthology of His Writings on the Country and Its People, ed. Donald Richie (North Clarendon, VT: Tuttle Publishing, 1997)

Nightmare-Touch, ed. Paul Murray (Leyburn: Tartarus Press, 2010; limited edition)

Insect Literature by Lafcadio Hearn (Dublin: Swan River Press, 2015)

Kwaidan: Ghost Stories of Lafcadio Hearn, ed. Paul Murray (Dublin: Little Museum, 2015; limited edition)

Books and Articles on Hearn

Chamberlain, Basil Hall, *Letters from Basil Hall Chamberlain to Lafcadio Hearn*, ed. Kazuo Koizumi (Tokyo: Hokuseido Press, 1936)

——, *More Letters from Basil Hall Chamberlain to Lafcadio Hearn*, ed. Kazuo Koizumi (Tokyo: Hokuseido Press, 1937)

Cott, Jonathan, *Wandering Ghost: The Odyssey of Lafcadio Hearn* (New York: Alfred A. Knopf, 1991)

Dawson, Carl, *Lafcadio Hearn and the Vision of Japan* (Baltimore and London: Johns Hopkins University Press, 1992)

Hasegawa, Yoji (ed.), *A Walk in Kumamoto: The Life and Times of Setsu Koizumi, Lafcadio Hearn's Japanese Wife* (Folkestone: Global Oriental, 1997)

Hirakawa, Sukehiro (ed.), *Rediscovering Lafcadio Hearn* (Folkestone: Global Oriental, 1997)

Kennard, Nina H., *Lafcadio Hearn* (London: Eveleigh Nash, 1912)

Koizumi, Kazuo, *Father and I: Memories of Lafcadio Hearn* (Boston and New York: Houghton Mifflin Company, 1935)

——, *Re-Echo* (Caldwell, Idaho: Caxton Printers, 1957)

McWilliams, Vera, *Lafcadio Hearn* (Boston: Houghton Mifflin Company, 1946)

Murray, Paul, *A Fantastic Journey: The Life and Literature of Lafcadio Hearn* (Folkestone: Japan Library, 1993; reprinted London and New York: Routledge, 2005)

——, 'Lafcadio Hearn, 1850–1904', in Ian Nish (ed.), *Britain and Japan: Biographical Portraits*, vol. 2 (Folkestone: Japan Library, 1997), pp. 137–50

——, 'Lafcadio Hearn and the Irish Horror Tradition', in Bruce Stewart (ed.), *That Other World: The Supernatural and the Fantastic in Irish Literature and Its Contexts*, vol. 2 (Gerrards Cross: Colin Smythe, 1998), pp. 238–54

——, 'Lafcadio Hearn's Interpretation of Japan', *Proceedings of the Japan Society London*, no. 124 (Autumn 1994), pp. 50–65

Noguchi, Yone, *Lafcadio Hearn in Japan, With Mrs Hearn's Reminiscences* (London: Elkin Matthews; Yokohama: Kelly and Walsh, 1910)

Ota, Yuzo, *Basil Hall Chamberlain: Portrait of a Japanologist* (Richmond, Surrey: Curzon Press/Japan Library, 1998)

Proceedings: International Symposium on 'The Open Mind of Lafcadio Hearn' (Lefkada, Greece, 2014): http://hearn2014.yakumokai. org/wp-content/uploads/2015/03/hearn2014proceedings.pdf

Ronan, Sean G. and Toki Koizumi, *Lafcadio Hearn (Koizumi Yakumo): His Life, Work and Irish Background* (Dublin: Ireland Japan Association, 1991)

Ronan, Sean G. (ed.), *Irish Writing on Lafcadio Hearn and Japan* (Folkestone: Global Oriental, 1997)

Stevenson, Elizabeth, *Lafcadio Hearn* (New York: Macmillan Company, 1961)

Thomas, Edward, *Lafcadio Hearn* (Boston: Houghton Mifflin Company, 1912)

JAPANESE GHOST STORIES

OF GHOSTS AND GOBLINS[1]

'A long time ago, in the days when Fox-women and goblins haunted this land, there came to the capital with her parents a samurai girl, so beautiful that all men who saw her fell enamored of her. And hundreds of young samurai desired and hoped to marry her, and made their desire known to her parents. For it has ever been the custom in Japan that marriages should be arranged by parents. But there are exceptions to all customs, and the case of this maiden was such an exception. Her parents declared that they intended to allow their daughter to choose her own husband, and that all who wished to win her would be free to woo her.

'Many men of high rank and of great wealth were admitted to the house as suitors; and each one courted her as he best knew how – with gifts, and with fair words, and with poems written in her honor, and with promises of eternal love. And to each one she spoke sweetly and hopefully; but she made strange conditions. For every suitor she obliged to bind himself by his word of honor as a samurai to submit to a test of his love for her, and never to divulge to living person what that test might be. And to this all agreed.

'But even the most confident suitors suddenly ceased their importunities after having been put to the test; and all of them appeared to have been greatly terrified by something. Indeed, not a few even fled away from the city, and could not be persuaded by their friends to return. But no one ever so much as hinted why. Therefore it was whispered by those who knew nothing of the mystery, that the beautiful girl must be either a Fox-woman or a goblin.

'Now, when all the wooers of high rank had abandoned their suit, there came a samurai who had no wealth but his sword. He was a good man and true, and of pleasing presence; and the girl seemed to like him. But she made him take the same pledge which the others had taken; and after he had taken it, she told him to return upon a certain evening.

'When that evening came, he was received at the house by none but the girl herself. With her own hands she set before him the repast of hospitality, and waited upon him, after which she told him that she wished him to go out with her at a late hour. To this he consented gladly, and inquired to what place she desired to go. But she replied nothing to his question, and all at once became very silent, and strange in her manner. And after a while she retired from the apartment, leaving him alone.

'Only long after midnight she returned, robed all in white – like a Soul – and, without uttering a word, signed to him to follow her. Out of the house they hastened while all the city slept. It was what is called an *oborozuki-yo* – "moon-clouded night". Always upon such a night, 'tis said, do ghosts wander. She swiftly led the way; and the dogs howled as she flitted by; and she passed beyond the confines of the city to a place of knolls shadowed by enormous trees, where an ancient cemetery was. Into it she glided – a white shadow into blackness. He followed, wondering, his hand upon his sword. Then his eyes became accustomed to the gloom; and he saw.

'By a new-made grave she paused and signed to him to wait. The tools of the grave-maker were still lying there. Seizing one, she began to dig furiously, with strange haste and strength. At last her spade smote a coffin-lid and made it boom: another moment and the fresh white wood of the *kwan*[2] was bare. She tore off the lid, revealing a corpse within – the corpse of a child. With goblin gestures she wrung an arm from the body, wrenched it in twain, and, squatting down, began to devour the upper half. Then, flinging to her lover the other half, she cried to him, *"Eat, if thou lovest me! this is what I eat!"*

'Not even for a single instant did he hesitate. He squatted down upon the other side of the grave, and ate the half of the arm, and said, *"Kekkō degozarimasu! mo sukoshi chōdai."** For that arm was made of the best *kwashi*† that Saikyō could produce.

---

* 'It is excellent: I pray you give me a little more.'
† *Kwashi*: Japanese confectionery.

'Then the girl sprang to her feet with a burst of laughter, and cried: "You only, of all my brave suitors, did not run away! And I wanted a husband who could not fear. I will marry you; I can love you: you are *a man!*"'[3]

'O Kinjurō,' I said, as we took our way home, 'I have heard and I have read many Japanese stories of the returning of the dead. Likewise you yourself have told me it is still believed the dead return, and why. But according both to that which I have read and that which you have told me, the coming back of the dead is never a thing to be desired. They return because of hate, or because of envy, or because they cannot rest for sorrow. But of any who return for that which is not evil – where is it written? Surely the common history of them is like that which we have this night seen: much that is horrible and much that is wicked and nothing of that which is beautiful or true.'

Now this I said that I might tempt him. And he made even the answer I desired, by uttering the story which is hereafter set down:

'Long ago, in the days of a *daimyō*[4] whose name has been forgotten, there lived in this old city a young man and a maid who loved each other very much. Their names are not remembered, but their story remains. From infancy they had been betrothed; and as children they played together, for their parents were neighbors. And as they grew up, they became always fonder of each other.

'Before the youth had become a man, his parents died. But he was able to enter the service of a rich samurai, an officer of high rank, who had been a friend of his people. And his protector soon took him into great favor, seeing him to be courteous, intelligent, and apt at arms. So the young man hoped to find himself shortly in a position that would make it possible for him to marry his betrothed. But war broke out in the north and east; and he was summoned suddenly to follow his master to the field. Before departing, however, he was able to see the girl; and they exchanged pledges in the presence of her parents; and he promised, should he remain alive, to return within a year from that day to marry his betrothed.

'After his going much time passed without news of him, for there was no post in that time as now; and the girl grieved so much for thinking of the chances of war that she became all white and thin and weak. Then at last she heard of him through a messenger sent from the army to bear news to the *daimyō*, and once again a letter was brought to her by another messenger. And thereafter there came no word. Long is a year to one who waits. And the year passed, and he did not return.

'Other seasons passed, and still he did not come; and she thought him dead; and she sickened and lay down, and died, and was buried. Then her old parents, who had no other child, grieved unspeakably, and came to hate their home for the lonesomeness of it. After a time they resolved to sell all they had, and to set out upon a *sengaji* – the great pilgrimage to the Thousand Temples of the Nichiren-Shū, which requires many years to perform. So they sold their small house with all that it contained, excepting the ancestral tablets, and the holy things which must never be sold, and the *ihai*[5] of their buried daughter, which were placed, according to the custom of those about to leave their native place, in the family temple. Now the family was of the Nichiren-Shū; and their temple was Myōkōji.

'They had been gone only four days when the young man who had been betrothed to their daughter returned to the city. He had attempted, with the permission of his master, to fulfil his promise. But the provinces upon his way were full of war, and the roads and passes were guarded by troops, and he had been long delayed by many difficulties. And when he heard of his misfortune he sickened for grief, and many days remained without knowledge of anything, like one about to die.

'But when he began to recover his strength, all the pain of memory came back again; and he regretted that he had not died. Then he resolved to kill himself upon the grave of his betrothed; and, as soon as he was able to go out unobserved, he took his sword and went to the cemetery where the girl was buried: it is a lonesome place – the cemetery of Myōkōji. There he found her tomb, and knelt before it, and prayed and wept, and whispered to her that which he was about to do. And suddenly he heard her voice cry to him: "*Anata!*"[6] and felt her hand upon his hand; and he turned, and saw her kneeling beside him, smiling, and beautiful as he remembered her, only a little pale. Then his heart leaped so that he could not speak for the wonder and the doubt and the joy of that moment. But she said: "Do not doubt: it is really I. I am not dead. It was all a mistake. I was buried, because my people thought me dead – buried too soon. And my own parents thought me dead, and went upon a pilgrimage. Yet you see, I am not dead – not a ghost. It is I: do not doubt it! And I have seen your heart, and that was worth all the waiting, and the pain . . . But now let us go away at once to another city, so that people may not know this thing and trouble us; for all still believe me dead."

'And they went away, no one observing them. And they went even to the village of Minobu, which is in the province of Kai. For there is a famous temple of the Nichiren-Shū in that place; and the girl had said: "I know that in the course of their pilgrimage my parents will surely visit Minobu: so that if we dwell there, they will find us, and we shall be all again together." And when they came to Minobu, she said: "Let us open a little shop." And they opened a little food-shop, on the wide way leading to the holy place; and there they sold cakes for children, and toys, and food for pilgrims. For two years they so lived and prospered; and there was a son born to them.

'Now when the child was a year and two months old, the parents of the wife came in the course of their pilgrimage to Minobu; and they stopped at the little shop to buy food. And seeing their daughter's betrothed, they cried out and wept and asked questions. Then he made them enter, and bowed down before them, and astonished them, saying: "Truly as I speak it, your daughter is not dead; and she is my wife; and we have a son. And she is even now within the farther room, lying down with the child. I pray you go in at once and gladden her, for her heart longs for the moment of seeing you again."

'So while he busied himself in making all things ready for their comfort, they entered the inner room very softly – the mother first.

'They found the child asleep; but the mother they did not find. She seemed to have gone out for a little while only: her pillow was still warm. They waited long for her: then they began to seek her. But never was she seen again.

'And they understood only when they found beneath the cover-ings which had covered the mother and child, something which they remembered having left years before in the temple of Myōkōji – a little mortuary tablet – the *ihai* of their buried daughter.'

I suppose I must have looked thoughtful after this tale; for the old man said:

'Perhaps the Master honorably thinks concerning the story that it is foolish?'

'Nay, Kinjurō, the story is in my heart.'

THE DREAM OF A SUMMER DAY

I

The hotel seemed to me a paradise, and the maids thereof celestial beings. This was because I had just fled away from one of the Open Ports, where I had ventured to seek comfort in a European hotel, supplied with all 'modern improvements'. To find myself at ease once more in a *yukata*,[1] seated upon cool, soft matting, waited upon by sweet-voiced girls, and surrounded by things of beauty, was therefore like a redemption from all the sorrows of the nineteenth century. Bamboo-shoots and lotus-bulbs were given me for breakfast, and a fan from heaven for a keepsake. The design upon that fan represented only the white rushing burst of one great wave on a beach, and sea-birds shooting in exultation through the blue overhead. But to behold it was worth all the trouble of the journey. It was a glory of light, a thunder of motion, a triumph of sea-wind – all in one. It made me want to shout when I looked at it.

Between the cedarn balcony pillars I could see the course of the pretty gray town following the shore-sweep – and yellow lazy junks asleep at anchor – and the opening of the bay between enormous green cliffs – and beyond it the blaze of summer to the horizon. In that horizon there were mountain shapes faint as old memories. And all things but the gray town, and the yellow junks, and the green cliffs, were blue.

Then a voice softly toned as a wind-bell began to tinkle words of courtesy into my reverie, and broke it; and I perceived that the mistress of the palace had come to thank me for the *chadai*,* and

---

* A little gift of money, always made to a hotel by the guest shortly after his arrival.

I prostrated myself before her. She was very young, and more than pleasant to look upon – like the moth maidens, like the butterfly-women, of Kunisada. And I thought at once of death; for the beautiful is sometimes a sorrow of anticipation.

She asked whither I honorably intended to go, that she might order a *kuruma*[2] for me.

And I made answer:

'To Kumamoto. But the name of your house I much wish to know, that I may always remember it.'

'My guest-rooms,' she said, 'are augustly insignificant, and my maidens honorably rude. But the house is called the House of Urashima. And now I go to order a *kuruma.*'

The music of her voice passed; and I felt enchantment falling all about me – like the thrilling of a ghostly web. For the name was the name of the story of a song that bewitches men.

II

Once you hear the story, you will never be able to forget it. Every summer when I find myself on the coast – especially of very soft, still days – it haunts me most persistently. There are many native versions of it which have been the inspiration for countless works of art. But the most impressive and the most ancient is found in the 'Manyefushifu',[3] a collection of poems dating from the fifth to the ninth century. From this ancient version the great scholar Aston[4] translated it into prose, and the great scholar Chamberlain[5] into both prose and verse. But for English readers I think the most charming form of it is Chamberlain's version written for children, in the 'Japanese Fairy-Tale Series' – because of the delicious colored pictures by native artists. With that little book before me, I shall try to tell the legend over again in my own words.

Fourteen hundred and sixteen years ago, the fisher-boy Urashima Tarō left the shore of Suminoyé in his boat.

Summer days were then as now – all drowsy and tender blue, with only some light, pure white clouds hanging over the mirror of the sea. Then, too, were the hills the same – far blue soft shapes melting into the blue sky. And the winds were lazy.

And presently the boy, also lazy, let his boat drift as he fished. It was a queer boat, unpainted and rudderless, of a shape you probably never saw. But still, after fourteen hundred years, there are such boats to be seen in front of the ancient fishing-hamlets of the coast of the Sea of Japan.

After long waiting, Urashima caught something, and drew it up to him. But he found it was only a tortoise.

Now a tortoise is sacred to the Dragon God of the Sea, and the period of its natural life is a thousand – some say ten thousand – years. So that to kill it is very wrong. The boy gently unfastened the creature from his line, and set it free, with a prayer to the gods.

But he caught nothing more. And the day was very warm; and sea and air and all things were very, very silent. And a great drowsiness grew upon him – and he slept in his drifting boat.

Then out of the dreaming of the sea rose up a beautiful girl – just as you can see her in the picture to Professor Chamberlain's 'Urashima' – robed in crimson and blue, with long black hair flowing down her back even to her feet, after the fashion of a prince's daughter fourteen hundred years ago.

Gliding over the waters she came, softly as air; and she stood above the sleeping boy in the boat, and woke him with a light touch, and said:

'Do not be surprised. My father, the Dragon King of the Sea, sent me to you, because of your kind heart. For to-day you set free a tortoise. And now we will go to my father's palace in the island where summer never dies; and I will be your flower-wife if you wish; and we shall live there happily forever.'

And Urashima wondered more and more as he looked upon her; for she was more beautiful than any human being, and he could not but love her. Then she took one oar, and he took another, and they rowed away together – just as you may still see, off the far western coast, wife and husband rowing together, when the fishing-boats flit into the evening gold.

They rowed away softly and swiftly over the silent blue water down into the south – till they came to the island where summer never dies – and to the palace of the Dragon King of the Sea.

[Here the text of the little book suddenly shrinks away as you read, and faint blue ripplings flood the page; and beyond them in a fairy horizon you can see the long low soft shore of the island, and peaked roofs rising through evergreen foliage – the roofs of the Sea God's palace – like the palace of the Mikado Yuriaku,[6] fourteen hundred and sixteen years ago.]

There strange servitors came to receive them in robes of ceremony – creatures of the Sea, who paid greeting to Urashima as the son-in-law of the Dragon King.

So the Sea God's daughter became the bride of Urashima; and it was a bridal of wondrous splendor; and in the Dragon Palace there was great rejoicing.

And each day for Urashima there were new wonders and new pleasures: wonders of the deepest deep brought up by the servants of the Ocean God; pleasures of that enchanted land where summer never dies. And so three years passed.

But in spite of all these things, the fisher-boy felt always a heaviness at his heart when he thought of his parents waiting alone. So that at last he prayed his bride to let him go home for a little while only, just to say one word to his father and mother – after which he would hasten back to her.

At these words she began to weep; and for a long time she continued to weep silently. Then she said to him: 'Since you wish to go, of course you must go. I fear your going very much; I fear we shall never see each other again. But I will give you a little box to take with you. It will help you to come back to me if you will do what I tell you. Do not open it. Above all things, do not open it – no matter what may happen! Because, if you open it, you will never be able to come back, and you will never see me again.'

Then she gave him a little lacquered box tied about with a silken cord. [And that box can be seen unto this day in the temple of Kanagawa, by the seashore; and the priests there also keep Urashima Tarō's fishing line, and some strange jewels which he brought back with him from the realm of the Dragon King.]

But Urashima comforted his bride, and promised her never, never to open the box – never even to loosen the silken string. Then he passed away through the summer light over the ever-sleeping sea; and the shape of the island where summer never dies faded behind him like a dream; and he saw again before him the blue mountains of Japan, sharpening in the white glow of the northern horizon.

Again at last he glided into his native bay; again he stood upon its beach. But as he looked, there came upon him a great bewilderment – a weird doubt.

For the place was at once the same, and yet not the same. The cottage of his fathers had disappeared. There was a village; but the shapes of the houses were all strange, and the trees were strange, and the fields, and even the faces of the people. Nearly all remembered landmarks were gone; the Shintō temple appeared to have been rebuilt in a new place; the woods had vanished from the neighboring slopes. Only the voice of the little stream flowing through the settlement, and the forms of the mountains, were still the same. All else was unfamiliar and new. In vain he tried to find the dwelling of his parents; and the fisherfolk stared wonderingly at him; and he could not remember having ever seen any of those faces before.

There came along a very old man, leaning on a stick, and Urashima asked him the way to the house of the Urashima family. But the old man looked quite astonished, and made him repeat the question many times, and then cried out:

'Urashima Tarō! Where do you come from that you do not know the story? Urashima Tarō! Why, it is more than four hundred years since he was drowned, and a monument is erected to his memory in the graveyard. The graves of all his people are in that graveyard – the old graveyard which is not now used any more. Urashima Tarō! How can you be so foolish as to ask where his house is?' And the old man hobbled on, laughing at the simplicity of his questioner.

But Urashima went to the village graveyard – the old graveyard that was not used any more – and there he found his own tombstone, and the tombstones of his father and his mother and his kindred, and the tombstones of many others he had known. So old they were, so moss-eaten, that it was very hard to read the names upon them.

Then he knew himself the victim of some strange illusion, and he took his way back to the beach – always carrying in his hand the box, the gift of the Sea God's daughter. But what was this illusion? And what could be in that box? Or might not that which was in the box be the cause of the illusion? Doubt mastered faith. Recklessly he broke the promise made to his beloved; he loosened the silken cord; he opened the box!

Instantly, without any sound, there burst from it a white cold spectral vapor that rose in air like a summer cloud, and began to drift away swiftly into the south, over the silent sea. There was nothing else in the box.

And Urashima then knew that he had destroyed his own happiness – that he could never again return to his beloved, the daughter of the Ocean King. So that he wept and cried out bitterly in his despair.

Yet for a moment only. In another, he himself was changed. An icy chill shot through all his blood; his teeth fell out; his face shriveled; his hair turned white as snow; his limbs withered; his strength ebbed; he sank down lifeless on the sand, crushed by the weight of four hundred winters.

Now in the official annals of the Emperors it is written that 'in the twenty-first year of the Mikado Yuriaku, the boy Urashima of Midzunoyé, in the district of Yosa, in the province of Tango, a descendant of the divinity Shimanemi, went to Elysium [Hōrai] in a fishing-boat.' After this there is no more news of Urashima during the reigns of thirty-one emperors and empresses – that is, from the fifth until the ninth century. And then the annals announce that 'in the second year of Tenchiyō, in the reign of the Mikado Go-Junwa,[7] the boy Urashima returned, and presently departed again, none knew whither.'*

III

The fairy mistress came back to tell me that everything was ready, and tried to lift my valise in her slender hands – which I

---

* See *The Classical Poetry of the Japanese*, by Professor Chamberlain, in Trübner's *Oriental Series*. According to Western chronology, Urashima went fishing in 477 A. D., and returned in 825.

prevented her from doing, because it was heavy. Then she laughed, but would not suffer that I should carry it myself, and summoned a sea-creature with Chinese characters upon his back. I made obeisance to her; and she prayed me to remember the unworthy house despite the rudeness of the maidens. 'And you will pay the *kurumaya*,'[8] she said, 'only seventy-five sen.'[9]

Then I slipped into the vehicle; and in a few minutes the little gray town had vanished behind a curve. I was rolling along a white road overlooking the shore. To the right were pale brown cliffs; to the left only space and sea.

Mile after mile I rolled along that shore, looking into the infinite light. All was steeped in blue – a marvelous blue, like that which comes and goes in the heart of a great shell. Glowing blue sea met hollow blue sky in a brightness of electric fusion; and vast blue apparitions – the mountains of Higo – angled up through the blaze, like masses of amethyst. What a blue transparency! The universal color was broken only by the dazzling white of a few high summer clouds, motionlessly curled above one phantom peak in the offing. They threw down upon the water snowy tremulous lights. Midges of ships creeping far away seemed to pull long threads after them – the only sharp lines in all that hazy glory. But what divine clouds! White purified spirits of clouds, resting on their way to the beatitude of Nirvana? Or perhaps the mists escaped from Urashima's box a thousand years ago?

The gnat of the soul of me flitted out into that dream of blue, 'twixt sea and sun – hummed back to the shore of Suminoyé through the luminous ghosts of fourteen hundred summers. Vaguely I felt beneath me the drifting of a keel. It was the time of the Mikado Yuriaku. And the Daughter of the Dragon King said tinklingly, 'Now we will go to my father's palace where it is always blue.' 'Why always blue?' I asked. 'Because,' she said, 'I put all the clouds into the Box.' 'But I must go home,' I answered resolutely. 'Then,' she said, 'you will pay the *kurumaya* only seventy-five sen.'

Wherewith I woke into Doyō, or the Period of Greatest Heat, in the twenty-sixth year of Meiji[11] – and saw proof of the era in a line of telegraph poles reaching out of sight on the land side of the way. The *kuruma* was still fleeing by the shore, before the same blue vision of sky, peak, and sea; but the white clouds were gone! – and there were no more cliffs close to the road, but fields of rice and of barley stretching to far-off hills. The telegraph lines absorbed my attention for a moment, because on the top wire, and only on the top wire, hosts of little birds were perched, all with their heads to the road, and nowise disturbed by our coming. They remained quite still, looking down upon us as mere passing phenomena. There were hundreds and hundreds in rank, for miles and miles. And I could not see one having its tail turned to the road. Why they sat thus, and what they were watching or waiting for, I could not guess. At intervals I waved my hat and shouted, to startle the ranks. Whereupon a few would rise up fluttering and chippering, and drop back again upon the wire in the same position as before. The vast majority refused to take me seriously.

The sharp rattle of the wheels was drowned by a deep booming; and as we whirled past a village I caught sight of an immense drum under an open shed, beaten by naked men.

'O *kurumaya*!' I shouted – 'that – what is it?'

He, without stopping, shouted back:

'Everywhere now the same thing is. Much time-in rain has not been: so the gods-to prayers are made, and drums are beaten.'

We flashed through other villages; and I saw and heard more drums of various sizes, and from hamlets invisible, over miles of parching rice-fields, yet other drums, like echoings, responded.

IV

Then I began to think about Urashima again. I thought of the pictures and poems and proverbs recording the influence of the legend upon the imagination of a race. I thought of an Izumo dancing-girl I saw at a banquet acting the part of Urashima, with a little lacquered box whence there issued at the tragical minute a mist of Kyōto incense. I thought about the antiquity of the beautiful dance – and therefore about vanished generations of dancing-girls – and therefore about dust in the abstract; which, again, led me to think of dust in the concrete, as bestirred by the sandals of the *kurumaya* to whom I was to pay only seventy-five sen. And I wondered how much of it might be old human dust, and whether in the eternal order of things the motion of hearts might be of more consequence than the motion of dust. Then my ancestral morality took alarm; and I tried to persuade myself that a story which had lived for a thousand years, gaining fresher charm with the passing of every century, could only have survived by virtue of some truth in it. But what truth? For the time being I could find no answer to this question.

The heat had become very great; and I cried,
'O *kurumaya*! the throat of Selfishness is dry; water desirable is.'
He, still running, answered:
'The Village of the Long Beach inside of – not far – a great gush-water is. There pure august water will be given.'
I cried again:
'O *kurumaya*! – those little birds as-for, why this way always facing?'
He, running still more swiftly, responded:
'All birds wind-to facing sit.'
I laughed first at my own simplicity; then at my forgetfulness – remembering I had been told the same thing, somewhere or other, when a boy. Perhaps the mystery of Urashima might also have been created by forgetfulness.

I thought again about Urashima. I saw the Daughter of the Dragon King waiting vainly in the palace made beautiful for his welcome – and the pitiless return of the Cloud, announcing what had happened – and the loving uncouth sea-creatures, in their garments of great ceremony, trying to comfort her. But in the real story there was nothing of all this; and the pity of the people seemed to be all for Urashima. And I began to discourse with myself thus:

Is it right to pity Urashima at all? Of course he was bewildered by the gods. But who is not bewildered by the gods? What is Life itself but a bewilderment? And Urashima in his bewilderment doubted the purpose of the gods, and opened the box. Then he died without any trouble, and the people built a shrine to him as Urashima Miō-jin.[12] Why, then, so much pity?

Things are quite differently managed in the West. After disobeying Western gods, we have still to remain alive and to learn the height and the breadth and the depth of superlative sorrow. We are not allowed to die quite comfortably just at the best possible time: much less are we suffered to become after death small gods in our own right. How can we pity the folly of Urashima after he had lived so long alone with visible gods.

Perhaps the fact that we do may answer the riddle. This pity must be self-pity; wherefore the legend may be the legend of a myriad souls. The thought of it comes just at a particular time of blue light and soft wind – and always like an old reproach. It has too intimate relation to a season and the feeling of a season not to be also related to something real in one's life, or in the lives of one's ancestors. But what was that real something? Who was the Daughter of the Dragon King? Where was the island of unending summer? And what was the cloud in the box?

I cannot answer all those questions. I know this only – which is not at all new:

I have memory of a place and a magical time in which the Sun and the Moon were larger and brighter than now. Whether it was of this life or of some life before I cannot tell. But I know the sky was very much more blue, and nearer to the world – almost as it seems to become above the masts of a steamer steaming into equatorial summer. The sea was alive, and used to talk – and the Wind made me cry out for joy when it touched me. Once or twice during other years, in divine days lived among the peaks, I have dreamed just for a moment that the same wind was blowing – but it was only a remembrance.

Also in that place the clouds were wonderful, and of colors for which there are no names at all – colors that used to make me hungry and thirsty. I remember, too, that the days were ever so much longer than these days – and that every day there were new wonders and new pleasures for me. And all that country and time were softly ruled by One who thought only of ways to make me happy. Sometimes I would refuse to be made happy, and that always caused her pain, although she was divine; and I remember that I tried very hard to be sorry. When day was done, and there fell the great hush of the light before moonrise, she would tell me stories that made me tingle from head to foot with pleasure. I have never heard any other stories half so beautiful. And when the pleasure became too great, she would sing a weird little song which always brought sleep. At last there came a parting day; and she wept, and told me of a charm she had given that I must never, never lose, because it would keep me young, and give me power to return. But I never returned. And the years went; and one day I knew that I had lost the charm, and had become ridiculously old.

V

The Village of the Long Beach is at the foot of a green cliff near the road, and consists of a dozen thatched cottages clustered about a rocky pool, shaded by pines. The basin overflows with cold water, supplied by a stream that leaps straight from the heart of the cliff – just as folks imagine that a poem ought to spring straight from the heart of a poet. It was evidently a favorite halting-place, judging by the number of *kuruma* and of people resting. There were benches under the trees; and, after having allayed thirst, I sat down to smoke and to look at the women washing clothes and the travelers refreshing themselves at the pool – while my *kurumaya* stripped, and proceeded to dash buckets of cold water over his body. Then tea was brought me by a young man with a baby on his back; and I tried to play with the baby, which said 'Ah, bah!'

Such are the first sounds uttered by a Japanese babe. But they are purely Oriental; and in Romaji[13] should be written *Aba*. And, as an utterance untaught, *Aba* is interesting. It is in Japanese child-speech the word for 'good-by' – precisely the last we would expect an infant to pronounce on entering into this world of illusion. To whom or to what is the little soul saying good-by? – to friends in a previous state of existence still freshly remembered? – to comrades of its shadowy journey from nobody-knows-where? Such theorizing is tolerably safe, from a pious point of view, since the child can never decide for us. What its thoughts were at that mysterious moment of first speech, it will have forgotten long before it has become able to answer questions.

Unexpectedly, a queer recollection came to me – resurrected, perhaps, by the sight of the young man with the baby – perhaps by the song of the water in the cliff; the recollection of a story:

Long, long ago there lived somewhere among the mountains a poor wood-cutter and his wife. They were very old, and had no children. Every day the husband went alone to the forest to cut wood, while the wife sat weaving at home.

One day the old man went farther into the forest than was his custom, to seek a certain kind of wood; and he suddenly found himself at the edge of a little spring he had never seen before. The water was strangely clear and cold, and he was thirsty; for the day was hot, and he had been working hard. So he doffed his great straw hat, knelt down, and took a long drink. That water seemed to refresh him in a most extraordinary way. Then he caught sight of his own face in the spring, and started back. It was certainly his own face, but not at all as he was accustomed to see it in the old mirror at home. It was the face of a very young man! He could not believe his eyes. He put up both hands to his head, which had been quite bald only a moment before. It was covered with thick black hair. And his face had become smooth as a boy's; every wrinkle was gone. At the same moment he discovered himself full of new strength. He stared in astonishment at the limbs that had been so long withered by age; they were now shapely and hard with dense young muscle. Unknowingly he had drunk at the Fountain of Youth; and that draught had transformed him.

First, he leaped high and shouted for joy; then he ran home faster than he had ever run before in his life. When he entered his house his wife was frightened – because she took him for a stranger; and when he told her the wonder, she could not at once believe him. But after a long time he was able to convince her that the young man she now saw before her was really her husband;

and he told her where the spring was, and asked her to go there with him.

Then she said: 'You have become so handsome and so young that you cannot continue to love an old woman; so I must drink some of that water immediately. But it will never do for both of us to be away from the house at the same time. Do you wait here while I go.' And she ran to the woods all by herself.

She found the spring and knelt down, and began to drink. Oh! how cool and sweet that water was! She drank and drank and drank, and stopped for breath only to begin again.

Her husband waited for her impatiently; he expected to see her come back changed into a pretty slender girl. But she did not come back at all. He got anxious, shut up the house, and went to look for her.

When he reached the spring, he could not see her. He was just on the point of returning when he heard a little wail in the high grass near the spring. He searched there and discovered his wife's clothes and a baby – a very small baby, perhaps six months old!

For the old woman had drunk too deeply of the magical water; she had drunk herself far back beyond the time of youth into the period of speechless infancy.

He took up the child in his arms. It looked at him in a sad, wondering way. He carried it home – murmuring to it – thinking strange, melancholy thoughts.

In that hour, after my reverie about Urashima, the moral of this story seemed less satisfactory than in former time. Because by drinking too deeply of life we do not become young.

Naked and cool my *kurumaya* returned, and said that because of the heat he could not finish the promised run of twenty-five miles, but that he had found another runner to take me the rest of the way. For so much as he himself had done, he wanted fifty-five sen.

It was really very hot – more than 100° I afterwards learned; and far away there throbbed continually, like a pulsation of the heat itself, the sound of great drums beating for rain. And I thought of the Daughter of the Dragon King.

'Seventy-five sen, she told me,' I observed; 'and that promised to be done has not been done. Nevertheless, seventy-five sen to you shall be given – because I am afraid of the gods.'

And behind a yet unwearied runner I fled away into the enormous blaze – in the direction of the great drums.

IN CHOLERA-TIME

I

China's chief ally in the late war,[1] being deaf and blind, knew nothing, and still knows nothing, of treaties or of peace. It followed the returning armies of Japan, invaded the victorious empire, and killed about thirty thousand people during the hot season. It is still slaying; and the funeral pyres burn continually. Sometimes the smoke and the odor come wind-blown into my garden down from the hills behind the town, just to remind me that the cost of burning an adult of my own size is eighty sen – about half a dollar in American money at the present rate of exchange.

From the upper balcony of my house, the whole length of a Japanese street, with its rows of little shops, is visible down to the bay. Out of various houses in that street I have seen cholera-patients conveyed to the hospital – the last one (only this morning) my neighbor across the way, who kept a porcelain shop. He was removed by force, in spite of the tears and cries of his family. The sanitary law forbids the treatment of cholera in private houses; yet people try to hide their sick, in spite of fines and other penalties, because the public cholera-hospitals are overcrowded and roughly managed, and the patients are entirely separated from all who love them. But the police are not often deceived: they soon discover unreported cases, and come with litters and coolies. It seems cruel; but sanitary law must be cruel. My neighbor's wife followed the litter, crying, until the police obliged her to return to her desolate little shop. It is now closed up, and will probably never be opened again by the owners.

Such tragedies end as quickly as they begin. The bereaved, so soon as the law allows, remove their pathetic belongings, and disappear; and the ordinary life of the street goes on, by day and by night, exactly as if nothing particular had happened. Itinerant venders, with their bamboo poles and baskets or buckets or boxes, pass the empty houses, and utter their accustomed cries; religious processions go by, chanting fragments of sutras; the blind shampooer blows his melancholy whistle; the private watchman makes his heavy staff boom upon the gutter-flags; the boy who sells confectionery still taps his drum, and sings a love-song with a plaintive sweet voice, like a girl's:

> 'You and I together . . . I remained long; yet in the moment of going I thought I had only just come.
> 'You and I together . . . Still I think of the tea. Old or new tea of Uji it might have seemed to others; but to me it was Gyokorō tea, of the beautiful yellow of the yamabuki flower.
> 'You and I together . . . I am the telegraph-operator; you are the one who waits the message. I send my heart, and you receive it. What care we now if the posts should fall, if the wires be broken?'

And the children sport as usual. They chase one another with screams and laughter; they dance in chorus; they catch dragon-flies and tie them to long strings; they sing burdens of the war, about cutting off Chinese heads:

> 'Chan-chan bozu no
> Kubi wo hane!'[2]

Sometimes a child vanishes; but the survivors continue their play. And this is wisdom.

It costs only forty-four sen to burn a child. The son of one of my neighbors was burned a few days ago. The little stones with which he used to play lie there in the sun just as he left them . . . Curious, this child-love of stones! Stones are the toys not only of the children of the poor, but of all children at one period of existence: no matter how well supplied with other playthings, every Japanese child wants sometimes to play with stones. To the child-mind a stone is a marvelous thing, and ought so to be, since even to the understanding of the mathematician there can be nothing more wonderful than a common stone. The tiny urchin suspects the stone to be much more than it seems, which is an excellent suspicion; and if stupid grown-up folk did not untruthfully tell him that his plaything is not worth thinking about, he would never tire of it, and would always be finding something new and extraordinary in it. Only a very great mind could answer all a child's questions about stones.

According to popular faith, my neighbor's darling is now playing with small ghostly stones in the Dry Bed of the River of Souls – wondering, perhaps, why they cast no shadows. The true poetry in the legend of the Sai-no-Kawara[3] is the absolute naturalness of its principal idea – the phantom-continuation of that play which all little Japanese children play with stones.

II

The pipe-stem seller used to make his round with two large boxes suspended from a bamboo pole balanced upon his shoulder: one box containing stems of various diameters, lengths, and colors, together with tools for fitting them into metal pipes; and the other box containing a baby – his own baby. Sometimes I saw it peeping over the edge of the box, and smiling at the passers-by; sometimes I saw it lying, well wrapped up and fast asleep, in the bottom of the box; sometimes I saw it playing with toys. Many people, I was told, used to give it toys. One of the toys bore a curious resemblance to a mortuary tablet (*ihai*); and this I always observed in the box, whether the child were asleep or awake.

The other day I discovered that the pipe-stem seller had abandoned his bamboo pole and suspended boxes. He was coming up the street with a little hand-cart just big enough to hold his wares and his baby, and evidently built for that purpose in two compartments. Perhaps the baby had become too heavy for the more primitive method of conveyance. Above the cart fluttered a small white flag, bearing in cursive characters the legend *Ki-seru-rao kae* (pipe-stems exchanged), and a brief petition for 'honorable help',

O-tasuké wo negaimasu. The child seemed well and happy; and I again saw the tablet-shaped object which had so often attracted my notice before. It was now fastened upright to a high box in the cart facing the infant's bed. As I watched the cart approaching, I suddenly felt convinced that the tablet was really an *ihai*: the sun shone full upon it, and there was no mistaking the conventional Buddhist text. This aroused my curiosity; and I asked Manyemon⁴ to tell the pipe-stem seller that we had a number of pipes needing fresh stems – which was true. Presently the cartlet drew up at our gate, and I went to look at it.

The child was not afraid, even of a foreign face – a pretty boy. He lisped and laughed and held out his arms, being evidently used to petting; and while playing with him I looked closely at the tablet. It was a Shinshū *ihai*, bearing a woman's *kaimyō*, or posthumous name; and Manyemon translated the Chinese characters for me: *Revered and of good rank in the Mansion of Excellence, the thirty-first day of the third month of the twenty-eighth year of Meiji.*⁵ Meantime a servant had fetched the pipes which needed new stems; and I glanced at the face of the artisan as he worked. It was the face of a man past middle age, with those worn, sympathetic lines about the mouth, dry beds of old smiles, which give to so many Japanese faces an indescribable expression of resigned gentleness. Presently Manyemon began to ask questions; and when Manyemon asks questions, not to reply is possible for the wicked only. Sometimes behind that dear innocent old head I think I see the dawning of an aureole – the aureole of the Bosatsu.⁶

The pipe-stem seller answered by telling his story. Two months after the birth of their little boy, his wife had died. In the last hour of her illness she had said: 'From what time I die till three full years be past I pray you to leave the child always united with the Shadow of me: never let him be separated from my *ihai*, so that I may continue to care for him and to nurse him – since thou knowest that he should have the breast for three years. This, my last asking, I entreat thee, do not forget.' But the mother being dead, the father could not labor as he had been wont to do, and also take care of so young a child, requiring continual attention both night and day; and he was too poor to hire a nurse. So he took to selling pipe-stems, as he could thus make a little money without leaving the child even for a minute alone. He could not afford to buy milk; but he had fed the boy for more than a year with rice gruel and *amé* syrup.[7]

I said that the child looked very strong, and none the worse for lack of milk.

'That,' declared Manyemon, in a tone of conviction bordering on reproof, 'is because the dead mother nurses him. How should he want for milk?'

And the boy laughed softly, as if conscious of a ghostly caress.

NINGYŌ-NO-HAKA

Manyemon had coaxed the child indoors, and made her eat. She appeared to be about eleven years old, intelligent, and pathetically docile. Her name was Iné, which means 'springing rice'; and her frail slimness made the name seem appropriate.

When she began, under Manyemon's gentle persuasion, to tell her story, I anticipated something queer from the accompanying change in her voice. She spoke in a high thin sweet tone, perfectly even – a tone changeless and unemotional as the chanting of the little kettle over its charcoal bed. Not unfrequently in Japan one may hear a girl or a woman utter something touching or cruel or terrible in just such a steady, level, penetrating tone, but never anything indifferent. It always means that feeling is being kept under control.

'There were six of us at home,' said Iné – 'mother and father and father's mother, who was very old, and my brother and myself, and a little sister. Father was a *hyōguya*, a paper-hanger: he papered sliding-screens and also mounted *kakémono*.[1] Mother was a hairdresser. My brother was apprenticed to a seal-cutter.

'Father and mother did well: mother made even more money than father. We had good clothes and good food; and we never had any real sorrow until father fell sick.

'It was the middle of the hot season. Father had always been healthy: we did not think that his sickness was dangerous, and he did not think so himself. But the very next day he died. We were very much surprised. Mother tried to hide her heart, and to wait upon her customers as before. But she was not very strong, and the pain of father's death came too quickly. Eight days after father's funeral mother also died. It was so sudden that everybody wondered. Then the neighbors told us that we must make a *ningyō-no-haka* at once – or else there would be another death in our house. My brother said they were right; but he put off doing what they told him. Perhaps he did not have money enough, I do not know; but the *haka* was not made.' . . .

'What is a *ningyō-no-haka*?' I interrupted.

'I think,' Manyemon made answer, 'that you have seen many *ningyō-no-haka* without knowing what they were; they look just like graves of children. It is believed that when two of a family die in the same year, a third also must soon die. There is a saying, *Always three graves*. So when two out of one family have been buried in the same year, a third grave is made next to the graves of those two, and in it is put a coffin containing only a little figure of straw – *wara-ningyō*; and over that grave a small tombstone is set up, bearing a *kaimyō*.* The priests of the temple to which the graveyard belongs write the *kaimyō* for these little gravestones. By making a *ningyō-no-haka* it is thought that a death may be prevented . . . We listen for the rest, Iné.'

The child resumed:

'There were still four of us – grandmother, brother, myself, and my little sister. My brother was nineteen years old. He had finished his apprenticeship just before father died: we thought that was like the pity of the gods for us. He had become the head of the house. He was very skillful in his business, and had many friends: therefore he could maintain us. He made thirteen yen the first month; that is very good for a seal-cutter. One evening he came home sick: he said that his head hurt him. Mother had then been dead forty-seven days. That evening he could not eat. Next morning he was not able to get up; he had a very hot fever: we nursed him as well as we could, and sat up at night to watch by him; but he did not get better. On the morning of the third day of his sickness we became frightened – because he began to talk to mother. It was the forty-ninth day after mother's death – the day the Soul

---

* The posthumous Buddhist name of the person buried is chiseled upon the tomb or *haka*.

leaves the house; and brother spoke as if mother was calling him: "Yes, mother, yes! – in a little while I shall come!" Then he told us that mother was pulling him by the sleeve. He would point with his hand and call to us: "There she is! – there! – do you not see her?" We would tell him that we could not see anything. Then he would say, "Ah! you did not look quick enough: she is hiding now; she has gone down under the floor-mats." All the morning he talked like that. At last grandmother stood up, and stamped her foot on the floor, and reproached mother – speaking very loud. "Taka!" she said, "Taka, what you do is very wrong. When you were alive we all loved you. None of us ever spoke unkind words to you. Why do you now want to take the boy? You know that he is the only pillar of our house. You know that if you take him there will not be any one to care for the ancestors. You know that if you take him, you will destroy the family name! O Taka, it is cruel! it is shameful! it is wicked!" Grandmother was so angry that all her body trembled. Then she sat down and cried; and I and my little sister cried. But our brother said that mother was still pulling him by the sleeve. When the sun went down, he died.

'Grandmother wept, and stroked us, and sang a little song that she made herself. I can remember it still:

> *Oya no nai ko to*
> *Hamabé no chidori:*
> *Higuré-higuré ni*
> *Sodé shiboru.**

So the third grave was made – but it was not a *ningyō-no-haka*; and that was the end of our house. We lived with kindred until winter, when grandmother died. She died in the night – when, nobody knew: in the morning she seemed to be sleeping, but she

* 'Children without parents, like the seagulls of the coast. Evening after evening the sleeves are wrung.' The word *chidori* – indiscriminately applied to many kinds of birds – is here used for seagull. The cries of the seagull are thought to express melancholy and desolation: hence the comparison. The long sleeve of the Japanese robe is used to wipe the eyes as well as to hide the face in moments of grief. To 'wring the sleeve' – that is, to wring the moisture from a tear-drenched sleeve – is a frequent expression in Japanese poetry.

was dead. Then I and my little sister were separated. My sister was adopted by a *tatamiya*, a mat-maker – one of father's friends. She is kindly treated: she even goes to school!'

'*Aa fushigi na koto da! – aa komatta ne?*'[2] murmured Manyemon. Then there was a moment or two of sympathetic silence. Iné prostrated herself in thanks, and rose to depart. As she slipped her feet under the thongs of her sandals, I moved toward the spot where she had been sitting, to ask the old man a question. She perceived my intention, and immediately made an indescribable sign to Manyemon, who responded by checking me just as I was going to sit down beside him.

'She wishes,' he said, 'that the master will honorably strike the matting first.'

'But why?' I asked in surprise – noticing only that under my unshod feet, the spot where the child had been kneeling felt comfortably warm.

Manyemon answered:

'She believes that to sit down upon the place made warm by the body of another is to take into one's own life all the sorrow of that other person – unless the place be stricken first.'

Whereat I sat down without performing the rite; and we both laughed.

'Iné,' said Manyemon, 'the master takes your sorrows upon him. He wants – (I cannot venture to render Manyemon's honorifics) – 'to understand the pain of other people. You need not fear for him, Iné.'

THE ETERNAL HAUNTER

This year the Tōkyō color-prints – *Nishiki-é* – seem to me of unusual interest. They reproduce, or almost reproduce, the color-charm of the early broadsides; and they show a marked improvement in line-drawing. Certainly one could not wish for anything prettier than the best prints of the present season.

My latest purchase has been a set of weird studies – spectres of all kinds known to the Far East, including many varieties not yet discovered in the West. Some are extremely unpleasant; but a few are really charming. Here, for example, is a delicious thing by 'Chikanobu',[1] just published, and for sale at the remarkable price of three sen!

Can you guess what it represents? . . . Yes, a girl, but what kind of a girl? Study it a little . . . Very lovely, is she not, with that shy sweetness in her downcast gaze – that light and dainty grace, as of a resting butterfly? . . . No, she is not some Psyche[2] of the most Eastern East, in the sense that you mean – but she is a soul. Observe that the cherry-flowers falling from the branch above, are passing *through* her form. See also the folds of her robe, below, melting into blue faint mist. How delicate and vapory the whole thing is! It gives you the feeling of spring; and all those fairy colors are the colors of a Japanese spring-morning . . . No, she is not the personification of any season. Rather she is a dream – such a dream as might haunt the slumbers of Far-Eastern youth; but the artist did not intend her to represent a dream . . . You cannot guess? Well, she is a tree-spirit – the Spirit of the Cherry-tree. Only in the twilight of morning or of evening she appears, gliding about her tree; and whoever sees her must love her. But, if approached, she vanishes back into the trunk, like a vapor absorbed. There is a legend of one tree-spirit who loved a man, and even gave him a son; but such conduct was quite at variance with the shy habits of her race . . .

You ask what is the use of drawing the Impossible? Your asking proves that you do not feel the charm of this vision of youth – this dream of spring. *I* hold that the Impossible bears a much closer relation to fact than does most of what we call the real and the commonplace. The Impossible may not be naked truth; but I think that it is usually truth – masked and veiled, perhaps, but eternal. Now to me this Japanese dream is true – true, at least, as human love is. Considered even as a ghost it is true. Whoever pretends not to believe in ghosts of any sort, lies to his own heart. Every man is haunted by ghosts. And this color-print reminds me of a ghost whom we all know – though most of us (poets excepted) are unwilling to confess the acquaintance.

Perhaps – for it happens to some of us – you may have seen this haunter, in dreams of the night, even during childhood. Then, of course, you could not know the beautiful shape bending above your rest: possibly you thought her to be an angel, or the soul of a dead sister. But in waking life we first become aware of her presence about the time when boyhood begins to ripen into youth.

This first of her apparitions is a shock of ecstasy, a breathless delight; but the wonder and the pleasure are quickly followed by a sense of sadness inexpressible – totally unlike any sadness ever felt before – though in her gaze there is only caress, and on her lips the most exquisite of smiles. And you cannot imagine the reason of that feeling until you have learned who she is – which is not an easy thing to learn.

Only a moment she remains; but during that luminous moment all the tides of your being set and surge to her with a longing for which there is not any word. And then – suddenly! – she is not; and you find that the sun has gloomed, the colors of the world turned grey.

Thereafter enchantment remains between you and all that you loved before – persons or things or places. None of them will ever seem again so near and dear as in other days.

Often she will return. Once that you have seen her she will never cease to visit you. And this haunting – ineffably sweet, inexplicably sad – may fill you with rash desire to wander over the world in search of somebody like her. But however long and far you wander, never will you find that somebody.

Later you may learn to fear her visits because of the pain they bring – the strange pain that you cannot understand. But the breadth of zones and seas cannot divide you from her; walls of iron cannot exclude her. Soundless and subtle as a shudder of ether is the motion of her.

Ancient her beauty as the heart of man – yet ever waxing fairer, forever remaining young. Mortals wither in Time as leaves in the frost of autumn; but Time only brightens the glow and the bloom of her endless youth.

All men have loved her; all must continue to love her. But none shall touch with his lips even the hem of her garment.

All men adore her; yet all she deceives, and many are the ways of her deception. Most often she lures her lover into the presence of some earthly maid, and blends herself incomprehensibly with the body of that maid, and works such sudden glamour that the human gaze becomes divine – that the human limbs shine through their raiment. But presently the luminous haunter detaches herself from the mortal, and leaves her dupe to wonder at the mockery of sense.

No man can describe her, though nearly all men have some time tried to do so. Pictured she cannot be – since her beauty itself is a ceaseless becoming, multiple to infinitude, and tremulous with perpetual quickening, as with flowing of light.

There is a story, indeed, that thousands of years ago some marvellous sculptor was able to fix in stone a single remembrance of her. But this doing became for many the cause of sorrow supreme; and the Gods decreed, out of compassion, that to no other mortal should ever be given power to work the like wonder. In these years we can worship only; we cannot portray.

But who is she? – what is she? ... Ah! that is what I wanted you to ask. Well, she has never had a name; but I shall call her a tree-spirit.

The Japanese say that you can exorcise a tree-spirit – if you are cruel enough to do it – simply by cutting down her tree.

But you cannot exorcise the Spirit of whom I speak – nor ever cut down her tree.

For her tree is the measureless, timeless, billion-branching Tree of Life – even the World-Tree, Yggdrasil,[3] whose roots are in Night and Death, whose head is above the Gods.

Seek to woo her – she is Echo.[4] Seek to clasp her – she is Shadow. But her smile will haunt you into the hour of dissolution and beyond – through numberless lives to come.

And never will you return her smile – never, because of that which it awakens within you – the pain that you cannot understand.

And never, never shall you win to her – because she is the phantom light of long-expired suns – because she was shaped by the beating of infinite millions of hearts that are dust – because her witchery was made in the endless ebb and flow of the visions and hopes of youth, through countless forgotten cycles of your own incalculable past.

FRAGMENT

And it was at the hour of sunset that they came to the foot of the mountain. There was in that place no sign of life – neither token of water, nor trace of plant, nor shadow of flying bird – nothing but desolation rising to desolation. And the summit was lost in heaven.

Then the Bodhisattva said to his young companion: 'What you have asked to see will be shown to you. But the place of the Vision is far; and the way is rude. Follow after me, and do not fear: strength will be given you.'

Twilight gloomed about them as they climbed. There was no beaten path, nor any mark of former human visitation; and the way was over an endless heaping of tumbled fragments that rolled or turned beneath the foot. Sometimes a mass dislodged would clatter down with hollow echoings; sometimes the substance trodden would burst like an empty shell ... Stars pointed and thrilled; and the darkness deepened.

'Do not fear, my son,' said the Bodhisattva, guiding: 'danger there is none, though the way be grim.'

Under the stars they climbed – fast, fast – mounting by help of power superhuman. High zones of mist they passed; and they saw below them, ever widening as they climbed, a soundless flood of cloud, like the tide of a milky sea.

Hour after hour they climbed; and forms invisible yielded to their tread with dull soft crashings; and faint cold fires lighted and died at every breaking.

And once the pilgrim-youth laid hand on a something smooth

that was not stone – and lifted it – and dimly saw the cheekless gibe of death.

'Linger not thus, my son!' urged the voice of the teacher; 'the summit that we must gain is very far away!'

On through the dark they climbed – and felt continually beneath them the soft strange breakings – and saw the icy fires worm and die – till the rim of the night turned grey, and the stars began to fail, and the east began to bloom.

Yet still they climbed – fast, fast – mounting by help of power superhuman. About them now was frigidness of death – and silence tremendous . . . A gold flame kindled in the east.

Then first to the pilgrim's gaze the steeps revealed their nakedness; and a trembling seized him – and a ghastly fear. For there was not any ground – neither beneath him nor about him nor above him – but a heaping only, monstrous and measureless, of skulls and fragments of skulls and dust of bone – with a shimmer of shed teeth strown through the drift of it, like the shimmer of scrags of shell in the wrack of a tide.

'Do not fear, my son!' cried the voice of the Bodhisattva; 'only the strong of heart can win to the place of the Vision!'

Behind them the world had vanished. Nothing remained but the clouds beneath, and the sky above, and the heaping of skulls between – upslanting out of sight.

Then the sun climbed with the climbers; and there was no warmth in the light of him, but coldness sharp as a sword. And the horror of stupendous height, and the nightmare of stupendous depth, and the terror of silence, ever grew and grew, and weighed upon the pilgrim, and held his feet – so that suddenly all power departed from him, and he moaned like a sleeper in dreams.

'Hasten, hasten, my son!' cried the Bodhisattva: 'the day is brief, and the summit is very far away.'

But the pilgrim shrieked,

'I fear! I fear unspeakably! – and the power has departed from me!'

'The power will return, my son,' made answer the

Bodhisattva . . . 'Look now below you and above you and about you, and tell me what you see.'

'I cannot,' cried the pilgrim, trembling and clinging; 'I dare not look beneath! Before me and about me there is nothing but skulls of men.'

'And yet, my son,' said the Bodhisattva, laughing softly – 'and yet you do not know of what this mountain is made.'

The other, shuddering, repeated:

'I fear! – unutterably I fear! . . . there is nothing but skulls of men!'

'A mountain of skulls it is,' responded the Bodhisattva. 'But know, my son, that all of them ARE YOUR OWN! Each has at some time been the nest of your dreams and delusions and desires. Not even one of them is the skull of any other being. All – all without exception – have been yours, in the billions of your former lives.'

A PASSIONAL KARMA

One of the never-failing attractions of the Tōkyō stage is the performance, by the famous Kikugorō[1] and his company, of the *Botan-Dōrō*, or 'Peony-Lantern'.[2] This weird play, of which the scenes are laid in the middle of the last century, is the dramatization of a romance by the novelist Enchō,[3] written in colloquial Japanese, and purely Japanese in local color, though inspired by a Chinese tale. I went to see the play; and Kikugorō made me familiar with a new variety of the pleasure of fear.

'Why not give English readers the ghostly part of the story?' – asked a friend who guides me betimes through the mazes of Eastern philosophy. 'It would serve to explain some popular ideas of the supernatural which Western people know very little about. And I could help you with the translation.'

I gladly accepted the suggestion; and we composed the following summary of the more extraordinary portion of Enchō's romance. Here and there we found it necessary to condense the original narrative; and we tried to keep close to the text only in the conversational passages – some of which happen to possess a particular quality of psychological interest.

*   *   *

This is the story of the Ghosts in the Romance of the Peony-Lantern:

I

There once lived in the district of Ushigomé, in Yedo, a *hatamoto**
called Iijima Heizayémon, whose only daughter, Tsuyu, was beautiful as her name, which signifies 'Morning Dew'. Iijima took a second
wife when his daughter was about sixteen; and, finding that O-
Tsuyu[4] could not be happy with her mother-in-law [sic], he had a pretty
villa built for the girl at Yanagijima, as a separate residence, and gave
her an excellent maidservant, called O-Yoné, to wait upon her.

O-Tsuyu lived happily enough in her new home until one day
when the family physician, Yamamoto Shijō, paid her a visit in
company with a young samurai named Hagiwara Shinzaburō, who
resided in the Nedzu quarter. Shinzaburō was an unusually handsome lad, and very gentle; and the two young people fell in love
with each other at sight. Even before the brief visit was over, they
contrived – unheard by the old doctor – to pledge themselves to
each other for life. And, at parting, O-Tsuyu whispered to the youth,
'Remember! if you do not come to see me again, I shall certainly die!'

Shinzaburō never forgot those words; and he was only too eager to
see more of O-Tsuyu. But etiquette forbade him to make the visit
alone: he was obliged to wait for some other chance to accompany
the doctor, who had promised to take him to the villa a second
time. Unfortunately the old man did not keep this promise. He had
perceived the sudden affection of O-Tsuyu; and he feared that her
father would hold him responsible for any serious results. Iijima
Heizayémon had a reputation for cutting off heads. And the more
Shijō thought about the possible consequences of his introduction
of Shinzaburō at the Iijima villa, the more he became afraid. Therefore he purposely abstained from calling upon his young friend.

---

* The *hatamoto* were samurai forming the special military force of the Shōgun.
The name literally signifies 'Banner-Supporters'. These were the highest class of
samurai – not only as the immediate vassals of the Shōgun, but as a military
aristocracy.

Months passed; and O-Tsuyu, little imagining the true cause of Shinzaburō's neglect, believed that her love had been scorned. Then she pined away, and died. Soon afterwards, the faithful servant O-Yoné also died, through grief at the loss of her mistress; and the two were buried side by side in the cemetery of Shin-Banzui-In – a temple which still stands in the neighborhood of Dango-Zaka, where the famous chrysanthemum-shows are yearly held.

II

Shinzaburō knew nothing of what had happened; but his disappointment and his anxiety had resulted in a prolonged illness. He was slowly recovering, but still very weak, when he unexpectedly received another visit from Yamamoto Shijō. The old man made a number of plausible excuses for his apparent neglect. Shinzaburō said to him:

'I have been sick ever since the beginning of spring; even now I cannot eat anything . . . Was it not rather unkind of you never to call? I thought that we were to make another visit together to the house of the Lady Iijima; and I wanted to take to her some little present as a return for our kind reception. Of course I could not go by myself.'

Shijō gravely responded, 'I am very sorry to tell you that the young lady is dead.'

'Dead!' repeated Shinzaburō, turning white – 'did you say that she is dead?'

The doctor remained silent for a moment, as if collecting himself: then he resumed, in the quick light tone of a man resolved not to take trouble seriously:

'My great mistake was in having introduced you to her; for it seems that she fell in love with you at once. I am afraid that you must have said something to encourage this affection – when you were in that little room together. At all events, I saw how she felt towards you; and then I became uneasy – fearing that her father might come to hear of the matter, and lay the whole blame upon me. So – to be quite frank with you – I decided that it would be better not to call upon you; and I purposely stayed away for a long time. But, only a few days ago, happening to visit Iijima's house, I heard, to my great surprise, that his daughter had died, and that her servant O-Yoné had also died. Then, remembering all that had taken place, I knew that the young lady must have died of love for you . . . [*Laughing*] Ah, you are really a sinful fellow! Yes, you are! [*Laughing*] Isn't it a sin to have been born so handsome that the girls die for love of you?* . . . [*Seriously*] Well, we must leave the dead to the dead. It is no use to talk further about the matter; all that you now can do for her is to repeat the *Nembutsu*.† . . . Good-bye.'

And the old man retired hastily – anxious to avoid further converse about the painful event for which he felt himself to have been unwittingly responsible.

III

Shinzaburō long remained stupefied with grief by the news of O-Tsuyu's death. But as soon as he found himself again able to think clearly, he inscribed the dead girl's name upon a mortuary tablet, and placed the tablet in the Buddhist shrine of his house, and set offerings before it, and recited prayers. Every day thereafter he presented offerings, and repeated the *Nembutsu*; and the memory of O-Tsuyu was never absent from his thought.

Nothing occurred to change the monotony of his solitude before the time of the Bon – the great Festival of the Dead – which begins upon the thirteenth day of the seventh month. Then he decorated his house, and prepared everything for the festival; hanging out the lanterns that guide the returning spirits, and setting the food of ghosts on the *shōryōdana*, or Shelf of Souls. And on the first evening of the Bon, after sundown, he kindled a small lamp before the tablet of O-Tsuyu, and lighted the lanterns.

---

* Perhaps this conversation may seem strange to the Western reader; but it is true to life. The whole of the scene is characteristically Japanese.

† The invocation *Namu Amida Butsu!* ('Hail to the Buddha Amitâbha!'), repeated, as a prayer, for the sake of the dead.

The night was clear, with a great moon – and windless, and very warm. Shinzaburō sought the coolness of his veranda. Clad only in a light summer-robe, he sat there thinking, dreaming, sorrowing; sometimes fanning himself; sometimes making a little smoke to drive the mosquitoes away. Everything was quiet. It was a lonesome neighborhood, and there were few passers-by. He could hear only the soft rushing of a neighboring stream, and the shrilling of night-insects.

But all at once this stillness was broken by a sound of women's *geta** approaching – *kara-kon, kara-kon*; and the sound drew nearer and nearer, quickly, till it reached the live-hedge surrounding the garden. Then Shinzaburō, feeling curious, stood on tiptoe, so as to look over the hedge; and he saw two women passing. One, who was carrying a beautiful lantern decorated with peony-flowers,† appeared to be a servant; the other was a slender girl of about seventeen, wearing a long-sleeved robe embroidered with designs of autumn-blossoms. Almost at the same instant both women turned their faces toward Shinzaburō; and to his utter astonishment, he recognized O-Tsuyu and her servant O-Yoné.

They stopped immediately; and the girl cried out – 'Oh, how strange! . . . Hagiwara Sama!'5

Shinzaburō simultaneously called to the maid:

'O-Yoné! Ah, you are O-Yoné! – I remember you very well.'

'Hagiwara Sama!' exclaimed O-Yoné in a tone of supreme amazement. 'Never could I have believed it possible! . . . Sir, we were told that you had died.'

'How extraordinary!' cried Shinzaburō. 'Why, I was told that both of you were dead!'

---

* *Komageta* in the original. The *geta* is a wooden sandal, or clog, of which there are many varieties – some decidedly elegant. The *komageta*, or 'pony-geta' is so-called because of the sonorous hoof-like echo which it makes on hard ground.

† The sort of lantern here referred to is no longer made [. . .]. It was totally unlike the modern domestic hand-lantern, painted with the owner's crest; but it was not altogether unlike some forms of lanterns still manufactured for the Festival of the Dead, and called *Bon-dōrō*. The flowers ornamenting it were not painted: they were artificial flowers of crêpe-silk, and were attached to the top of the lantern.

'Ah, what a hateful story!' returned O-Yoné. 'Why repeat such unlucky words? . . . Who told you?'

'Please to come in,' said Shinzaburō; 'here we can talk better. The garden-gate is open.'

So they entered, and exchanged greeting; and when Shinzaburō had made them comfortable, he said:

'I trust that you will pardon my discourtesy in not having called upon you for so long a time. But Shijō, the doctor, about a month ago, told me that you had both died.'

'So it was he who told you?' exclaimed O-Yoné. 'It was very wicked of him to say such a thing. Well, it was also Shijō who told us that you were dead. I think that he wanted to deceive you – which was not a difficult thing to do, because you are so confiding and trustful. Possibly my mistress betrayed her liking for you in some words which found their way to her father's ears; and, in that case, O-Kuni – the new wife – might have planned to make the doctor tell you that we were dead, so as to bring about a separation. Anyhow, when my mistress heard that you had died, she wanted to cut off her hair immediately, and to become a nun. But I was able to prevent her from cutting off her hair; and I persuaded her at last to become a nun only in her heart. Afterwards her father wished her to marry a certain young man; and she refused. Then there was a great deal of trouble – chiefly caused by O-Kuni; and we went away from the villa, and found a very small house in Yanaka-no-Sasaki. There we are now just barely able to live, by doing a little private work . . . My mistress has been constantly repeating the *Nembutsu* for your sake. Today, being the first day of the Bon, we went to visit the temples; and we were on our way home – thus late – when this strange meeting happened.'

'Oh, how extraordinary!' cried Shinzaburō. 'Can it be true? – or is it only a dream? Here I, too, have been constantly reciting the *Nembutsu* before a tablet with her name upon it! Look!' And he showed them O-Tsuyu's tablet in its place upon the Shelf of Souls.

'We are more than grateful for your kind remembrance,' returned O-Yoné, smiling . . . 'Now as for my mistress' – she continued, turning towards O-Tsuyu, who had all the while remained demure and silent, half-hiding her face with her sleeve – 'as for my mistress, she actually says that she would not mind being disowned by her father for the time of seven existences,* or even being killed by him, for your sake! . . . Come! will you not allow her to stay here to-night?'

Shinzaburō turned pale for joy. He answered in a voice trembling with emotion:

'Please remain; but do not speak loud – because there is a troublesome fellow living close by – a *ninsomi*† called Hakuōdō Yusai, who tells people's fortunes by looking at their faces. He is inclined to be curious; and it is better that he should not know.'

The two women remained that night in the house of the young samurai, and returned to their own home a little before daybreak. And after that night they came every night for seven nights – whether the weather were foul or fair – always at the same hour. And Shinzaburō became more and more attached to the girl; and the twain were fettered, each to each, by that bond of illusion which is stronger than bands of iron.

IV

Now there was a man called Tomozō, who lived in a small cottage adjoining Shinzaburō's residence. Tomozō and his wife O-Miné were both employed by Shinzaburō as servants. Both seemed to be devoted to their young master; and by his help they were able to live in comparative comfort.

One night, at a very late hour, Tomozō heard the voice of a woman in his master's apartment; and this made him uneasy. He feared that Shinzaburō, being very gentle and affectionate, might

* 'For the time of seven existences' – that is to say, for the time of seven successive lives. In Japanese drama and romance it is not uncommon to represent a father as disowning his child 'for the time of seven lives'. Such a disowning is called *shichi-shō madé no mandō*, a disinheritance for seven lives – signifying that in six future lives after the present the erring son or daughter will continue to feel the parental displeasure.

† The profession is not yet extinct. The *ninsomi* uses a kind of magnifying glass (or magnifying-mirror sometimes), called *tengankyō* or *ninsomégané*.

be made the dupe of some cunning wanton – in which event the domestics would be the first to suffer. He therefore resolved to watch; and on the following night he stole on tiptoe to Shinzaburō's dwelling, and looked through a chink in one of the sliding shutters. By the glow of a night-lantern within the sleeping-room, he was able to perceive that his master and a strange woman were talking together under the mosquito-net. At first he could not see the woman distinctly. Her back was turned to him; he only observed that she was very slim, and that she appeared to be very young – judging from the fashion of her dress and hair.* Putting his ear to the chink, he could hear the conversation plainly. The woman said:

'And if I should be disowned by my father, would you then let me come and live with you?'

Shinzaburō answered:

'Most assuredly I would – nay, I should be glad of the chance. But there is no reason to fear that you will ever be disowned by your father; for you are his only daughter, and he loves you very much. What I do fear is that some day we shall be cruelly separated.'

She responded softly:

'Never, never could I even think of accepting any other man for my husband. Even if our secret were to become known, and my father were to kill me for what I have done, still – after death itself – I could never cease to think of you. And I am now quite sure that you yourself would not be able to live very long without me.' . . . Then clinging closely to him, with her lips at his neck, she caressed him; and he returned her caresses.

Tomozō wondered as he listened – because the language of the woman was not the language of a common woman, but the language of a lady of rank.† Then he determined at all hazards to get

---

* The color and form of the dress, and the style of wearing the hair, are by Japanese custom regulated according to the age of the woman.
† The forms of speech used by the samurai, and other superior classes, differed considerably from those of the popular idiom; but these differences could not be effectively rendered into English.

one glimpse of her face; and he crept round the house, backwards and forwards, peering through every crack and chink. And at last he was able to see; but therewith an icy trembling seized him; and the hair of his head stood up.

For the face was the face of a woman long dead – and the fingers caressing were fingers of naked bone – and of the body below the waist there was not anything: it melted off into thinnest trailing shadow. Where the eyes of the lover deluded saw youth and grace and beauty, there appeared to the eyes of the watcher horror only, and the emptiness of death. Simultaneously another woman's figure, and a weirder, rose up from within the chamber, and swiftly made toward the watcher, as if discerning his presence. Then, in uttermost terror, he fled to the dwelling of Hakuōdō Yusai, and, knocking frantically at the doors, succeeded in arousing him.

V

Hakuōdō Yusai, the *ninsomi*, was a very old man; but in his time he had travelled much, and he had heard and seen so many things that he could not be easily surprised. Yet the story of the terrified Tomozō both alarmed and amazed him. He had read in ancient Chinese books of love between the living and the dead; but he had never believed it possible. Now, however, he felt convinced that the statement of Tomozō was not a falsehood, and that something very strange was really going on in the house of Hagiwara. Should the truth prove to be what Tomozō imagined, then the young samurai was a doomed man.

'If the woman be a ghost,' said Yusai to the frightened servant, '– if the woman be a ghost, your master must die very soon –unless something extraordinary can be done to save him. And if the woman be a ghost, the signs of death will appear upon his face. For the spirit of the living is *yōki*, and pure – the spirit of the dead is *inki*, and unclean: the one is Positive, the other Negative. He whose bride is a ghost cannot live. Even though in his blood there existed the force of a life of one hundred years, that force must quickly perish ... Still, I shall do all that I can to save

Hagiwara Sama. And in the meantime, Tomozō, say nothing to
any other person – not even to your wife – about this matter. At
sunrise I shall call upon your master.'

VI

When questioned next morning by Yusai, Shinzaburō at first
attempted to deny that any women had been visiting the house;
but finding this artless policy of no avail, and perceiving that the
old man's purpose was altogether unselfish, he was finally persuaded
to acknowledge what had really occurred, and to give his reasons
for wishing to keep the matter a secret. As for the lady Iijima, he
intended, he said, to make her his wife as soon as possible.

'Oh, madness!' cried Yusai – losing all patience in the intensity
of his alarm. 'Know, sir, that the people who have been coming
here, night after night, are dead! Some frightful delusion is upon
you! . . . Why, the simple fact that you long supposed O-Tsuyu to
be dead, and repeated the *Nembutsu* for her, and made offerings
before her tablet, is itself the proof! . . . The lips of the dead have
touched you! – the hands of the dead have caressed you! . . . Even
at this moment I see in your face the signs of death – and you will
not believe! . . . Listen to me now, sir – I beg of you – if you wish
to save yourself: otherwise you have less than twenty days to live.
They told you – those people – that they were residing in the district of Shitaya, in Yanaka-no-Sasaki. Did you ever visit them at
that place? No! – of course you did not! Then go to-day – as soon
as you can – to Yanaka-no-Sasaki, and try to find their home! . . .'

And having uttered this counsel with the most vehement earn-
estness, Hakuōdō Yusai abruptly took his departure.

Shinzaburō, startled though not convinced, resolved after a
moment's reflection to follow the advice of the *ninsomi*, and to go
to Shitaya. It was yet early in the morning when he reached the
quarter of Yanaka-no-Sasaki, and began his search for the dwelling of O-Tsuyu. He went through every street and side-street, read
all the names inscribed at the various entrances, and made inquiries whenever an opportunity presented itself. But he could not

find anything resembling the little house mentioned by O-Yoné; and none of the people whom he questioned knew of any house in the quarter inhabited by two single women. Feeling at last certain that further research would be useless, he turned homeward by the shortest way, which happened to lead through the grounds of the temple Shin-Banzui-In.

Suddenly his attention was attracted by two new tombs, placed side by side, at the rear of the temple. One was a common tomb, such as might have been erected for a person of humble rank: the other was a large and handsome monument; and hanging before it was a beautiful peony-lantern, which had probably been left there at the time of the Festival of the Dead. Shinzaburō remembered that the peony-lantern carried by O-Yoné was exactly similar; and the coincidence impressed him as strange. He looked again at the tombs; but the tombs explained nothing. Neither bore any personal name – only the Buddhist *kaimyō* or posthumous appellation. Then he determined to seek information at the temple. An acolyte stated, in reply to his questions, that the large tomb had been recently erected for the daughter of Iijima Heizayémon, the *hatamoto* of Ushigomé; and that the small tomb next to it was that of her servant O-Yoné, who had died of grief soon after the young lady's funeral.

Immediately to Shinzaburō's memory there recurred, with another and sinister meaning, the words of O-Yoné: 'We went away, and found a very small house in Yanaka-no-Sasaki. There we are now just barely able to live – by doing a little private work ...' Here was indeed the very small house – and in Yanaka-no-Sasaki. But the little *private work* ... ?

Terror-stricken, the samurai hastened with all speed to the house of Yusai, and begged for his counsel and assistance. But Yusai declared himself unable to be of any aid in such a case. All that he could do was to send Shinzaburō to the high-priest Ryōseki, of Shin-Banzui-In, with a letter praying for immediate religious help.

VII

The high-priest Ryōseki was a learned and a holy man. By spirit-ual vision he was able to know the secret of any sorrow, and the nature of the karma that had caused it. He heard unmoved the story of Shinzaburō, and said to him:

'A very great danger now threatens you, because of an error committed in one of your former states of existence. The karma that binds you to the dead is very strong; but if I tried to explain its character, you would not be able to understand. I shall there-fore tell you only this – that the dead person has no desire to injure you out of hate, feels no enmity towards you: she is influ-enced, on the contrary, by the most passionate affection for you. Probably the girl has been in love with you from a time long preceding your present life – from a time of not less than three or four past existences; and it would seem that, although necessarily changing her form and condition at each succeeding birth, she has not been able to cease from following after you. Therefore it will not be an easy thing to escape from her influence ... But now I am going to lend you this powerful *mamori*.* It is a pure gold image of that Buddha called the Sea-Sounding Tathâgata – *Kai-On-Nyōrai* – because his preaching of the Law sounds through the world like the sound of the sea. And this little image is espe-cially a *shiryō-yoké*† – which protects the living from the dead.

---

* The Japanese word *mamori* has significations at least as numerous as those attaching to our own term 'amulet'. It would be impossible, in a mere footnote, even to suggest the variety of Japanese religious objects to which the name is given. In this instance, the *mamori* is a very small image, probably enclosed in a miniature shrine of lacquer-work or metal, over which a silk cover is drawn. Such little images were often worn by samurai on the person. I was recently shown a miniature figure of Kwannon,[6] in an iron case, which had been carried by an officer through the Satsuma war.[7] He observed, with good reason, that it had probably saved his life; for it had stopped a bullet of which the dent was plainly visible.

† From *shiryō*, a ghost, and *yokeru*, to exclude. The Japanese have two kinds of ghosts proper in their folklore: the spirits of the dead, *shiryō*; and the spirits of the living, *ikiryō*. A house or a person may be haunted by an *ikiryō* as well as by a *shiryō*.

This you must wear, in its covering, next to your body – under the girdle . . . Besides, I shall presently perform in the temple, a *ségaki*-service* for the repose of the troubled spirit . . . And here is a holy sutra, called *Ubō-Darani-Kyō*, or "Treasure-Raining Sutra":† you must be careful to recite it every night in your house without fail . . . Furthermore I shall give you this package of *o-fuda*;‡ you must paste one of them over every opening of your house – no matter how small. If you do this, the power of the holy texts will prevent the dead from entering. But – whatever may happen – do not fail to recite the sutra.'

Shinzaburō humbly thanked the high-priest and then, taking with him the image, the sutra, and the bundle of sacred texts, he made all haste to reach his home before the hour of sunset.

VIII

With Yusai's advice and help, Shinzaburō was able before dark to fix the holy texts over all the apertures of his dwelling. Then the *ninsomi* returned to his own house – leaving the youth alone.

Night came, warm and clear. Shinzaburō made fast the doors, bound the precious amulet about his waist, entered his

* A special service – accompanying offerings of food, etc., to those dead having no living relatives or friends to care for them – is thus termed. In this case, however, the service would be of a particular and exceptional kind.

† The name would be more correctly written *Uhō-Darani-Kyō*. It is the Japanese pronunciation of the title of a very short sutra translated out of Sanscrit into Chinese by the Indian priest Amoghavajra, probably during the eighth century. The Chinese text contains transliterations of some mysterious Sanscrit words – apparently talismanic words – like those to be seen in Kern's translation of the Saddharma-Pundarika, ch. xxvi.[8]

‡ *O-fuda* is the general name given to religious texts used as charms or talismans. They are sometimes stamped or burned upon wood, but more commonly written or printed upon narrow strips of paper. *O-fuda* are pasted above house-entrances, on the walls of rooms, upon tablets placed in household shrines, etc., etc. Some kinds are worn about the person; others are made into pellets, and swallowed as spiritual medicine. The text of the larger *o-fuda* is often accompanied by curious pictures or symbolic illustrations.

mosquito-net, and by the glow of a night-lantern began to recite
the *Ubō-Darani-Kyō*. For a long time he chanted the words, com-
prehending little of their meaning; then he tried to obtain some
rest. But his mind was still too much disturbed by the strange
events of the day. Midnight passed; and no sleep came to him. At
last he heard the boom of the great temple-bell of Dentsu-In
announcing the eighth hour.*

It ceased; and Shinzaburō suddenly heard the sound of *geta*
approaching from the old direction – but this time more slowly:
karan-koron, karan-koron! At once a cold sweat broke over his forehead. Opening the sutra hastily, with trembling hand, he began
again to recite it aloud. The steps came nearer and nearer – reached
the live hedge – stopped! Then, strange to say, Shinzaburō felt
unable to remain under his mosquito-net: something stronger
even than his fear impelled him to look; and, instead of continu-
ing to recite the *Ubō-Darani-Kyō*, he foolishly approached the
shutters, and through a chink peered out into the night. Before
the house be saw O-Tsuyu standing, and O-Yoné with the peony-
lantern; and both of them were gazing at the Buddhist texts pasted
above the entrance. Never before – not even in what time she
lived – had O-Tsuyu appeared so beautiful; and Shinzaburō felt his
heart drawn towards her with a power almost resistless. But the
terror of death and the terror of the unknown restrained; and
there went on within him such a struggle between his love and his
fear that he became as one suffering in the body the pains of the
Shō-netsu hell.† Presently he heard the voice of the maid-servant,
saying: 'My dear mistress, there is no way to enter. The heart of
Hagiwara Sama must have changed. For the promise that he made

* According to the old Japanese way of counting time, this *yatsudoki* or eighth
hour was the same as our two o'clock in the morning. Each Japanese hour was
equal to two European hours, so that there were only six hours instead of our
twelve; and these six hours were counted backwards in the order, 9, 8, 7, 6, 5, 4.
Thus the ninth hour corresponded to our midday, or midnight; half-past nine to
our one o'clock; eight to our two o'clock. Two o'clock in the morning, also called
'the Hour of the Ox', was the Japanese hour of ghosts and goblins.
† *En-netsu* or *Shō-netsu* (Sanscrit 'Tapana') is the sixth of the Eight Hot Hells of
Japanese Buddhism. One day of life in this hell is equal in duration to thousands
(some say millions) of human years.

last night has been broken; and the doors have been made fast to keep us out . . . We cannot go in to-night . . . It will be wiser for you to make up your mind not to think any more about him, because his feeling towards you has certainly changed. It is evident that he does not want to see you. So it will be better not to give yourself any more trouble for the sake of a man whose heart is so unkind.'

But the girl answered, weeping:

'Oh, to think that this could happen after the pledges which we made to each other! . . . Often I was told that the heart of a man changes as quickly as the sky of autumn; yet surely the heart of Hagiwara Sama cannot be so cruel that he should really intend to exclude me in this way! . . . Dear Yoné, please find some means of taking me to him . . . Unless you do, I will never, never go home again.'

Thus she continued to plead, veiling her face with her long sleeves – and very beautiful she looked, and very touching; but the fear of death was strong upon her lover.

O-Yoné at last made answer,

'My dear young lady, why will you trouble your mind about a man who seems to be so cruel? . . . Well, let us see if there be no way to enter at the back of the house: come with me!'

And taking O-Tsuyu by the hand, she led her away toward the rear of the dwelling; and there the two disappeared as suddenly as the light disappears when the flame of a lamp is blown out.

IX

Night after night the shadows came at the Hour of the Ox; and nightly Shinzaburō heard the weeping of O-Tsuyu. Yet he believed himself saved – little imagining that his doom had already been decided by the character of his dependants.

Tomozō had promised Yusai never to speak to any other person – not even to O-Miné – of the strange events that were taking place. But Tomozō was not long suffered by the haunters to rest in peace. Night after night O-Yoné entered into his dwelling, and roused him from his sleep, and asked him to remove the *o-fuda* placed over one very small window at the back of his master's house. And Tomozō, out of fear, as often promised her to take away the *o-fuda* before the next sundown; but never by day could he make up his mind to remove it – believing that evil was intended to Shinzaburō. At last, in a night of storm, O-Yoné startled him from slumber with a cry of reproach, and stooped above his pillow, and said to him: 'Have a care how you trifle with us! If, by to-morrow night, you do not take away that text, you shall learn how I can hate!' And she made her face so frightful as she spoke that Tomozō nearly died of terror.

O-Miné, the wife of Tomozō, had never till then known of these visits: even to her husband they had seemed like bad dreams. But on this particular night it chanced that, waking suddenly, she heard the voice of a woman talking to Tomozō. Almost in the same moment the talking ceased; and when O-Miné looked about her, she saw, by the light of the night-lamp, only her husband, shuddering and white with fear. The stranger was gone; the doors were fast: it seemed impossible that anybody could have entered. Nevertheless the jealousy of the wife had been aroused; and she began to chide and to question Tomozō in such a manner that he thought himself obliged to betray the secret, and to explain the terrible dilemma in which he had been placed.

Then the passion of O-Miné yielded to wonder and alarm; but she was a subtle woman, and she devised immediately a plan to save her husband by the sacrifice of her master. And she gave Tomozō a cunning counsel – telling him to make conditions with the dead.

They came again on the following night at the Hour of the Ox; and O-Miné hid herself on hearing the sound of their coming – *karan-koron, karan-koron!* But Tomozō went out to meet them in the dark, and even found courage to say to them what his wife had told him to say:

'It is true that I deserve your blame; but I had no wish to cause you anger. The reason that the *o-fuda* has not been taken away is that my wife and I are able to live only by the help of Hagiwara Sama, and that we cannot expose him to any danger without bringing misfortune upon ourselves. But if we could obtain the sum of a hundred *ryō*⁹ in gold, we should be able to please you, because we should then need no help from anybody. Therefore if you will give us a hundred *ryō*, I can take the *o-fuda* away without being afraid of losing our only means of support.'

When he had uttered these words, O-Yoné and O-Tsuyu looked at each other in silence for a moment. Then O-Yoné said:

'Mistress, I told you that it was not right to trouble this man – as we have no just cause of ill will against him. But it is certainly useless to fret yourself about Hagiwara Sama, because his heart has changed towards you. Now once again, my dear young lady, let me beg you not to think any more about him!'

But O-Tsuyu, weeping, made answer:

'Dear Yoné, whatever may happen, I cannot possibly keep myself from thinking about him! . . . You know that you can get a hundred *ryō* to have the *o-fuda* taken off . . . Only once more, I pray, dear Yoné! – only once more bring me face to face with Hagiwara Sama – I beseech you!' And hiding her face with her sleeve, she thus continued to plead.

'Oh! why will you ask me to do these things?' responded O-Yoné. 'You know very well that I have no money. But since you will persist in this whim of yours, in spite of all that I can say, I suppose that I must try to find the money somehow, and to bring it here to-morrow night . . .' Then, turning to the faithless Tomozō, she said: 'Tomozō, I must tell you that Hagiwara Sama now wears upon his body a *mamori* called by the name of *Kai-On-Nyōrai*, and that so long as he wears it we cannot approach him. So you will have to get that *mamori* away from him, by some means or other, as well as to remove the *o-fuda*.'

Tomozō feebly made answer:

'That also I can do, if you will promise to bring me the hundred *ryō*.'

'Well, mistress,' said O-Yoné, 'you will wait – will you not – until to-morrow night?'

'Oh, dear Yoné!' sobbed the other – 'have we to go back to-night again without seeing Hagiwara Sama? Ah! it is cruel!'

And the shadow of the mistress, weeping, was led away by the shadow of the maid.

X

Another day went, and another night came, and the dead came with it. But this time no lamentation was heard without the house of Hagiwara; for the faithless servant found his reward at the Hour of the Ox, and removed the *o-fuda*. Moreover he had been able, while his master was at the bath, to steal from its case the golden *mamori*, and to substitute for it an image of copper; and he had buried the *Kai-On-Nyōrai* in a desolate field. So the visitants found nothing to oppose their entering. Veiling their faces with their sleeves they rose and passed, like a streaming of vapor, into the little window from over which the holy text had been torn away. But what happened thereafter within the house Tomozō never knew.

The sun was high before he ventured again to approach his master's dwelling, and to knock upon the sliding-doors. For the first time in years he obtained no response; and the silence made him afraid. Repeatedly he called, and received no answer. Then, aided by O-Miné, he succeeded in effecting an entrance and making his way alone to the sleeping-room, where he called again in vain. He rolled back the rumbling shutters to admit the light; but still within the house there was no stir. At last he dared to lift a corner of the mosquito-net. But no sooner had he looked beneath than he fled from the house, with a cry of horror.

Shinzaburō was dead – hideously dead; and his face was the face of a man who had died in the uttermost agony of fear; and lying beside him in the bed were the bones of a woman! And the bones of the arms, and the bones of the hands, clung fast about his neck.

XI

Hakuōdō Yusai, the fortune-teller, went to view the corpse at the prayer of the faithless Tomozō. The old man was terrified and astonished at the spectacle, but looked about him with a keen eye. He soon perceived that the *o-fuda* had been taken from the little window at the back of the house; and on searching the body of Shinzaburō, he discovered that the golden *mamori* had been taken from its wrapping, and a copper image of Fudō[10] put in place of it. He suspected Tomozō of the theft; but the whole occurrence was so very extraordinary that he thought it prudent to consult with the priest Ryōseki before taking further action. Therefore, after having made a careful examination of the premises, he betook himself to the temple Shin-Banzui-In, as quickly as his aged limbs could bear him.

Ryōseki, without waiting to hear the purpose of the old man's visit, at once invited him into a private apartment.

'You know that you are always welcome here,' said Ryōseki. 'Please seat yourself at ease ... Well, I am sorry to tell you that Hagiwara Sama is dead.'

Yusai wonderingly exclaimed:

'Yes, he is dead; but how did you learn of it?'

The priest responded:

'Hagiwara Sama was suffering from the results of an evil karma; and his attendant was a bad man. What happened to Hagiwara Sama was unavoidable; his destiny had been determined from a time long before his last birth. It will be better for you not to let your mind be troubled by this event.'

Yusai said:

'I have heard that a priest of pure life may gain power to see into the future for a hundred years; but truly this is the first time in my existence that I have had proof of such power ... Still, there is another matter about which I am very anxious ...'

'You mean,' interrupted Ryōseki, 'the stealing of the holy *mamori*, the *Kai-On-Nyōrai*. But you must not give yourself any concern about that. The image has been buried in a field; and it will be found there and returned to me during the eighth month of the coming year. So please do not be anxious about it.'

More and more amazed, the old *ninsomi* ventured to observe:

'I have studied the *In-Yō*,* and the science of divination; and I

* The Male and Female principles of the universe, the Active and Passive forces of Nature. Yusai refers here to the old Chinese nature-philosophy – better known to Western readers by the name FENG-SHUI.

make my living by telling people's fortunes; but I cannot possibly understand how you know these things.'

Ryōseki answered gravely:

'Never mind how I happen to know them ... I now want to speak to you about Hagiwara's funeral. The House of Hagiwara has its own family-cemetery, of course; but to bury him there would not be proper. He must be buried beside O-Tsuyu, the Lady Iijima; for his karma-relation to her was a very deep one. And it is but right that you should erect a tomb for him at your own cost, because you have been indebted to him for many favors.'

Thus it came to pass that Shinzaburō was buried beside O-Tsuyu, in the cemetery of Shin-Banzui-In, in Yanaka-no-Sasaki.

Here ends the story of the Ghosts in the Romance of the Peony-Lantern.

*   *   *

My friend asked me whether the story had interested me; and I answered by telling him that I wanted to go to the cemetery of Shin-Banzui-In, so as to realize more definitely the local color of the author's studies.

'I shall go with you at once,' he said. 'But what did you think of the personages?'

'To Western thinking,' I made answer, 'Shinzaburō is a despicable creature. I have been mentally comparing him with the true lovers of our old ballad-literature. They were only too glad to follow a dead sweetheart into the grave; and nevertheless, being Christians, they believed that they had only one human life to enjoy in this world. But Shinzaburō was a Buddhist – with a million lives behind him and a million lives before him; and he was too selfish to give up even one miserable existence for the sake of the girl that came back to him from the dead. Then he was even more cowardly than selfish. Although a samurai by birth and training, he had to beg a priest to save him from ghosts. In every way he proved himself contemptible; and O-Tsuyu did quite right in choking him to death.'

'From the Japanese point of view, likewise,' my friend responded, 'Shinzaburō is rather contemptible. But the use of this weak character helped the author to develop incidents that could not otherwise, perhaps, have been so effectively managed. To my thinking, the only attractive character in the story is that of O-Yoné: type of the old-time loyal and loving servant – intelligent, shrewd, full of resource – faithful not only unto death, but beyond death ... Well, let us go to Shin-Banzui-In.'

We found the temple uninteresting, and the cemetery an abomination of desolation. Spaces once occupied by graves had been turned into potato-patches. Between were tombs leaning at all angles out of the perpendicular, tablets made illegible by scurf, empty pedestals, shattered water-tanks, and statues of Buddhas without heads or hands. Recent rains had soaked the black soil, leaving here and there small pools of slime about which swarms of tiny frogs were hopping. Everything – excepting the potato-patches – seemed to have been neglected for years. In a shed just within the gate, we observed a woman cooking; and my companion presumed to ask her if she knew anything about the tombs described in the Romance of the Peony-Lantern.

'Ah! the tombs of O-Tsuyu and O-Yoné?' she responded, smiling; 'you will find them near the end of the first row at the back of the temple – next to the statue of Jizō.'[11]

Surprises of this kind I had met with elsewhere in Japan.

We picked our way between the rain-pools and between the green ridges of young potatoes – whose roots were doubtless feeding on the substance of many another O-Tsuyu and O-Yoné; and we reached at last two lichen-eaten tombs of which the inscriptions seemed almost obliterated. Beside the larger tomb was a statue of Jizō, with a broken nose.

'The characters are not easy to make out,' said my friend – 'but wait!' ... He drew from his sleeve a sheet of soft white paper, laid it over the inscription, and began to rub the paper with a lump of clay. As he did so, the characters appeared in white on the blackened surface.

' "*Eleventh day, third month – Rat, Elder Brother, Fire – Sixth year of Horéki* [A. D. 1756]." ... This would seem to be the grave of some innkeeper of Nedzu, named Kichibei. Let us see what is on the other monument.'

With a fresh sheet of paper he presently brought out the text of a *kaïmyō*, and read,

' "*En-myō-In, Hō-yō-I-tei-ken-shi, Hō-ni*": "Nun-of-the-Law, Illustrious, Pure-of-heart-and-will, Famed-in-the-Law – inhabiting the Mansion-of-the-Preaching-of-Wonder" ... The grave of some Buddhist nun.'

'What utter humbug!' I exclaimed. 'That woman was only making fun of us.'

'Now,' my friend protested, 'you are unjust to the woman! You came here because you wanted a sensation; and she tried her very best to please you. You did not suppose that ghost-story was true, did you?'

INGWA-BANASHI[1]

The daimyō's wife was dying, and knew that she was dying. She had not been able to leave her bed since the early autumn of the tenth Bunsei. It was now the fourth month of the twelfth Bunsei[2] – the year 1829 by Western counting; and the cherry-trees were blossoming. She thought of the cherry-trees in her garden, and of the gladness of spring. She thought of her children. She thought of her husband's various concubines – especially the Lady Yukiko, nineteen years old.

'My dear wife,' said the *daimyō*, 'you have suffered very much for three long years. We have done all that we could to get you well – watching beside you night and day, praying for you, and often fasting for your sake. But in spite of our loving care, and in spite of the skill of our best physicians, it would now seem that the end of your life is not far off. Probably we shall sorrow more than you will sorrow because of your having to leave what the Buddha so truly termed "this burning-house of the world". I shall order to be performed – no matter what the cost – every religious rite that can serve you in regard to your next rebirth; and all of us will pray without ceasing for you, that you may not have to wander in the Black Space, but may quickly enter Paradise, and attain to Buddhahood.'

He spoke with the utmost tenderness, caressing her the while. Then, with eyelids closed, she answered him in a voice thin as the voice of an insect:

'I am grateful – most grateful – for your kind words . . . Yes, it is true, as you say, that I have been sick for three long years, and that I have been treated with all possible care and affection . . . Why, indeed, should I turn away from the one true Path at the very moment of my death? . . . Perhaps to think of worldly matters at such a time is not right; but I have one last request to make – only one . . . Call here to me the Lady Yukiko; you know that I love her like a sister. I want to speak to her about the affairs of this household.'

Yukiko came at the summons of the lord, and, in obedience to a sign from him, knelt down beside the couch. The *daimyō*'s wife opened her eyes, and looked at Yukiko, and spoke:

'Ah, here is Yukiko! . . . I am so pleased to see you, Yukiko! . . . Come a little closer – so that you can hear me well: I am not able to speak loud . . . Yukiko, I am going to die. I hope that you will be faithful in all things to our dear lord; for I want you to take my place when I am gone . . . I hope that you will always be loved by him – yes, even a hundred times more than I have been – and that you will very soon be promoted to a higher rank, and become his honored wife . . . And I beg of you always to cherish our dear lord: never allow another woman to rob you of his affection . . . This is what I wanted to say to you, dear Yukiko . . . Have you been able to understand?'

'Oh, my dear Lady,' protested Yukiko, 'do not, I entreat you, say such strange things to me! You well know that I am of poor and mean condition: how could I ever dare to aspire to become the wife of our lord!'

'Nay, nay!' returned the wife, huskily – 'this is not a time for words of ceremony: let us speak only the truth to each other. After my death, you will certainly be promoted to a higher place; and I now assure you again that I wish you to become the wife of our lord – yes, I wish this, Yukiko, even more than I wish to become a Buddha! . . . Ah, I had almost forgotten! – I want you to do something for me, Yukiko. You know that in the garden there is a *yaë-zakura*,* which was brought here, the year before last, from Mount Yoshino in Yamato. I have been told that it is now in full bloom; and I wanted so much to see it in flower! In a little while I shall be dead; I must see that tree before I die. Now I wish you to

* *Yaë-zakura*, *yaë-no-sakura*, a variety of Japanese cherry-tree that bears double-blossoms.

carry me into the garden – at once, Yukiko – so that I can see it . . .
Yes, upon your back, Yukiko; take me upon your back . . .'

While thus asking, her voice had gradually become clear and
strong – as if the intensity of the wish had given her new force:
then she suddenly burst into tears. Yukiko knelt motionless, not
knowing what to do; but the lord nodded assent.

'It is her last wish in this world,' he said. 'She always loved
cherry-flowers; and I know that she wanted very much to see that
Yamato-tree in blossom. Come, my dear Yukiko, let her have
her will.'

As a nurse turns her back to a child, that the child may cling to
it, Yukiko offered her shoulders to the wife, and said:

'Lady, I am ready: please tell me how I best can help you.'

'Why, this way!' – responded the dying woman, lifting herself
with an almost superhuman effort by clinging to Yukiko's shoulders. But as she stood erect, she quickly slipped her thin hands
down over the shoulders, under the robe, and clutched the breasts
of the girl, and burst into a wicked laugh.

'I have my wish!' she cried – 'I have my wish for the cherry-
bloom* – but not the cherry-bloom of the garden! . . . I could not
die before I got my wish. Now I have it! – oh, what a delight!' And
with these words she fell forward upon the crouching girl, and died.

The attendants at once attempted to lift the body from Yukiko's
shoulders, and to lay it upon the bed. But – strange to say! – this
seemingly easy thing could not be done. The cold hands had
attached themselves in some unaccountable way to the breasts of
the girl – appeared to have grown into the quick flesh. Yukiko
became senseless with fear and pain.

Physicians were called. They could not understand what had
taken place. By no ordinary methods could the hands of the dead
woman be unfastened from the body of her victim; they so clung
that any effort to remove them brought blood. This was not because

---

* In Japanese poetry and proverbial phraseology, the physical beauty of a woman
is compared to the cherry-flower; while feminine moral beauty is compared to
the plum-flower.

the fingers held: it was because the flesh of the palms had united itself in some inexplicable manner to the flesh of the breasts!

At that time the most skilful physician in Yedo was a foreigner – a Dutch surgeon. It was decided to summon him. After a careful examination he said that he could not understand the case, and that for the immediate relief of Yukiko there was nothing to be done except to cut the hands from the corpse. He declared that it would be dangerous to attempt to detach them from the breasts. His advice was accepted; and the hands were amputated at the wrists. But they remained clinging to the breasts; and there they soon darkened and dried up – like the hands of a person long dead.

Yet this was only the beginning of the horror.

Withered and bloodless though they seemed, those hands were not dead. At intervals they would stir – stealthily, like great grey spiders. And nightly thereafter – beginning always at the Hour of the Ox* – they would clutch and compress and torture. Only at the Hour of the Tiger the pain would cease.

Yukiko cut off her hair, and became a mendicant-nun – taking the religious name of Dassetsu. She had an *ihai* (mortuary tablet) made, bearing the *kaimyō* of her dead mistress – '*Myō-Kō-In-Den Chizan-Ryō-Fu Daishi*'; and this she carried about with her in all her wanderings; and every day before it she humbly besought the dead for pardon, and performed a Buddhist service in order that the jealous spirit might find rest. But the evil karma that had rendered such an affliction possible could not soon be exhausted. Every night at the Hour of the Ox, the hands never failed to torture her, during more than seventeen years – according to the testimony of those persons to whom she last told her story, when she stopped for one evening at the house of Noguchi Dengozayémon, in the village of Tanaka in the district of Kawachi in the province of Shimotsuké. This was in the third year of Kōkwa[3] (1846). Thereafter nothing more was ever heard of her.

* In ancient Japanese time, the Hour of the Ox was the special hour of ghosts. It began at 2 A.M., and lasted until 4 A.M. – for the old Japanese hour was double the length of the modern hour. The Hour of the Tiger began at 4 A.M.

STORY OF A TENGU

In the days of the Emperor Go-Reizei,[1] there was a holy priest living in the temple of Saito, on the mountain called Hiyei-Zan, near Kyōto. One summer day this good priest, after a visit to the city, was returning to his temple by way of Kita-no-Ōji, when he saw some boys ill-treating a kite. They had caught the bird in a snare, and were beating it with sticks. 'Oh, the poor creature!' compassionately exclaimed the priest; 'why do you torment it so, children?' One of the boys made answer: 'We want to kill it to get the feathers.' Moved by pity, the priest persuaded the boys to let him have the kite in exchange for a fan that he was carrying; and he set the bird free. It had not been seriously hurt, and was able to fly away.

Happy at having performed this Buddhist act of merit, the priest then resumed his walk. He had not proceeded very far when he saw a strange monk come out of a bamboo-grove by the road-side, and hasten towards him. The monk respectfully saluted him, and said: 'Sir, through your compassionate kindness my life has been saved; and I now desire to express my gratitude in a fitting manner.' Astonished at hearing himself thus addressed, the priest replied: 'Really, I cannot remember to have ever seen you before: please tell me who you are.' 'It is not wonderful that you cannot recognize me in this form,' returned the monk: 'I am the kite that those cruel boys were tormenting at Kita-no-Ōji. You saved my life; and there is nothing in this world more precious than life. So I now wish to return your kindness in some way or other. If there be anything that you would like to have, or to know, or to see – anything that I can do for you, in short – please

to tell me; for as I happen to possess, in a small degree, the Six
Supernatural Powers, I am able to gratify almost any wish that
you can express.' On hearing these words, the priest knew that he
was speaking with a Tengu;[2] and he frankly made answer: 'My
friend, I have long ceased to care for the things of this world: I am
now seventy years of age; neither fame nor pleasure has any
attraction for me. I feel anxious only about my future birth; but
as that is a matter in which no one can help me, it were useless to
ask about it. Really, I can think of but one thing worth wishing
for. It has been my life-long regret that I was not in India in the
time of the Lord Buddha, and could not attend the great assembly on the holy mountain Gridhrakûta.[3] Never a day passes in
which this regret does not come to me, in the hour of morning or
of evening prayer. Ah, my friend! if it were possible to conquer
Time and Space, like the Bodhisattvas, so that I could look upon
that marvellous assembly, how happy should I be!' – 'Why,' the
Tengu exclaimed, 'that pious wish of yours can easily be satisfied.
I perfectly well remember the assembly on the Vulture Peak;[4] and
I can cause everything that happened there to reappear before
you, exactly as it occurred. It is our greatest delight to represent
such holy matters . . . Come this way with me!'

And the priest suffered himself to be led to a place among
pines, on the slope of a hill. 'Now,' said the Tengu, 'you have only
to wait here for awhile, with your eyes shut. Do not open them
until you hear the voice of the Buddha preaching the Law. Then
you can look. But when you see the appearance of the Buddha,
you must not allow your devout feelings to influence you in any
way; you must not bow down, nor pray, nor utter any such
exclamation as, *"Even so, Lord!"* or *"O thou Blessed One!"* You must
not speak at all. Should you make even the least sign of reverence,
something very unfortunate might happen to me.' The priest
gladly promised to follow these injunctions; and the Tengu hurried away as if to prepare the spectacle.

The day waned and passed, and the darkness came; but the old
priest waited patiently beneath a tree, keeping his eyes closed. At
last a voice suddenly resounded above him – a wonderful voice,
deep and clear like the pealing of a mighty bell – the voice of the

Buddha Sâkyamuni proclaiming the Perfect Way. Then the priest, opening his eyes in a great radiance, perceived that all things had been changed: the place was indeed the Vulture Peak – the holy Indian mountain Gridhrakûta; and the time was the time of the Sûtra of the Lotos of the Good Law. Now there were no pines about him, but strange shining trees made of the Seven Precious Substances, with foliage and fruit of gems; and the ground was covered with Mandârava and Manjûshaka flowers[5] showered from heaven; and the night was filled with fragrance and splendour and the sweetness of the great Voice. And in mid-air, shining as a moon above the world, the priest beheld the Blessed One seated upon the Lion-throne, with Samantabhadra at his right hand, and Mañjusrî at his left – and before them assembled – immeasurably spreading into Space, like a flood of stars – the hosts of the Mahâttvas and the Bodhisattvas with their countless following: 'gods, demons, Nâgas, goblins, men, and beings not human.' Sâriputra he saw, and Kâsyapa, and Ânanda, with all the disciples of the Tathâgata – and the Kings of the Devas – and the Kings of the Four Directions, like pillars of fire – and the great Dragon-Kings – and the Gandharvas and Garudas – and the Gods of the Sun and the Moon and the Wind – and the shining myriads of Brahma's heaven. And incomparably further than even the measureless circling of the glory of these, he saw – made visible by a single ray of light that shot from the forehead of the Blessed One to pierce beyond uttermost Time – the eighteen hundred thousand Buddha-fields of the Eastern Quarter with all their habitants – and the beings in each of the Six States of Existence – and even the shapes of the Buddhas extinct, that had entered into Nirvana. These, and all the gods, and all the demons, he saw bow down before the Lion-throne; and he heard that multitude incalculable of beings praising the Sutra of the Lotos of the Good Law – like the roar of a sea before the Lord. Then forgetting utterly his pledge – foolishly dreaming that he stood in the very presence of the very Buddha – he cast himself down in worship with tears of love and thanksgiving; crying out with a loud voice, *'O thou Blessed One!'* . . .

Instantly with a shock as of earthquake the stupendous spectacle disappeared; and the priest found himself alone in the dark,

kneeling upon the grass of the mountain-side. Then a sadness unspeakable fell upon him, because of the loss of the vision, and because of the thoughtlessness that had caused him to break his word. As he sorrowfully turned his steps homeward, the goblin-monk once more appeared before him, and said to him in tones of reproach and pain: 'Because you did not keep the promise which you made to me, and heedlessly allowed your feelings to overcome you, the Gohōtendo, who is the Guardian of the Doctrine, swooped down suddenly from heaven upon us, and smote us in great anger, crying out, "How do ye dare thus to deceive a pious person?" Then the other monks, whom I had assembled, all fled in fear. As for myself, one of my wings has been broken – so that now I cannot fly.' And with these words the Tengu vanished forever.

THE RECONCILIATION

There was a young samurai of Kyōto who had been reduced to poverty by the ruin of his lord, and found himself obliged to leave his home, and to take service with the Governor of a distant province. Before quitting the capital, this samurai divorced his wife – a good and beautiful woman – under the belief that he could better obtain promotion by another alliance. He then married the daughter of a family of some distinction, and took her with him to the district whither he had been called.

But it was in the time of the thoughtlessness of youth, and the sharp experience of want, that the samurai could not understand the worth of the affection so lightly cast away. His second marriage did not prove a happy one; the character of his new wife was hard and selfish; and he soon found every cause to think with regret of Kyōto days. Then he discovered that he still loved his first wife – loved her more than he could ever love the second; and he began to feel how unjust and how thankless he had been. Gradually his repentance deepened into a remorse that left him no peace of mind. Memories of the woman he had wronged – her gentle speech, her smiles, her dainty, pretty ways, her faultless patience – continually haunted him. Sometimes in dreams he saw her at her loom, weaving as when she toiled night and day to help him during the years of their distress: more often he saw her kneeling alone in the desolate little room where he had left her, veiling her tears with her poor worn sleeve. Even in the hours of official duty, his thoughts would wander back to her: then he would ask himself how she was living, what she was doing. Something in his heart assured him that she could not accept another husband, and that she never would refuse to pardon him. And he secretly resolved to seek her out as soon as he could return to Kyōto – then to beg her forgiveness, to take her back, to do everything that a man could do to make atonement. But the years went by.

At last the Governor's official term expired, and the samurai was free. 'Now I will go back to my dear one,' he vowed to himself. 'Ah, what a cruelty – what a folly to have divorced her!' He sent his second wife to her own people (she had given him no children); and hurrying to Kyōto, he went at once to seek his former companion – not allowing himself even the time to change his traveling-garb.

When he reached the street where she used to live, it was late in the night – the night of the tenth day of the ninth month; and the city was silent as a cemetery. But a bright moon made everything visible; and he found the house without difficulty. It had a deserted look: tall weeds were growing on the roof. He knocked at the sliding-doors, and no one answered. Then, finding that the doors had not been fastened from within, he pushed them open, and entered. The front room was matless and empty: a chilly wind was blowing through crevices in the planking; and the moon shone through a ragged break in the wall of the alcove. Other rooms presented a like forlorn condition. The house, to all seeming, was unoccupied. Nevertheless, the samurai determined to visit one other apartment at the farther end of the dwelling; – a very small room that had been his wife's favorite resting-place. Approaching the sliding-screen that closed it, he was startled to perceive a glow within. He pushed the screen aside, and uttered a cry of joy; for he saw her there – sewing by the light of a paper-lamp. Her eyes at the same instant met his own; and with a happy smile she greeted him – asking only: 'When did you come back to Kyōto? How did you find your way here to me, through all those black rooms?' The years had not changed her. Still she seemed as fair and young as in his fondest memory of her; but sweeter than any memory there came to him the music of her voice, with its trembling of pleased wonder.

Then joyfully he took his place beside her, and told her all: how deeply he repented his selfishness – how wretched he had been without her – how constantly he had regretted her – how long he had hoped and planned to make amends; caressing her the while, and asking her forgiveness over and over again. She answered him, with loving gentleness, according to his heart's desire – entreating him to cease all self-reproach. It was wrong, she said, that he should have allowed himself to suffer on her account: she had always felt that she was not worthy to be his wife. She knew that he had separated from her, notwithstanding, only because of poverty; and while he lived with her, he had always been kind; and she had never ceased to pray for his happiness. But even if there had been a reason for speaking of amends, this honorable visit would be ample amends: what greater happiness than thus to see him again, though it were only for a moment? 'Only for a moment?' he replied, with a glad laugh – 'say, rather, for the time of seven existences!¹ My loved one, unless you forbid, I am coming back to live with you always – always – always! Nothing shall ever separate us again. Now I have means and friends: we need not fear poverty. To-morrow my goods will be brought here, and my servants will come to wait upon you, and we shall make this house beautiful . . . To-night,' he added, apologetically, 'I came thus late – without even changing my dress – only because of the longing I had to see you, and to tell you this.' She seemed greatly pleased by these words; and in her turn she told him about all that had happened in Kyōto since the time of his departure; excepting her own sorrows, of which she sweetly refused to speak. They chatted far into the night: then she conducted him to a warmer room, facing south – a room that had been their bridal chamber in former time. 'Have you no one in the house to help you?' he asked, as she began to prepare the couch for him. 'No,' she answered, laughing cheerfully: 'I could not afford a servant; – so I have been living all alone.' 'You will have plenty of servants to-morrow,' he said – 'good servants – and every-thing else that you need!' They lay down to rest – not to sleep: they had too much to tell each other; and they talked of the past and the present and the future, until the dawn was grey. Then, involuntar-ily, the samurai closed his eyes, and slept.

When he awoke, the daylight was streaming through the chinks of the sliding-shutters; and he found himself, to his utter amazement, lying upon the naked boards of a mouldering floor . . . Had he only dreamed a dream? No: she was there; she slept . . . He bent above her – and looked – and shrieked; for the sleeper had no face! . . . Before him, wrapped in its grave-sheet only, lay the corpse of a woman – a corpse so wasted that little remained save the bones, and the long black tangled hair.

Slowly – as he stood shuddering and sickening in the sun – the icy horror yielded to a despair so intolerable, a pain so atrocious, that he clutched at the mocking shadow of a doubt. Feigning ignorance of the neighborhood, he ventured to ask his way to the house in which his wife had lived.

'There is no one in that house,' said the person questioned. 'It used to belong to the wife of a samurai who left the city several years ago. He divorced her in order to marry another woman before he went away; and she fretted a great deal, and so became sick. She had no relatives in Kyōto, and nobody to care for her, and she died in the autumn of the same year; on the tenth day of the ninth month . . .'

A LEGEND OF
FUGEN-BOSATSU

There was once a very pious and learned priest, called Shōku Shōnin, who lived in the province of Harima. For many years he meditated daily upon the chapter of Fugen-Bosatsu [the Bodhisattva Samantabhadra] in the Sûtra of the Lotos of the Good Law; and he used to pray, every morning and evening, that he might at some time be permitted to behold Fugen-Bosatsu as a living presence, and in the form described in the holy text.*

One evening, while he was reciting the Sûtra, drowsiness overcame him; and he fell asleep leaning upon his *kyōsoku*.† Then he dreamed; and in his dream a voice told him that, in order to see Fugen-Bosatsu, he must go to the house of a certain courtesan, known as the 'Yujō-no-Chōja',‡ who lived in the town of Kanzaki. Immediately upon awakening he resolved to go to Kanzaki;

---

* The priest's desire was probably inspired by the promises recorded in the chapter entitled 'The Encouragement of Samantabhadra' (see Kern's translation of the Saddharma Pundarîka in the *Sacred Books of the East*, pp. 433–434): 'Then the Bodhisattva Mahâsattva Samantabhadra said to the Lord: ... "When a preacher who applies himself to this Dharmaparyâya shall take a walk, then, O Lord, will I mount a white elephant with six tusks, and betake myself to the place where that preacher is walking, in order to protect this Dharmaparyâya. And when that preacher, applying himself to this Dharmaparyâya, forgets, be it but a single word or syllable, then will I mount the white elephant with six tusks, and show my face to that preacher, and repeat this entire Dharmaparyâya." – But these promises refer to "the end of time".'
† The *kyōsoku* is a kind of padded arm-rest, or arm-stool, upon which the priest leans one arm while reading. The use of such an arm-rest is not confined, however, to the Buddhist clergy.
‡ A *yujō*, in old days, was a singing-girl as well as a courtesan. The term 'Yujō-no-Chōja', in this case, would mean simply 'the first (or best) of *yujō*.'

and, making all possible haste, he reached the town by the evening of the next day.

When he entered the house of the *yujō*, he found many persons already there assembled – mostly young men of the capital, who had been attracted to Kanzaki by the fame of the woman's beauty. They were feasting and drinking; and the *yujō* was playing a small hand-drum (*tsu-zumi*), which she used very skilfully, and singing a song. The song which she sang was an old Japanese song about a famous shrine in the town of Murozumi; and the words were these:

> *Within the sacred water-tank* of Murozumi in Suwō,*
> *Even though no wind be blowing,*
> *The surface of the water is always rippling.*

The sweetness of the voice filled everybody with surprise and delight. As the priest, who had taken a place apart, listened and wondered, the girl suddenly fixed her eyes upon him; and in the same instant he saw her form change into the form of Fugen-Bosatsu, emitting from her brow a beam of light that seemed to pierce beyond the limits of the universe, and riding a snow-white elephant with six tusks. And still she sang – but the song also was now transformed; and the words came thus to the ears of the priest:

> *On the vast Sea of Cessation,*
> *Though the Winds of the Six Desires and of the Five*
>   *Corruptions never blow,*
> *Yet the surface of that deep is always covered*
> *With the billowings of Attainment to the Reality-in-Itself.*

Dazzled by the divine ray, the priest closed his eyes: but through their lids he still distinctly saw the vision. When he opened them

---

* *Mitarai. Mitarai* (or *mitarashi*) is the name especially given to the water-tanks, or water-fonts – of stone or bronze – placed before Shintō shrines in order that the worshipper may purify his lips and hands before making prayer. Buddhist tanks are not so named.

again, it was gone: he saw only the girl with her hand-drum, and heard only the song about the water of Murozumi. But he found that as often as he shut his eyes he could see Fugen-Bosatsu on the six-tusked elephant, and could hear the mystic Song of the Sea of Cessation. The other persons present saw only the *yujō*: they had not beheld the manifestation.

Then the singer suddenly disappeared from the banquet-room – none could say when or how. From that moment the revelry ceased; and gloom took the place of joy. After having waited and sought for the girl to no purpose, the company dispersed in great sorrow. Last of all, the priest departed, bewildered by the emotions of the evening. But scarcely had he passed beyond the gate, when the *yujō* appeared before him, and said: 'Friend, do not speak yet to any one of what you have seen this night.' And with these words she vanished away – leaving the air filled with a delicious fragrance.

*   *   *

The monk by whom the foregoing legend was recorded, comments upon it thus: The condition of a *yujō* is low and miserable, since she is condemned to serve the lusts of men. Who therefore could imagine that such a woman might be the *nirmaṇakya*, or incarnation, of a Bodhisattva. But we must remember that the Buddhas and the Bodhisattvas may appear in this world in countless different forms; choosing, for the purpose of their divine compassion, even the most humble or contemptible shapes when such shapes can serve them to lead men into the true path, and to save them from the perils of illusion.

THE CORPSE-RIDER

The body was cold as ice; the heart had long ceased to beat: yet there were no other signs of death. Nobody even spoke of burying the woman. She had died of grief and anger at having been divorced. It would have been useless to bury her – because the last undying wish of a dying person for vengeance can burst asunder any tomb and lift the heaviest graveyard stone. People who lived near the house in which she was lying fled from their homes. They knew that she was only *waiting for the return of the man who had divorced her.*

At the time of her death he was on a journey. When he came back and was told what had happened, terror seized him. 'If I can find no help before dark,' he thought to himself, 'she will tear me to pieces.' It was yet only the Hour of the Dragon;* but he knew that he had no time to lose.

He went at once to an *inyōshi*† and begged for succor. The *inyōshi* knew the story of the dead woman; and he had seen the body. He said to the supplicant: 'A very great danger threatens you. I will try to save you. But you must promise to do whatever I shall tell you to do. There is only one way by which you can be saved. It is a fearful way. But unless you find the courage to attempt it, she will tear you limb from limb. If you can be brave, come to

---

* *Tatsu no Koku*, or the Hour of the Dragon, by old Japanese time, began at about eight o'clock in the morning.
† *Inyōshi*, a professor or master of the science of *in-yō* – the old Chinese nature-philosophy, based upon the theory of a male and a female principle pervading the universe.

me again in the evening before sunset.' The man shuddered; but he promised to do whatever should be required of him.

At sunset the *inyōshi* went with him to the house where the body was lying. The *inyōshi* pushed open the sliding-doors, and told his client to enter. It was rapidly growing dark. 'I dare not!' gasped the man, quaking from head to foot; 'I dare not even look at her!' 'You will have to do much more than look at her,' declared the *inyōshi*; 'and you promised to obey. Go in!' He forced the trembler into the house and led him to the side of the corpse.

The dead woman was lying on her face. 'Now you must get astride upon her,' said the *inyōshi*, 'and sit firmly on her back, as if you were riding a horse . . . Come! – you must do it!' The man shivered so that the *inyōshi* had to support him – shivered horribly; but he obeyed. 'Now take her hair in your hands,' commanded the *inyōshi* – 'half in the right hand, half in the left . . . So! . . . You must grip it like a bridle. Twist your hands in it – both hands – tightly. That is the way! . . . Listen to me! You must stay like that till morning. You will have reason to be afraid in the night – plenty of reason. But whatever may happen, never let go of her hair. If you let go – even for one second – she will tear you into gobbets!'
    The *inyōshi* then whispered some mysterious words into the ear of the body, and said to its rider: 'Now, for my own sake, I must leave you alone with her . . . Remain as you are! . . . Above all things, remember that you must not let go of her hair.' And he went away – closing the doors behind him.

Hour after hour the man sat upon the corpse in black fear; and the hush of the night deepened and deepened about him till he screamed to break it. Instantly the body sprang beneath him, as to cast him off; and the dead woman cried out loudly, 'Oh, how heavy it is! Yet I shall bring that fellow here now!'
    Then tall she rose, and leaped to the doors, and flung them open, and rushed into the night – always bearing the weight of the man. But he, shutting his eyes, kept his hands twisted in her

long hair – tightly, tightly – though fearing with such a fear that he could not even moan. How far she went, he never knew. He saw nothing: he heard only the sound of her naked feet in the dark – *picha-picha, picha-picha* – and the hiss of her breathing as she ran.

At last she turned, and ran back into the house, and lay down upon the floor exactly as at first. Under the man she panted and moaned till the cocks began to crow. Thereafter she lay still.

But the man, with chattering teeth, sat upon her until the *inyōshi* came at sunrise. 'So you did not let go of her hair!' – observed the *inyōshi*, greatly pleased. 'That is well ... Now you can stand up.' He whispered again into the ear of the corpse, and then said to the man: 'You must have passed a fearful night; but nothing else could have saved you. Hereafter you may feel secure from her vengeance.'

*   *   *

The conclusion of this story I do not think to be morally satisfying. It is not recorded that the corpse-rider became insane, or that his hair turned white: we are told only that 'he worshipped the *inyōshi* with tears of gratitude.' A note appended to the recital is equally disappointing. 'It is reported,' the Japanese author says, 'that a grandchild of the man [*who rode the corpse*] still survives, and that a grandson of the *inyōshi* is at this very time living in a village called Otokunoi-mura [*probably pronounced Otonoi-mura*].'

This village-name does not appear in any Japanese directory of today. But the names of many towns and villages have been changed since the foregoing story was written.

THE SYMPATHY OF BENTEN

In Kyōto there is a famous temple called Amadera. Sadazumi Shinnō, the fifth son of the Emperor Seiwa,[1] passed the greater part of his life there as a priest; and the graves of many celebrated persons are to be seen in the temple-grounds.

But the present edifice is not the ancient Amadera. The original temple, after the lapse of ten centuries, fell into such decay that it had to be entirely rebuilt in the fourteenth year of Genroku[2] (1701 A. D.).

A great festival was held to celebrate the re-building of the Amadera; and among the thousands of persons who attended that festival there was a young scholar and poet named Hanagaki Baishū. He wandered about the newly-laid-out grounds and gardens, delighted by all that he saw, until he reached the place of a spring at which he had often drunk in former times. He was then surprised to find that the soil about the spring had been dug away, so as to form a square pond, and that at one corner of this pond there had been set up a wooden tablet bearing the words *Tanjō-Sui* ('Birth-Water').* He also saw that a small, but very handsome temple of the Goddess Benten[3] had been erected beside the pond. While he was looking at this new temple, a sudden gust of wind blew to his feet a *tanzaku*† on which the following poem had been written:

---

* The word *tanjō* (birth) should here be understood in its mystical Buddhist meaning of new life or rebirth, rather than in the western signification of birth.
† *Tanzaku* is the name given to the long strips or ribbons of paper, usually colored, upon which poems are written perpendicularly. Poems written upon *tanzaku* are suspended to trees in flower, to wind-bells, to any beautiful object in which the poet has found an inspiration.

Shirushi aréto
Iwai zo somuru
Tama hōki,
Toruté bakari no
Chigiri narétomo.[4]

This poem – a poem on first love (*hatsu koi*), composed by the famous Shunrei Kyō – was not unfamiliar to him; but it had been written upon the *tanzaku* by a female hand, and so exquisitely that he could scarcely believe his eyes. Something in the form of the characters – an indefinite grace – suggested that period of youth between childhood and womanhood; and the pure rich color of the ink seemed to bespeak the purity and goodness of the writer's heart.*

Baishū carefully folded up the *tanzaku*, and took it home with him. When he looked at it again the writing appeared to him even more wonderful than at first. His knowledge in calligraphy assured him only that the poem had been written by some girl who was very young, very intelligent, and probably very gentle-hearted. But this assurance sufficed to shape within his mind the image of a very charming person; and he soon found himself in love with the unknown. Then his first resolve was to seek out the writer of the verses, and, if possible, make her his wife ... Yet how was he to find her? Who was she? Where did she live? Certainly he could hope to find her only through the favor of the Gods.

But presently it occurred to him that the Gods might be very willing to lend their aid. The *tanzaku* had come to him while he was standing in front of the temple of Benten-Sama;[5] and it was to this divinity in particular that lovers were wont to pray for happy

---

* It is difficult for the inexperienced European eye to distinguish in Chinese or Japanese writing those characteristics implied by our term 'hand' – in the sense of individual style. But the Japanese scholar never forgets the peculiarities of a handwriting once seen; and he can even guess at the approximate age of the writer. Chinese and Japanese authors claim that the color (quality) of the ink used tells something of the character of the writer. As every person grounds or prepares his or her own ink, the deeper and clearer black would at least indicate something of personal carefulness and of the sense of beauty.

union. This reflection impelled him to beseech the Goddess for assistance. He went at once to the temple of Benten-of-the-Birth-Water (*Tanjō-sui-no-Benten*) in the grounds of the Amadera; and there, with all the fervor of his heart, he made his petition: 'O Goddess, pity me! – help me to find where the young person lives who wrote the *tanzaku*! – vouchsafe me but one chance to meet her – even if only for a moment!' And after having made this prayer, he began to perform a seven days' religious service (*nanuka-mairi*)* in honor of the Goddess; vowing at the same time to pass the seventh night in ceaseless worship before her shrine.

Now on the seventh night – the night of his vigil – during the hour when the silence is most deep, he heard at the main gateway of the temple-grounds a voice calling for admittance. Another voice from within answered; the gate was opened; and Baishū saw an old man of majestic appearance approaching with slow steps. This venerable person was clad in robes of ceremony; and he wore upon his snow-white head a black cap (*eboshi*) of the form indicating high rank. Reaching the little temple of Benten, he knelt down in front of it, as if respectfully awaiting some order. Then the outer door of the temple was opened; the hanging curtain of bamboo behind it, concealing the inner sanctuary, was rolled half-way up; and a *chigo*† came forward – a beautiful boy, with long hair tied back in the ancient manner. He stood at the threshold, and said to the old man in a clear loud voice:

'There is a person here who has been praying for a love-union not suitable to his present condition, and otherwise difficult to bring about. But as the young man is worthy of Our pity, you have been called to see whether something can be done for him. If there should prove to be any relation between the parties from the period of a former birth, you will introduce them to each other.'

* There are many kinds of religious exercises called *mairi*. The performer of a *nanuka-mairi* pledges himself to pray at a certain temple every day for seven days in succession.

† The term *chigo* usually means the page of a noble household, especially an Imperial page. The *chigo* who appears in this story is of course a supernatural being – the court-messenger of the Goddess, and her mouthpiece.

On receiving this command, the old man bowed respectfully
to the *chigo*: then, rising, he drew from the pocket of his long left
sleeve a crimson cord. One end of this cord he passed round
Baishū's body, as if to bind him with it. The other end he put into
the flame of one of the temple-lamps; and while the cord was
there burning, he waved his hand three times, as if to summon
somebody out of the dark.

Immediately, in the direction of the Amadera, a sound of coming steps was heard; and in another moment a girl appeared – a
charming girl, fifteen or sixteen years old. She approached gracefully, but very shyly – hiding the lower part of her face with a fan;
and she knelt down beside Baishū. The *chigo* then said to Baishū:

'Recently you have been suffering much heart-pain; and this
desperate love of yours has even impaired your health. We could
not allow you to remain in so unhappy a condition; and We therefore summoned the Old-Man-under-the-Moon* to make you
acquainted with the writer of that *tanzaku*. She is now beside you.'

With these words, the *chigo* retired behind the bamboo curtain. Then the old man went away as he had come; and the young
girl followed him. Simultaneously Baishū heard the great bell of
the Amadera sounding the hour of dawn. He prostrated himself
in thanksgiving before the shrine of Benten-of-the-Birth-Water,
and proceeded homeward – feeling as if awakened from some
delightful dream – happy at having seen the charming person
whom he had so fervently prayed to meet – unhappy also because
of the fear that he might never meet her again.

But scarcely had he passed from the gateway into the street,
when he saw a young girl walking alone in the same direction
that he was going; and, even in the dusk of the dawn, he recognized her at once as the person to whom he had been introduced
before the temple of Benten. As he quickened his pace to overtake
her, she turned and saluted him with a graceful bow. Then for the
first time he ventured to speak to her; and she answered him in a
voice of which the sweetness filled his heart with joy. Through

* *Gekkawō*. This is a poetical appellation for the God of Marriage, more usually
known as *Musubi-no-kami*. Throughout this story there is an interesting min-
gling of Shintō and Buddhist ideas.

the yet silent streets they walked on, chatting happily, till they found themselves before the house where Baishū lived. There he paused – spoke to the girl of his hopes and fears. Smiling, she asked: 'Do you not know that I was sent for to become your wife?' And she entered with him.

Becoming his wife, she delighted him beyond expectation by the charm of her mind and heart. Moreover, he found her to be much more accomplished than he had supposed. Besides being able to write so wonderfully, she could paint beautiful pictures; she knew the art of arranging flowers, the art of embroidery, the art of music; she could weave and sew; and she knew everything in regard to the management of a house.

It was in the early autumn that the young people had met; and they lived together in perfect accord until the winter season began. Nothing, during those months, occurred to disturb their peace. Baishū's love for his gentle wife only strengthened with the passing of time. Yet, strangely enough, he remained ignorant of her history – knew nothing about her family. Of such matters she had never spoken; and, as the Gods had given her to him, he imagined that it would not be proper to question her. But neither the Old-Man-under-the-Moon nor any one else came – as he had feared – to take her away. Nobody even made any inquiries about her. And the neighbors, for some undiscoverable reason, acted as if totally unaware of her presence.

Baishū wondered at all this. But stranger experiences were awaiting him.

One winter morning he happened to be passing through a somewhat remote quarter of the city, when he heard himself loudly called by name, and saw a man-servant making signs to him from the gateway of a private residence. As Baishū did not know the man's face, and did not have a single acquaintance in that part of Kyōto, he was more than startled by so abrupt a summons. But the servant, coming forward, saluted him with the utmost respect, and said: 'My master greatly desires the honor of speaking with you: deign to enter for a moment.' After an instant of hesitation, Baishū allowed himself to be conducted to the house. A dignified and richly dressed person, who seemed to be the master, welcomed him at the entrance, and led him to the guest-room. When the courtesies due upon a first meeting had been fully exchanged, the host apologized for the informal manner of his invitation, and said:

'It must have seemed to you very rude of us to call you in such a way. But perhaps you will pardon our impoliteness when I tell you that we acted thus upon what I firmly believe to have been an inspiration from the Goddess Benten. Now permit me to explain.

'I have a daughter, about sixteen years old, who can write rather well,* and do other things in the common way: she has the ordinary nature of woman. As we were anxious to make her happy by finding a good husband for her, we prayed the Goddess Benten to help us; and we sent to every temple of Benten in the city a *tanzaku* written by the girl. Some nights later, the Goddess appeared to me in a dream, and said: "We have heard your prayer, and have already introduced your daughter to the person who is to become her husband. During the coming winter he will visit you." As I did not understand this assurance that a presentation had been made, I felt some doubt; I thought that the dream might have been only a common dream, signifying nothing. But last night again I saw Benten-Sama in a dream; and she said to me: "To-morrow the young man, of whom I once spoke to you, will come to this street: then you can call him into your house, and ask him to become the husband of your daughter. He is a good young man; and later in life he will obtain a much higher rank than he now holds." Then Benten-Sama told me your name, your age, your birthplace, and described your features and dress so exactly that my servant found no difficulty in recognizing you by the indications which I was able to give him.'

This explanation bewildered Baishū instead of reassuring him; and his only reply was a formal return of thanks for the honor

---

* As it is the old Japanese rule that parents should speak depreciatingly of their children's accomplishments the phrase 'rather well' in this connection would mean, for the visitor, 'wonderfully well'. For the same reason the expressions 'common way' and 'ordinary nature', as subsequently used, would imply almost the reverse of the literal meaning.

which the master of the house had spoken of doing him. But when the host invited him to another room, for the purpose of presenting him to the young lady, his embarrassment became extreme. Yet he could not reasonably decline the introduction. He could not bring himself, under such extraordinary circumstances, to announce that he already had a wife – a wife given to him by the Goddess Benten herself; a wife from whom he could not even think of separating. So, in silence and trepidation, he followed his host to the apartment indicated.

Then what was his amazement to discover, when presented to the daughter of the house, that she was the very same person whom he had already taken to wife!

The same – yet not the same.

She to whom he had been introduced by the Old-Man-under-the-Moon, was only the soul of the beloved.

She to whom he was now to be wedded, in her father's house, was the body.

Benten had wrought this miracle for the sake of her worshippers.

*   *   *

The original story breaks off suddenly at this point, leaving several matters unexplained. The ending is rather unsatisfactory. One would like to know something about the mental experiences of the real maiden during the married life of her phantom. One would also like to know what became of the phantom – whether it continued to lead an independent existence; whether it waited patiently for the return of its husband; whether it paid a visit to the real bride. And the book says nothing about these things. But a Japanese friend explains the miracle thus:

'The spirit-bride was really formed out of the *tanzaku*. So it is possible that the real girl did not know anything about the meeting at the temple of Benten. When she wrote those beautiful characters upon the *tanzaku*, something of her spirit passed into them. Therefore it was possible to evoke from the writing the double of the writer.'

THE GRATITUDE OF
THE SAMÉBITO

There was a man named Tawaraya Tōtarō, who lived in the Province of Ōmi. His house was situated on the shore of Lake Biwa, not far from the famous temple called Ishiyamadera. He had some property, and lived in comfort; but at the age of twenty-nine he was still unmarried. His greatest ambition was to marry a very beautiful woman; and he had not been able to find a girl to his liking.

One day, as he was passing over the Long Bridge of Séta* he saw a strange being crouching close to the parapet. The body of this being resembled the body of a man, but was black as ink; its face was like the face of a demon; its eyes were green as emeralds; and its beard was like the beard of a dragon. Tōtarō was at first very much startled. But the green eyes looked at him so gently that after a moment's hesitation he ventured to question the creature. Then it answered him, saying: 'I am a *Samébito*† – a Shark-Man of the sea; and until a short time ago I was in the service of the Eight Great Dragon-Kings [*Hachi-Dai-Ryū-Ō*] as a subordinate

---

* The Long Bridge of Séta (*Séta-no-Naga-Hashi*), famous in Japanese legend, is nearly eight hundred feet in length, and commands a beautiful view. This bridge crosses the waters of the Setagawa near the junction of the stream with Lake Biwa. Ishiyamadera, one of the most picturesque Buddhist temples in Japan, is situated within a short distance from the bridge.

† Literally, 'a Shark-Person', but in this story the *Samébito* is a male. The characters for *Samébito* can also be read *Kōjin* – which is the usual reading. In dictionaries the word is loosely rendered by 'merman' or 'mermaid'; but as the above description shows, the *Samébito* or *Kōjin* of the Far East is a conception having little in common with the Western idea of a merman or mermaid.

officer in the Dragon-Palace [*Ryūgū*].* But because of a small fault which I committed, I was dismissed from the Dragon-Palace, and also banished from the Sea. Since then I have been wandering about here – unable to get any food, or even a place to lie down. If you can feel any pity for me, do, I beseech you, help me to find a shelter, and let me have something to eat!'

This petition was uttered in so plaintive a tone, and in so humble a manner, that Tōtarō's heart was touched. 'Come with me,' he said. 'There is in my garden a large and deep pond where you may live as long as you wish; and I will give you plenty to eat.'

The *Samébito* followed Tōtarō home, and appeared to be much pleased with the pond.

Thereafter, for nearly half a year, this strange guest dwelt in the pond, and was every day supplied by Tōtarō with such food as sea-creatures like.

[*From this point of the original narrative the Shark-Man is referred to, not as a monster, but as a sympathetic Person of the male sex.*]

Now, in the seventh month of the same year, there was a female pilgrimage (*nyonin-mōdé*) to the great Buddhist temple called Miidera, in the neighboring town of Ōtsu; and Tōtarō went to Ōtsu to attend the festival. Among the multitude of women and young girls there assembled, he observed a person of extraordinary beauty. She seemed about sixteen years old; her face was fair and pure as snow; and the loveliness of her lips assured the beholder that their every utterance would sound 'as sweet as the voice of a nightingale singing upon a plum-tree'. Tōtarō fell in love with her at sight. When she left the temple he followed her at a respectful distance, and discovered that she and her mother were staying for a few days at a certain house in the neighboring village of Séta. By questioning some of the village folk, he was able also to learn that her name was Tamana; that she was unmarried; and that her family appeared to be unwilling that she should

* *Ryūgū* is also the name given to the whole of that fairy-realm beneath the sea which figures in so many Japanese legends.

marry a man of ordinary rank – for they demanded as a betrothal-gift a casket containing ten thousand jewels.*

Tōtarō returned home very much dismayed by this information. The more that he thought about the strange betrothal-gift demanded by the girl's parents, the more he felt that he could never expect to obtain her for his wife. Even supposing that there were as many as ten thousand jewels in the whole country, only a great prince could hope to procure them.

But not even for a single hour could Tōtarō banish from his mind the memory of that beautiful being. It haunted him so that he could neither eat nor sleep; and it seemed to become more and more vivid as the days went by. And at last he became ill – so ill that he could not lift his head from the pillow. Then he sent for a doctor.

The doctor, after having made a careful examination, uttered an exclamation of surprise. 'Almost any kind of sickness,' he said, 'can be cured by proper medical treatment, except the sickness of love. Your ailment is evidently love-sickness. There is no cure for it. In ancient times Rōya-Ō Hakuyo died of that sickness; and you must prepare yourself to die as he died.' So saying, the doctor went away, without even giving any medicine to Tōtarō.

About this time the Shark-Man that was living in the garden-pond heard of his master's sickness, and came into the house to wait upon Tōtarō. And he tended him with the utmost affection both by day and by night. But he did not know either the cause or the serious nature of the sickness until nearly a week later, when Tōtarō, thinking himself about to die, uttered these words of farewell:

'I suppose that I have had the pleasure of caring for you thus long, because of some relation that grew up between us in a

---

* *Tama* in the original. This word *tama* has a multitude of meanings; and as here used it is quite as indefinite as our own terms 'jewel', 'gem', or 'precious stone'. Indeed, it is more indefinite, for it signifies also a bead of coral, a ball of crystal, a polished stone attached to a hairpin, etc., etc. Later on, however, I venture to render it by 'ruby' – for reasons which need no explanation.

former state of existence. But now I am very sick indeed, and every day my sickness becomes worse; and my life is like the morning dew which passes away before the setting of the sun. For your sake, therefore, I am troubled in mind. Your existence has depended upon my care; and I fear that there will be no one to care for you and to feed you when I am dead . . . My poor friend! Alas! our hopes and our wishes are always disappointed in this unhappy world!'

No sooner had Tōtarō spoken these words than the Samébito uttered a strange wild cry of pain, and began to weep bitterly. And as he wept, great tears of blood streamed from his green eyes and rolled down his black cheeks and dripped upon the floor. And, falling, they were blood; but, having fallen, they became hard and bright and beautiful – became jewels of inestimable price, rubies splendid as crimson fire. For when men of the sea weep, their tears become precious stones.

Then Tōtarō, beholding this marvel, was so amazed and over-joyed that his strength returned to him. He sprang from his bed, and began to pick up and to count the tears of the Shark-Man, crying out the while: 'My sickness is cured! I shall live! I shall live!'

Therewith, the Shark-Man, greatly astonished, ceased to weep, and asked Tōtarō to explain this wonderful cure; and Tōtarō told him about the young person seen at Miidera, and about the extra-ordinary marriage-gift demanded by her family. 'As I felt sure,' added Tōtarō, 'that I should never be able to get ten thousand jewels, I supposed that my suit would be hopeless. Then I became very unhappy, and at last fell sick. But now, because of your generous weeping, I have many precious stones; and I think that I shall be able to marry that girl. Only – there are not yet quite enough stones; and I beg that you will be good enough to weep a little more, so as to make up the full number required.'

But at this request the Samébito shook his head, and answered in a tone of surprise and of reproach:

'Do you think that I am like a harlot – able to weep whenever I wish? Oh, no! Harlots shed tears in order to deceive men; but creatures of the sea cannot weep without feeling real sorrow. I wept for you because of the true grief that I felt in my heart at the thought that you were going to die. But now I cannot weep for you, because you have told me that your sickness is cured.'

'Then what am I to do?' plaintively asked Tōtarō. 'Unless I can get ten thousand jewels, I cannot marry the girl!'

The *Samébito* remained for a little while silent, as if thinking. Then he said:

'Listen! To-day I cannot possibly weep any more. But to-morrow let us go together to the Long Bridge of Séta, taking with us some wine and some fish. We can rest for a time on the bridge; and while we are drinking the wine and eating the fish, I shall gaze in the direction of the Dragon-Palace, and try, by thinking of the happy days that I spent there, to make myself feel homesick – so that I can weep.'

Tōtarō joyfully assented.

Next morning the two, taking plenty of wine and fish with them, went to the Séta bridge, and rested there, and feasted. After having drunk a great deal of wine, the *Samébito* began to gaze in the direction of the Dragon-Kingdom, and to think about the past. And gradually, under the softening influence of the wine, the memory of happier days filled his heart with sorrow, and the pain of homesickness came upon him, so that he could weep profusely. And the great red tears that he shed fell upon the bridge in a shower of rubies; and Tōtarō gathered them as they fell, and put them into a casket, and counted them until he had counted the full number of ten thousand. Then he uttered a shout of joy.

Almost in the same moment, from far away over the lake, a delightful sound of music was heard; and there appeared in the offing, slowly rising from the waters, like some fabric of cloud, a palace of the color of the setting sun.

At once the *Samébito* sprang upon the parapet of the bridge, and looked, and laughed for joy. Then, turning to Tōtarō, he said:

'There must have been a general amnesty proclaimed in the Dragon-Realm; the Kings are calling me. So now I must bid you farewell. I am happy to have had one chance of befriending you in return for your goodness to me.'

With these words he leaped from the bridge; and no man ever saw him again. But Tōtarō presented the casket of red jewels to the parents of Tamana, and so obtained her in marriage.

OF A PROMISE KEPT*

'I shall return in the early autumn,' said Akana Soyëmon several hundred years ago, – when bidding good-bye to his brother by adoption, young Hasébé Samon. The time was spring; and the place was the village of Kato in the province of Harima. Akana was an Izumo samurai; and he wanted to visit his birthplace.

Hasébé said:

'Your Izumo – the Country of the Eight-Cloud Rising† – is very distant. Perhaps it will therefore be difficult for you to promise to return here upon any particular day. But, if we were to know the exact day, we should feel happier. We could then prepare a feast of welcome; and we could watch at the gateway for your coming.'

'Why, as for that,' responded Akana, 'I have been so much accustomed to travel that I can usually tell beforehand how long it will take me to reach a place; and I can safely promise you to be here upon a particular day. Suppose we say the day of the festival Chōyō?'[1]

'That is the ninth day of the ninth month,' said Hasébé; 'then the chrysanthemums will be in bloom, and we can go together to look at them. How pleasant! . . . So you promise to come back on the ninth day of the ninth month?'

'On the ninth day of the ninth month,' repeated Akana, smiling farewell. Then he strode away from the village of Kato in the

* Related in the *Ugétsu Monogatari*.[2]
† One of the old poetical names for the Province of Izumo, or Unshū.

province of Harima; and Hasébé Samon and the mother of
Hasébé looked after him with tears in their eyes.

'Neither the Sun nor the Moon,' says an old Japanese proverb,
'ever halt upon their journey.' Swiftly the months went by; and the
autumn came – the season of chrysanthemums. And early upon
the morning of the ninth day of the ninth month Hasébé prepared to welcome his adopted brother. He made ready a feast of
good things, bought wine, decorated the guest-room, and filled
the vases of the alcove with chrysanthemums of two colors. Then
his mother, watching him, said: 'The province of Izumo, my son,
is more than one hundred *ri** from this place; and the journey
thence over the mountains is difficult and weary; and you cannot
be sure that Akana will be able to come to-day. Would it not be
better, before you take all this trouble, to wait for his coming?'
'Nay, mother!' Hasébé made answer – 'Akana promised to be here
to-day: he could not break a promise! And if he were to see us
beginning to make preparation after his arrival, he would know
that we had doubted his word; and we should be put to shame.'

The day was beautiful, the sky without a cloud, and the air so
pure that the world seemed to be a thousand miles wider than
usual. In the morning many travellers passed through the
village – some of them samurai; and Hasébé, watching each as he
came, more than once imagined that he saw Akana approaching.
But the temple-bells sounded the hour of midday; and Akana did
not appear. Through the afternoon also Hasébé watched and
waited in vain. The sun set; and still there was no sign of Akana.
Nevertheless Hasébé remained at the gate, gazing down the road.
Later his mother went to him, and said: 'The mind of a man, my
son – as our proverb declares – may change as quickly as the sky
of autumn. But your chrysanthemum-flowers will still be fresh
to-morrow. Better now to sleep; and in the morning you can
watch again for Akana, if you wish.' 'Rest well, mother,' returned
Hasébé; 'but I still believe that he will come.' Then the mother
went to her own room; and Hasébé lingered at the gate.

* A *ri* is about equal to two and a half English miles.

The night was pure as the day had been: all the sky throbbed with stars; and the white River of Heaven shimmered with unusual splendor. The village slept; the silence was broken only by the noise of a little brook, and by the far-away barking of peasants' dogs. Hasébé still waited – waited until he saw the thin moon sink behind the neighboring hills. Then at last he began to doubt and to fear. Just as he was about to re-enter the house, he perceived in the distance a tall man approaching – very lightly and quickly; and in the next moment he recognized Akana.

'Oh!' cried Hasébé, springing to meet him – 'I have been waiting for you from the morning until now! ... So you really did keep your promise after all ... But you must be tired, poor brother! – come in; everything is ready for you.' He guided Akana to the place of honor in the guest-room, and hastened to trim the lights, which were burning low. 'Mother,' continued Hasébé, 'felt a little tired this evening, and she has already gone to bed; but I shall awaken her presently.' Akana shook his head, and made a little gesture of disapproval. 'As you will, brother,' said Hasébé; and he set warm food and wine before the traveller. Akana did not touch the food or the wine, but remained motionless and silent for a short time. Then, speaking in a whisper – as if fearful of awakening the mother, he said:

'Now I must tell you how it happened that I came thus late. When I returned to Izumo I found that the people had almost forgotten the kindness of our former ruler, the good Lord Enya, and were seeking the favor of the usurper Tsunéhisa, who had possessed himself of the Tonda Castle. But I had to visit my cousin, Akana Tanji, though he had accepted service under Tsunéhisa, and was living, as a retainer, within the castle grounds. He persuaded me to present myself before Tsunéhisa: I yielded chiefly in order to observe the character of the new ruler, whose face I had never seen. He is a skilled soldier, and of great courage; but he is cunning and cruel. I found it necessary to let him know that I could never enter into his service. After I left his presence he ordered my cousin to detain me – to keep me confined within the house. I protested that I had promised to return to Harima upon the ninth day of the ninth month; but I was refused permission to go. I then hoped to escape from the castle at night; but I was

伊賀局

constantly watched; and until to-day I could find no way to fulfil my promise . . .'

'Until to-day!' exclaimed Hasébé in bewilderment; 'the castle is more than a hundred *ri* from here!'

'Yes,' returned Akana; 'and no living man can travel on foot a hundred *ri* in one day. But I felt that, if I did not keep my promise, you could not think well of me; and I remembered the ancient proverb, *Tama yoku ichi nichi ni sen ri wo yuku* ['The soul of a man can journey a thousand *ri* in a day']. Fortunately I had been allowed to keep my sword; thus only was I able to come to you . . . Be good to our mother.'

With these words he stood up, and in the same instant disappeared.

Then Hasébé knew that Akana had killed himself in order to fulfil the promise.

At earliest dawn Hasébé Samon set out for the Castle Tonda, in the province of Izumo. Reaching Matsué, he there learned that, on the night of the ninth day of the ninth month, Akana Soyë-mon had performed *harakiri*[3] in the house of Akana Tanji, in the grounds of the castle. Then Hasébé went to the house of Akana Tanji, and reproached Akana Tanji for the treachery done, and slew him in the midst of his family, and escaped without hurt. And when the Lord Tsunéhisa had heard the story, he gave commands that Hasébé should not be pursued. For, although an unscrupulous and cruel man himself, the Lord Tsunéhisa could respect the love of truth in others, and could admire the friendship and the courage of Hasébé Samon.

OF A PROMISE BROKEN*

I

'I am not afraid to die,' said the dying wife; 'there is only one thing that troubles me now. I wish that I could know who will take my place in this house.'

'My dear one,' answered the sorrowing husband, 'nobody shall ever take your place in my home. I will never, never marry again.'

At the time that he said this he was speaking out of his heart; for he loved the woman whom he was about to lose.

'On the faith of a samurai?' she questioned, with a feeble smile.

'On the faith of a samurai,' he responded – stroking the pale thin face.

'Then, my dear one,' she said, 'you will let me be buried in the garden – will you not? – near those plum-trees that we planted at the further end? I wanted long ago to ask this; but I thought, that if you were to marry again, you would not like to have my grave so near you. Now you have promised that no other woman shall take my place; so I need not hesitate to speak of my wish ... I want so much to be buried in the garden! I think that in the garden I should sometimes hear your voice, and that I should still be able to see the flowers in the spring.'

'It shall be as you wish,' he answered. 'But do not now speak of burial: you are not so ill that we have lost all hope.'

'I have,' she returned; 'I shall die this morning ... But you will bury me in the garden?'

* Izumo legend.

'Yes,' he said – 'under the shade of the plum-trees that we planted; and you shall have a beautiful tomb there.'

'And will you give me a little bell?'

'Bell – ?'

'Yes: I want you to put a little bell in the coffin – such a little bell as the Buddhist pilgrims carry. Shall I have it?'

'You shall have the little bell – and anything else that you wish.'

'I do not wish for anything else,' she said . . . 'My dear one, you have been very good to me always. Now I can die happy.'

Then she closed her eyes and died – as easily as a tired child falls asleep. She looked beautiful when she was dead; and there was a smile upon her face.

She was buried in the garden, under the shade of the trees that she loved; and a small bell was buried with her. Above the grave was erected a handsome monument, decorated with the family crest, and bearing the *kaimyō*: '*Great Elder Sister, Luminous-Shadow-of-the-Plum-Flower-Chamber, dwelling in the Mansion of the Great Sea of Compassion.*'

*   *   *

But, within a twelve-month after the death of his wife, the relatives and friends of the samurai began to insist that he should marry again. 'You are still a young man,' they said, 'and an only son; and you have no children. It is the duty of a samurai to marry. If you die childless, who will there be to make the offerings and to remember the ancestors?'

By many such representations he was at last persuaded to marry again. The bride was only seventeen years old; and he found that he could love her dearly, notwithstanding the dumb reproach of the tomb in the garden.

II

Nothing took place to disturb the happiness of the young wife until the seventh day after the wedding – when her husband was ordered to undertake certain duties requiring his presence at the castle by night. On the first evening that he was obliged to leave her alone, she felt uneasy in a way that she could not explain – vaguely afraid without knowing why. When she went to bed she could not sleep. There was a strange oppression in the air – an indefinable heaviness like that which sometimes precedes the coming of a storm.

About the Hour of the Ox she heard, outside in the night, the clanging of a bell – a Buddhist pilgrim's bell; and she wondered what pilgrim could be passing through the samurai quarter at such a time. Presently, after a pause, the bell sounded much nearer. Evidently the pilgrim was approaching the house; but why approaching from the rear, where no road was? ... Suddenly the dogs began to whine and howl in an unusual and horrible way; and a fear came upon her like the fear of dreams ... That ringing was certainly in the garden ... She tried to get up to waken a servant. But she found that she could not rise – could not move – could not call ... And nearer, and still more near, came the clang of the bell; and oh! how the dogs howled! ... Then, lightly as a shadow steals, there glided into the room a Woman – though every door stood fast, and every screen unmoved – a Woman robed in a grave-robe, and carrying a pilgrim's bell. Eyeless she came – because she had long been dead; and her loosened hair streamed down about her face; and she looked without eyes through the tangle of it, and spoke without a tongue:

'Not in this house – not in this house shall you stay! Here I am mistress still. You shall go; and you shall tell to none the reason of your going. If you tell HIM, I will tear you into pieces!'

So speaking, the haunter vanished. The bride became senseless with fear. Until the dawn she so remained.

Nevertheless, in the cheery light of day, she doubted the reality of what she had seen and heard. The memory of the warning still weighed upon her so heavily that she did not dare to speak of the vision, either to her husband or to any one else; but she was almost able to persuade herself that she had only dreamed an ugly dream, which had made her ill.

On the following night, however, she could not doubt. Again, at the Hour of the Ox, the dogs began to howl and whine; again the bell resounded – approaching slowly from the garden; again the listener vainly strove to rise and call; again the dead came into the room, and hissed,

'You shall go; and you shall tell to no one why you must go! If you even whisper it to HIM, I will tear you in pieces!' . . .

This time the haunter came close to the couch – and bent and muttered and mowed above it . . .

Next morning, when the samurai returned from the castle, his young wife prostrated herself before him in supplication:

'I beseech you,' she said, 'to pardon my ingratitude and my great rudeness in thus addressing you: but I want to go home; I want to go away at once.'

'Are you not happy here?' he asked, in sincere surprise. 'Has any one dared to be unkind to you during my absence?'

'It is not that –' she answered, sobbing. 'Everybody here has been only too good to me . . . But I cannot continue to be your wife; I must go away . . .'

'My dear,' he exclaimed, in great astonishment, 'it is very painful to know that you have had any cause for unhappiness in this house. But I cannot even imagine why you should want to go away – unless somebody has been very unkind to you . . . Surely you do not mean that you wish for a divorce?'

She responded, trembling and weeping,

'If you do not give me a divorce, I shall die!'

He remained for a little while silent – vainly trying to think of some cause for this amazing declaration. Then, without betraying any emotion, he made answer:

'To send you back now to your people, without any fault on your part, would seem a shameful act. If you will tell me a good reason for your wish – any reason that will enable me to explain matters honorably – I can write you a divorce. But unless you give me a reason, a good reason, I will not divorce you – for the honor of our house must be kept above reproach.'

And then she felt obliged to speak; and she told him everything – adding, in an agony of terror –

'Now that I have let you know, she will kill me! – she will kill me! . . .'

Although a brave man, and little inclined to believe in phantoms, the samurai was more than startled for the moment. But a simple and natural explanation of the matter soon presented itself to his mind.

'My dear,' he said, 'you are now very nervous; and I fear that some one has been telling you foolish stories. I cannot give you a divorce merely because you have had a bad dream in this house. But I am very sorry indeed that you should have been suffering in such a way during my absence. To-night, also, I must be at the castle; but you shall not be alone. I will order two of the retainers to keep watch in your room; and you will be able to sleep in peace. They are good men; and they will take all possible care of you.'

Then he spoke to her so considerately and so affectionately that she became almost ashamed of her terrors, and resolved to remain in the house.

III

The two retainers left in charge of the young wife were big, brave, simple-hearted men – experienced guardians of women and children. They told the bride pleasant stories to keep her cheerful. She talked with them a long time, laughed at their good-humored fun, and almost forgot her fears. When at last she lay down to sleep, the men-at-arms took their places in a corner of the room, behind a screen, and began a game of *go** – speaking only in whispers, that she might not be disturbed. She slept like an infant.

But again at the Hour of the Ox she awoke with a moan of terror – for she heard the bell! . . . It was already near, and was coming nearer. She started up; she screamed; but in the room there was no stir – only a silence as of death – a silence growing – a silence thickening. She rushed to the men-at-arms: they sat before their checker-table – motionless – each staring at the other with fixed eyes. She shrieked to them: she shook them: they remained as if frozen . . .

*

* A game resembling draughts, but much more complicated.

Afterwards they said that they had heard the bell – heard also the cry of the bride – even felt her try to shake them into wakefulness; and that, nevertheless, they had not been able to move or speak. From the same moment they had ceased to hear or to see: a black sleep had seized upon them.

*   *   *

Entering his bridal-chamber at dawn, the samurai beheld, by the light of a dying lamp, the headless body of his young wife, lying in a pool of blood. Still squatting before their unfinished game, the two retainers slept. At their master's cry they sprang up, and stupidly stared at the horror on the floor . . .

The head was nowhere to be seen; and the hideous wound showed that it had not been cut off, but *torn off.* A trail of blood led from the chamber to an angle of the outer gallery, where the storm-doors appeared to have been riven apart. The three men followed that trail into the garden – over reaches of grass – over spaces of sand – along the bank of an iris-bordered pond – under heavy shadowings of cedar and bamboo. And suddenly, at a turn, they found themselves face to face with a nightmare-thing that chippered like a bat: the figure of the long-buried woman, erect before her tomb – in one hand clutching a bell, in the other the dripping head . . . For a moment the three stood numbed. Then one of the men-at-arms, uttering a Buddhist invocation, drew, and struck at the shape. Instantly it crumbled down upon the soil – an empty scattering of grave-rags, bones, and hair; and the bell rolled clanking out of the ruin. But the fleshless right hand, though parted from the wrist, still writhed; and its fingers still gripped at the bleeding head – and tore, and mangled – as the claws of the yellow crab cling fast to a fallen fruit . . .

*   *   *

['That is a wicked story,' I said to the friend who had related it. 'The vengeance of the dead – if taken at all – should have been taken upon the man.'

'Men think so,' he made answer. 'But that is not the way that a woman feels . . .'

He was right.]

BEFORE THE
SUPREME COURT

The great Buddhist priest, Mongaku Shōnin, says in his book *Kyō-gyō Shin-shō*:[1] 'Many of those gods whom the people worship are unjust gods [*jajin*]: therefore such gods are not worshipped by persons who revere the Three Precious Things.* And even persons who obtain favors from those gods, in answer to prayer, usually find at a later day that such favors cause misfortune.' This truth is well exemplified by a story recorded in the book *Nihon-Rei-Iki*.[2]

During the time of the Emperor Shōmu† there lived in the district called Yamadagori, in the province of Sanuki, a man named Fushiki no Shin. He had but one child, a daughter called Kinumé.‡ Kinumé was a fine-looking girl, and very strong; but, shortly after she had reached her eighteenth year, a dangerous sickness began to prevail in that part of the country, and she was attacked by it. Her parents and friends then made offerings on her behalf to a certain Pest-God, and performed great austerities in honor of the Pest-God – beseeching him to save her.

After having lain in a stupor for several days, the sick girl one evening came to herself, and told her parents a dream that she had dreamed. She had dreamed that the Pest-God appeared to her, and said: 'Your people have been praying to me so earnestly for you, and have been worshipping me so devoutly, that I really wish to save you. But I cannot do so except by giving you the life of some other person. Do you happen to know of any other girl

* Sambō (Ratnatraya) – the Buddha, the Doctrine, and the Priesthood.
† He reigned during the second quarter of the eighth century.
‡ 'Golden Plum-Flower'.

who has the same name as yours?' 'I remember,' answered Kinumé, 'that in Utarigori there is a girl whose name is the same as mine.' 'Point her out to me,' the God said, touching the sleeper; and at the touch she rose into the air with him; and, in less than a second, the two were in front of the house of the other Kinumé, in Utarigori. It was night; but the family had not yet gone to bed, and the daughter was washing something in the kitchen. 'That is the girl,' said Kinumé of Yamadagori. The Pest-God took out of a scarlet bag at his girdle a long sharp instrument shaped like a chisel; and, entering the house, he drove the sharp instrument into the forehead of Kinumé of Utarigori. Then Kinumé of Utarigori sank to the floor in great agony; and Kinumé of Yamadagori awoke, and related the dream.

Immediately after having related it, however, she again fell into a stupor. For three days she remained without knowledge of the world; and her parents began to despair of her recovery. Then once more she opened her eyes, and spoke. But almost in the same moment she rose from her bed, looked wildly about the room, and rushed out of the house, exclaiming: 'This is not my home! – you are not my parents!' . . .

Something strange had happened.

Kinumé of Utarigori had died after having been stricken by the Pest-God. Her parents sorrowed greatly; and the priests of their parish-temple performed a Buddhist service for her; and her body was burned in a field outside the village. Then her spirit descended to the Meido, the world of the dead, and was summoned to the tribunal of Emma-Dai-Ō – the King and Judge of Souls. But no sooner had the Judge cast eyes upon her than he exclaimed: 'This girl is the Utarigori-Kinumé: she ought not to have been brought here so soon! Send her back at once to the *Shaba*-world,* and fetch me the other Kinumé – the Yamadagori girl!' Then the spirit of Kinumé of Utarigori made moan before King Emma, and complained, saying: 'Great Lord, it is more than three days since I died; and by this time my body must have been burned;

---

* The *Shaba*-world (*Sahaloka*), in common parlance, signifies the world of men – the region of human existence.

and, if you now send me back to the *Shaba*-world, what shall I do? My body has been changed into ashes and smoke; I shall have no body!' 'Do not be anxious,' the terrible King answered; 'I am going to give you the body of Kinumé of Yamadagori – for her spirit must be brought here to me at once. You need not fret about the burning of your body: you will find the body of the other Kinumé very much better.' And scarcely had he finished speaking when the spirit of Kinumé of Utarigori revived in the body of Kinumé of Yamadagori.

Now when the parents of Kinumé of Yamadagori saw their sick girl spring up and run away, exclaiming, 'This is not my home!' – they imagined her to be out of her mind, and they ran after her, calling out: 'Kinumé, where are you going? – wait for a moment, child! you are much too ill to run like that!' But she escaped from them, and ran on without stopping, until she came to Utarigori, and to the house of the family of the dead Kinumé. There she entered, and found the old people; and she saluted them, crying: 'Oh, how pleasant to be again at home! . . . Is it well with you, dear parents?' They did not recognize her, and thought her mad; but the mother spoke to her kindly, asking: 'Where have you come from, child?' 'From the Meido I have come,' Kinumé made answer. 'I am your own child, Kinumé, returned to you from the dead. But I have now another body, mother.' And she related all that had happened; and the old people wondered exceedingly, yet did not know what to believe. Presently the parents of Kinumé of Yamadagori also came to the house, looking for their daughter; and then the two fathers and the two mothers consulted together, and made the girl repeat her story, and questioned her over and over again. But she replied to every question in such a way that the truth of her statements could not be doubted. At last the mother of the Yamadagori Kinumé, after having related the strange dream which her sick daughter had dreamed, said to the parents of the Utarigori Kinumé: 'We are satisfied that the spirit of this girl is the spirit of your child. But you know that her body is the body of our child; and we think that both families ought to have a share in her. So we would ask you to agree that she be considered henceforward the daughter of both families.' To this proposal the Utarigori parents joyfully consented; and it is recorded that in after-time Kinumé inherited the property of both households.

'This story,' says the Japanese author of the *Bukkyō-Hyakkwa-Zenshō*,[3] 'may be found on the left side of the twelfth sheet of the first volume of the *Nihon-Rei-Iki*.'

THE STORY OF
KWASHIN KOJI*

During the period of Tenshō† there lived, in one of the northern districts of Kyōto, an old man whom the people called Kwashin Koji. He wore a long white beard, and was always dressed like a Shintō priest; but he made his living by exhibiting Buddhist pictures and by preaching Buddhist doctrine. Every fine day he used to go to the grounds of the temple Gion, and there suspend to some tree a large *kakémono*¹ on which were depicted the punishments of the various hells. This *kakémono* was so wonderfully painted that all things represented in it seemed to be real; and the old man would discourse to the people crowding to see it, and explain to them the Law of Cause and Effect, pointing out with a Buddhist staff [*nyoi*], which he always carried, each detail of the different torments, and exhorting everybody to follow the teachings of the Buddha. Multitudes assembled to look at the picture and to hear the old man preach about it; and sometimes the mat which he spread before him, to receive contributions, was covered out of sight by the heaping of coins thrown upon it.

Oda Nobunaga was at that time ruler of Kyōto and of the surrounding provinces. One of his retainers, named Arakawa, during a visit to the temple of Gion, happened to see the picture being displayed there; and he afterwards talked about it at the palace. Nobunaga was interested by Arakawa's description, and sent orders to Kwashin Koji to come at once to the palace, and to bring the picture with him.

---

* Related in the curious old book *Yasō-Kidan*.²
† The period of Tenshō lasted from 1573 to 1591 (A. D.). The death of the great captain, Oda Nobunaga,³ who figures in this story, occurred in 1582.

When Nobunaga saw the *kakémono* he was not able to conceal his surprise at the vividness of the work: the demons and the tortured spirits actually appeared to move before his eyes; and he heard voices crying out of the picture; and the blood there represented seemed to be really flowing – so that he could not help putting out his finger to feel if the painting was wet. But the finger was not stained – for the paper proved to be perfectly dry. More and more astonished, Nobunaga asked who had made the wonderful picture. Kwashin Koji answered that it had been painted by the famous Oguri Sōtan* – after he had performed the rite of self-purification every day for a hundred days, and practised great austerities, and made earnest prayer for inspiration to the divine Kwannon[4] of Kiyomidzu Temple.

Observing Nobunaga's evident desire to possess the *kakémono*, Arakawa then asked Kwashin Koji whether he would 'offer it up', as a gift to the great lord. But the old man boldly answered: 'This painting is the only object of value that I possess; and I am able to make a little money by showing it to the people. Were I now to present this picture to the lord, I should deprive myself of the only means which I have to make my living. However, if the lord be greatly desirous to possess it, let him pay me for it the sum of one hundred *ryō*[5] of gold. With that amount of money I should be able to engage in some profitable business. Otherwise, I must refuse to give up the picture.'

Nobunaga did not seem to be pleased at this reply; and he remained silent. Arakawa presently whispered something in the ear of the lord, who nodded assent; and Kwashin Koji was then dismissed, with a small present of money.

But when the old man left the palace, Arakawa secretly followed him – hoping for a chance to get the picture by foul means. The chance came; for Kwashin Koji happened to take a road leading directly to the heights beyond the town. When he reached a certain lonesome spot at the foot of the hills, where the road made a sudden turn, he was seized by Arakawa, who said to him: 'Why

---

* Oguri Sōtan was a great religious artist who flourished in the early part of the fifteenth century. He became a Buddhist priest in the later years of his life.

were you so greedy as to ask a hundred *ryō* of gold for that picture? Instead of a hundred *ryō* of gold, I am now going to give you one piece of iron three feet long.' Then Arakawa drew his sword, and killed the old man, and took the picture.

The next day Arakawa presented the *kakémono* – still wrapped up as Kwashin Koji had wrapped it before leaving the palace – to Oda Nobunaga, who ordered it to be hung up forthwith. But, when it was unrolled, both Nobunaga and his retainer were astounded to find that there was no picture at all – nothing but a blank surface. Arakawa could not explain how the original painting had disappeared; and as he had been guilty – whether willingly or unwillingly – of deceiving his master, it was decided that he should be punished. Accordingly he was sentenced to remain in confinement for a considerable time.

Scarcely had Arakawa completed his term of imprisonment, when news was brought to him that Kwashin Koji was exhibiting the famous picture in the grounds of Kitano Temple. Arakawa could hardly believe his ears; but the information inspired him with a vague hope that he might be able, in some way or other, to secure the *kakémono*, and thereby redeem his recent fault. So he quickly assembled some of his followers, and hurried to the temple; but when he reached it he was told that Kwashin Koji had gone away.

Several days later, word was brought to Arakawa that Kwashin Koji was exhibiting the picture at Kiyomidzu Temple, and preaching about it to an immense crowd. Arakawa made all haste to Kiyomidzu; but he arrived there only in time to see the crowd disperse – for Kwashin Koji had again disappeared.

At last one day Arakawa unexpectedly caught sight of Kwashin Koji in a wine-shop, and there captured him. The old man only laughed good-humoredly on finding himself seized, and said: 'I will go with you; but please wait until I drink a little wine.' To this request Arakawa made no objection; and Kwashin Koji thereupon drank, to the amazement of the bystanders, twelve bowls of wine. After drinking the twelfth he declared himself satisfied; and Arakawa ordered him to be bound with a rope, and taken to Nobunaga's residence.

In the court of the palace Kwashin Koji was examined at once by the Chief Officer, and sternly reprimanded. Finally the Chief Officer said to him: 'It is evident that you have been deluding people by magical practices; and for this offence alone you deserve to be heavily punished. However, if you will now respectfully offer up that picture to the Lord Nobunaga, we shall this time overlook your fault. Otherwise we shall certainly inflict upon you a very severe punishment.'

At this menace Kwashin Koji laughed in a bewildered way, and exclaimed: 'It is not I who have been guilty of deluding people.' Then, turning to Arakawa, he cried out: 'You are the deceiver! You wanted to flatter the lord by giving him that picture; and you tried to kill me in order to steal it. Surely, if there be any such thing as crime, that was a crime! As luck would have it, you did not succeed in killing me; but if you had succeeded, as you wished, what would you have been able to plead in excuse for such an act? You stole the picture, at all events. The picture that I now have is only a copy. And after you stole the picture, you changed your mind about giving it to Lord Nobunaga; and you devised a plan to keep it for yourself. So you gave a blank *kaké-mono* to Lord Nobunaga; and, in order to conceal your secret act and purpose, you pretended that I had deceived you by substituting a blank *kakémono* for the real one. Where the real picture now is, I do not know. You probably do.'

At these words Arakawa became so angry that he rushed towards the prisoner, and would have struck him but for the interference of the guards. And this sudden outburst of anger caused the Chief Officer to suspect that Arakawa was not altogether innocent. He ordered Kwashin Koji to be taken to prison for the time being; and he then proceeded to question Arakawa closely. Now Arakawa was naturally slow of speech; and on this occasion, being greatly excited, he could scarcely speak at all; and he stammered, and contradicted himself, and betrayed every sign of guilt. Then the Chief Officer ordered that Arakawa should be beaten with a stick until he told the truth. But it was not possible for him even to seem to tell the truth. So he was beaten with a bamboo until his senses departed from him, and he lay as if dead.

*

Kwashin Koji was told in the prison about what had happened to Arakawa; and he laughed. But after a little while he said to the jailer: 'Listen! That fellow Arakawa really behaved like a rascal; and I purposely brought this punishment upon him, in order to correct his evil inclinations. But now please say to the Chief Officer that Arakawa must have been ignorant of the truth, and that I shall explain the whole matter satisfactorily.'

Then Kwashin Koji was again taken before the Chief Officer, to whom he made the following declaration: 'In any picture of real excellence there must be a ghost; and such a picture, having a will of its own, may refuse to be separated from the person who gave it life, or even from its rightful owner. There are many stories to prove that really great pictures have souls. It is well known that some sparrows, painted upon a sliding-screen [*fusuma*] by Hōgen Yenshin, once flew away, leaving blank the spaces which they had occupied upon the surface. Also it is well known that a horse, painted upon a certain *kakémono*, used to go out at night to eat grass. Now, in this present case, I believe the truth to be that, inasmuch as the Lord Nobunaga never became the rightful owner of my *kakémono*, the picture voluntarily vanished from the paper when it was unrolled in his presence. But if you will give me the price that I first asked – one hundred *ryō* of gold – I think that the painting will then reappear, of its own accord, upon the now blank paper. At all events, let us try! There is nothing to risk – since, if the picture does not reappear, I shall at once return the money.'

On hearing of these strange assertions, Nobunaga ordered the hundred *ryō* to be paid, and came in person to observe the result. The *kakémono* was then unrolled before him; and, to the amazement of all present, the painting reappeared, with all its details. But the colors seemed to have faded a little; and the figures of the souls and the demons did not look really alive, as before. Perceiving this difference, the lord asked Kwashin Koji to explain the reason of it; and Kwashin Koji replied: 'The value of the painting, as you first saw it, was the value of a painting beyond all price. But the value of the painting, as you now see it, represents exactly what you paid for it – one hundred *ryō* of gold ... How could it be otherwise?' On hearing this answer, all present felt that it would be worse than useless to oppose the old man any further. He was immediately set at liberty; and Arakawa was also liberated, as he had more than expiated his fault by the punishment which he had undergone.

Now Arakawa had a younger brother named Buichi – also a retainer in the service of Nobunaga. Buichi was furiously angry because Arakawa had been beaten and imprisoned; and he resolved to kill Kwashin Koji. Kwashin Koji no sooner found himself again at liberty than he went straight to a wine-shop, and called for wine. Buichi rushed after him into the shop, struck him down, and cut off his head. Then, taking the hundred *ryō* that had been paid to the old man, Buichi wrapped up the head and the gold together in a cloth, and hurried home to show them to Arakawa. But when he unfastened the cloth he found, instead of the head, only an empty wine-gourd, and only a lump of filth instead of the gold . . . And the bewilderment of the brothers was presently increased by the information that the headless body had disappeared from the wine-shop – none could say how or when.

Nothing more was heard of Kwashin Koji until about a month later, when a drunken man was found one evening asleep in the gateway of Lord Nobunaga's palace, and snoring so loud that every snore sounded like the rumbling of distant thunder. A retainer discovered that the drunkard was Kwashin Koji. For this insolent offence, the old fellow was at once seized and thrown into the prison. But he did not awake; and in the prison he continued to sleep without interruption for ten days and ten nights – all the while snoring so that the sound could be heard to a great distance.

About this time, the Lord Nobunaga came to his death through the treachery of one of his captains, Akéchi Mitsuhidé,[6] who thereupon usurped rule. But Mitsuhidé's power endured only for a period of twelve days.

Now when Mitsuhidé became master of Kyōto, he was told of the case of Kwashin Koji; and he ordered that the prisoner should be brought before him. Accordingly Kwashin Koji was

summoned into the presence of the new lord; but Mitsuhidé
spoke to him kindly, treated him as a guest, and commanded that
a good dinner should be served to him. When the old man had
eaten, Mitsuhidé said to him: 'I have heard that you are very fond
of wine; how much wine can you drink at a single sitting?'
Kwashin Koji answered: 'I do not really know how much; I stop
drinking only when I feel intoxication coming on.' Then the lord
set a great wine-cup* before Kwashin Koji, and told a servant to
fill the cup as often as the old man wished. And Kwashin Koji
emptied the great cup ten times in succession, and asked for
more; but the servant made answer that the wine-vessel was
exhausted. All present were astounded by this drinking-feat; and
the lord asked Kwashin Koji, 'Are you not yet satisfied, Sir?' 'Well,
yes,' replied Kwashin Koji, 'I am somewhat satisfied; and now, in
return for your august kindness, I shall display a little of my art.
Be therefore so good as to observe that screen.' He pointed to a
large eight-folding screen upon which were painted the Eight
Beautiful Views of the Lake of Ōmi (*Ōmi-Hakkei*); and everybody
looked at the screen. In one of the views the artist had represented, far away on the lake, a man rowing a boat – the boat
occupying, upon the surface of the screen, a space of less than an
inch in length. Kwashin Koji then waved his hand in the direction of the boat; and all saw the boat suddenly turn, and begin to
move toward the foreground of the picture. It grew rapidly larger
and larger as it approached; and presently the features of the
boatman became clearly distinguishable. Still the boat drew
nearer – always becoming larger – until it appeared to be only a
short distance away. And, all of a sudden, the water of the lake
seemed to overflow – out of the picture into the room; – and the
room was flooded; and the spectators girded up their robes in
haste, as the water rose above their knees. In the same moment
the boat appeared to glide out of the screen – a real fishing-boat;
and the creaking of the single oar could be heard. Still the flood

* The term 'bowl' would better indicate the kind of vessel to which the story-teller
refers. Some of the so-called cups, used on festival occasions, were very large –
shallow lacquered basins capable of holding considerably more than a quart. To
empty one of the largest size, at a draught, was considered to be no small feat.

in the room continued to rise, until the spectators were standing up to their girdles in water. Then the boat came close up to Kwashin Koji; and Kwashin Koji climbed into it; and the boatman turned about, and began to row away very swiftly. And, as the boat receded, the water in the room began to lower rapidly – seeming to ebb back into the screen. No sooner had the boat passed the apparent foreground of the picture than the room was dry again! But still the painted vessel appeared to glide over the painted water – retreating further into the distance, and ever growing smaller – till at last it dwindled to a dot in the offing. And then it disappeared altogether; and Kwashin Koji disappeared with it. He was never again seen in Japan.

THE STORY OF
UMÉTSU CHŪBEI*

Umétsu Chūbei was a young samurai of great strength and courage. He was in the service of the Lord Tomura Jūdayū,[1] whose castle stood upon a lofty hill in the neighbourhood of Yokoté, in the province of Dewa. The houses of the lord's retainers formed a small town at the base of the hill.

Umétsu was one of those selected for night-duty at the castle-gates. There were two night-watches; the first beginning at sunset and ending at midnight; the second beginning at midnight and ending at sunrise.

Once, when Umétsu happened to be on the second watch, he met with a strange adventure. While ascending the hill at midnight, to take his place on guard, he perceived a woman standing at the last upper turn of the winding road leading to the castle. She appeared to have a child in her arms, and to be waiting for somebody. Only the most extraordinary circumstances could account for the presence of a woman in that lonesome place at so late an hour; and Umétsu remembered that goblins were wont to assume feminine shapes after dark, in order to deceive and destroy men. He therefore doubted whether the seeming woman before him was really a human being; and when he saw her hasten towards him, as if to speak, he intended to pass her by without a word. But he was too much surprised to do so when the woman called him by name, and said, in a very sweet voice: 'Good Sir Umétsu, to-night I am in great trouble, and I have a most painful duty to perform: will you not kindly help me by holding this baby for one little moment?' And she held out the child to him.

* Related in the *Bukkyō-Hyakkwa-Zenshō*.[2]

Umétsu did not recognize the woman, who appeared to be very young: he suspected the charm of the strange voice, suspected a supernatural snare, suspected everything; but he was naturally kind; and he felt that it would he unmanly to repress a kindly impulse through fear of goblins. Without replying, he took the child. 'Please hold it till I come back,' said the woman: 'I shall return in a very little while.' 'I will hold it,' he answered; and immediately the woman turned from him, and, leaving the road, sprang soundlessly down the hill so lightly and so quickly that he could scarcely believe his eyes. She was out of sight in a few seconds.

Umétsu then first looked at the child. It was very small, and appeared to have been just born. It was very still in his hands; and it did not cry at all.

Suddenly it seemed to be growing larger. He looked at it again . . . No: it was the same small creature; and it had not even moved. Why had he imagined that it was growing larger?

In another moment he knew why; and he felt a chill strike through him. The child was not growing larger; *but it was growing heavier* . . . At first it had seemed to weigh only seven or eight pounds: then its weight had gradually doubled – tripled – quadrupled. Now it could not weigh less than fifty pounds; and still it was getting heavier and heavier . . . A hundred pounds! – a hundred and fifty! – two hundred! . . . Umétsu knew that he had been deluded – that he had not been speaking with any mortal woman – that the child was not human. But he had made a promise; and a samurai was bound by his promise. So he kept the infant in his arms; and it continued to grow heavier. And heavier . . . two hundred and fifty! – three hundred! – four hundred pounds! . . . What was going to happen he could not imagine; but he resolved not to be afraid, and not to let the child go while his strength lasted . . . Five hundred! – five hundred and fifty! – six hundred pounds! All his muscles began to quiver with the strain; and still the weight increased . . . 'Namu Amida Butsu!' he groaned – 'Namu Amida Butsu! – Namu Amida Butsu!' Even as he uttered the holy invocation for the third time, the weight passed away from him with a shock; and he stood stupefied, with empty hands – for the child had unaccountably disappeared. But almost in the same instant he saw the mysterious woman returning as quickly as she had gone. Still panting she came to him; and he then first saw that she was very fair; but her brow dripped with sweat; and her sleeves were bound back with *tasuki*-cords,[2] as if she had been working hard.

'Kind Sir Umétsu,' she said, 'you do not know how great a service you have done me. I am the *Ujigami** of this place; and to-night one of my *Ujiko* found herself in the pains of childbirth, and prayed to me for aid. But the labour proved to be very diffi-cult; and I soon saw that by my own power alone I might not be able to save her: therefore I sought for the help of your strength and courage. And the child that I laid in your hands was the child that had not yet been born; and in the time that you first felt the child becoming heavier and heavier, the danger was very great – for the Gates of Birth were closed. And when you felt the child become so heavy that you despaired of being able to bear the weight much longer – in that same moment the mother seemed to be dead, and the family wept for her. Then you three times repeated the prayer, *Namu Amida Butsu!* – and the third time that you uttered it the power of the Lord Buddha came to our aid, and the Gates of Birth were opened ... And for that which you have done you shall be fitly rewarded. To a brave samurai no gift can be more serviceable than strength: therefore, not only to you, but likewise to your children and to your children's children, great strength shall be given.'

And, with this promise, the divinity disappeared.

Umétsu Chūbei, wondering greatly, resumed his way to the castle. At sunrise, on being relieved from duty, he proceeded as usual to wash his face and hands before making his morning prayer. But when he began to wring the towel which had served him, he was surprised to feel the tough material snap asunder in his hands. He attempted to twist together the separated portions; and again the stuff parted – like so much wet paper. He tried to wring the four thicknesses; and the result was the same. Presently, after handling

---

* *Ujigami* is the title given to the tutelary Shintō divinity of a parish or district. All persons living in that parish or district, and assisting in the maintenance of the temple (*miya*) of the deity, are called *Ujiko*.

various objects of bronze and of iron which yielded to his touch like clay, he understood that he had come into full possession of the great strength promised, and that he would have to be careful thenceforward when touching things, lest they should crumble in his fingers.

On returning home, he made inquiry as to whether any child had been born in the settlement during the night. Then he learned that a birth had actually taken place at the very hour of his adventure, and that the circumstances had been exactly as related to him by the *Ujigami*.

The children of Umétsu Chūbei inherited their father's strength. Several of his descendants – all remarkably powerful men – were still living in the province of Dewa at the time when this story was written.

THE LEGEND OF YUREI-DAKI

Near the village of Kurosaka, in the province of Hōki, there is a waterfall called Yurei-Daki, or The Cascade of Ghosts. Why it is so called I do not know. Near the foot of the fall there is a small Shintō shrine of the god of the locality, whom the people name Taki-Daimyōjin; and in front of the shrine is a little wooden money-box – *saisen-bako* – to receive the offerings of believers. And there is a story about that money-box.

One icy winter's evening, thirty-five years ago, the women and girls employed at a certain *asa-toriba*, or hemp-factory, in Kurosaka, gathered around the big brazier in the spinning-room after their day's work had been done. Then they amused themselves by telling ghost-stories. By the time that a dozen stories had been told, most of the gathering felt uncomfortable; and a girl cried out, just to heighten the pleasure of fear, 'Only think of going this night, all by one's self, to the Yurei-Daki!' The suggestion provoked a general scream, followed by nervous bursts of laughter . . . 'I'll give all the hemp I spun to-day,' mockingly said one of the party, 'to the person who goes!' 'So will I,' exclaimed another. 'And I,' said a third. 'All of us,' affirmed a fourth . . . Then from among the spinners stood up one Yasumoto O-Katsu, the wife of a carpenter; she had her only son, a boy of two years old, snugly wrapped up and asleep upon her back. 'Listen,' said O-Katsu; 'if you will all really agree to make over to me all the hemp spun today, I will go to the Yurei-Daki.' Her proposal was received with cries of astonishment and of defiance. But after having been several times repeated, it was seriously taken. Each of the spinners in turn agreed to give up her share of the day's work to O-Katsu, providing that O-Katsu should go to the Yurei-Daki. 'But how are we to know if she really goes there?' a sharp voice asked. 'Why, let her bring back the money-box of the god,' answered an old woman whom the spinners called Obaa-San, the Grandmother; 'that will be proof enough.' 'I'll bring it,' cried O-Katsu. And out she darted into the street, with her sleeping boy upon her back.

The night was frosty, but clear. Down the empty street O-Katsu hurried; and she saw that all the house fronts were tightly closed, because of the piercing cold. Out of the village, and along the high road she ran – *pichà-pichà* – with the great silence of frozen rice-fields on either hand, and only the stars to light her. Half an hour she followed the open road; then she turned down a narrower way, winding under cliffs. Darker and rougher the path became as she proceeded; but she knew it well, and she soon heard the dull roar of the water. A few minutes more, and the way widened into a glen, and the dull roar suddenly became a loud clamor, and before her she saw, looming against a mass of blackness, the long glimmering of the fall. Dimly she perceived the shrine, the money-box. She rushed forward – put out her hand . . .

'*Oi!* O-Katsu-San!'* suddenly called a warning voice above the crash of the water.

O-Katsu stood motionless, stupefied by terror.

'*Oi!* O-Katsu-San!' again pealed the voice, this time with more of menace in its tone.

But O-Katsu was really a bold woman. At once recovering from her stupefaction, she snatched up the money-box and ran. She neither heard nor saw anything more to alarm her until she reached the highroad, where she stopped a moment to take breath. Then she ran on steadily – *pichà-pichà* – till she got to Kurosaka, and thumped at the door of the *asa-toriba*.

How the women and the girls cried out as she entered, panting, with the money-box of the god in her hand! Breathlessly they heard her story; sympathetically they screeched when she told

---

* The exclamation *Oi!* is used to call the attention of a person: it is the Japanese equivalent for such English exclamations as 'Halloa!' 'Ho, there!' etc.

them of the Voice that had called her name, twice, out of the haunted water . . . What a woman! Brave O-Katsu! – well had she earned the hemp! . . . 'But your boy must be cold, O-Katsu!' cried the Obaa-San, 'let us have him here by the fire!'

'He ought to be hungry,' exclaimed the mother; 'I must give him his milk presently.' . . . 'Poor O-Katsu!' said the Obaa-San, helping to remove the wraps in which the boy had been carried – 'why, you are all wet behind!' Then, with a husky scream, the helper vociferated, *'Ara! it is blood!'*

And out of the wrappings unfastened there fell to the floor a blood-soaked bundle of baby clothes that left exposed two very small brown feet, and two very small brown hands – nothing more. The child's head had been torn off! . . .

IN A CUP OF TEA

Have you ever attempted to mount some old tower stairway, spiring up through darkness, and in the heart of that darkness found yourself at the cobwebbed edge of nothing? Or have you followed some coast path, cut along the face of a cliff, only to discover yourself, at a turn, on the jagged verge of a break. The emotional worth of such experience – from a literary point of view – is proved by the force of the sensations aroused, and by the vividness with which they are remembered.

Now there have been curiously preserved, in old Japanese storybooks, certain fragments of fiction that produce an almost similar emotional experience . . . Perhaps the writer was lazy; perhaps he had a quarrel with the publisher; perhaps he was suddenly called away from his little table, and never came back; perhaps death stopped the writing-brush in the very middle of a sentence.

But no mortal man can ever tell us exactly why these things were left unfinished . . . I select a typical example.

* * *

On the fourth day of the first month of the third Tenwa,[1] – that is to say, about two hundred and twenty years ago, – the lord Nakagawa Sado, while on his way to make a New Year's visit, halted with his train at a tea-house in Hakusan, in the Hongō district of Yedo. While the party were resting there, one of the lord's attendants – a *wakatō** named Sekinai – feeling very thirsty, filled for himself a large water-cup with tea. He was raising the cup to his

---

* The armed attendant of a samurai was thus called. The relation of the *wakatō* to the samurai was that of squire to knight.

lips when he suddenly perceived, in the transparent yellow infusion, the image or reflection of a face that was not his own. Startled, he looked around, but could see no one near him. The face in the tea appeared, from the coiffure, to be the face of a young samurai: it was strangely distinct, and very handsome – delicate as the face of a girl. And it seemed the reflection of a living face; for the eyes and the lips were moving. Bewildered by this mysterious apparition, Sekinai threw away the tea, and carefully examined the cup. It proved to be a very cheap water-cup, with no artistic devices of any sort. He found and filled another cup; and again the face appeared in the tea. He then ordered fresh tea, and refilled the cup; and once more the strange face appeared – this time with a mocking smile. But Sekinai did not allow himself to be frightened. 'Whoever you are,' he muttered, 'you shall delude me no further!' – then he swallowed the tea, face and all, and went his way, wondering whether he had swallowed a ghost.

Late in the evening of the same day, while on watch in the palace of the lord Nakagawa, Sekinai was surprised by the soundless coming of a stranger into the apartment. This stranger, a richly dressed young samurai, seated himself directly in front of Sekinai, and, saluting the *wakatō* with a slight bow, observed:

'I am Shikibu Heinai – met you to-day for the first time . . . You do not seem to recognize me.'

He spoke in a very low, but penetrating voice. And Sekinai was astonished to find before him the same sinister, handsome face of which he had seen, and swallowed, the apparition in a cup of tea. It was smiling now, as the phantom had smiled; but the steady gaze of the eyes, above the smiling lips, was at once a challenge and an insult.

'No, I do not recognize you,' returned Sekinai, angry but cool; 'and perhaps you will now be good enough to inform me how you obtained admission to this house?'

[In feudal times the residence of a lord was strictly guarded at all hours; and no one could enter unannounced, except through some unpardonable negligence on the part of the armed watch.]

'Ah, you do not recognize me!' exclaimed the visitor, in a tone of irony, drawing a little nearer as he spoke. 'No, you do not recognize me! Yet you took upon yourself this morning to do me a deadly injury! . . .'

Sekinai instantly seized the *tantō** at his girdle, and made a fierce thrust at the throat of the man. But the blade seemed to touch no substance. Simultaneously and soundlessly the intruder leaped sideward to the chamber-wall, *and through it!* . . . The wall showed no trace of his exit. He had traversed it only as the light of a candle passes through lantern-paper.

When Sekinai made report of the incident, his recital astonished and puzzled the retainers. No stranger had been seen either to enter or to leave the palace at the hour of the occurrence; and no one in the service of the lord Nakagawa had ever heard of the name 'Shikibu Heinai'.

On the following night Sekinai was off duty, and remained at home with his parents. At a rather late hour he was informed that some strangers had called at the house, and desired to speak with him for a moment. Taking his sword, he went to the entrance, and there found three armed men – apparently retainers – waiting in front of the doorstep. The three bowed respectfully to Sekinai; and one of them said:

'Our names are Matsuoka Bungō, Tsuchibashi Bungō, and Okamura Heiroku. We are retainers of the noble Shikibu Heinai. When our master last night deigned to pay you a visit, you struck him with a sword. He was much hurt, and has been obliged to go to the hot springs, where his wound is now being treated. But on the sixteenth day of the coming month he will return; and he will then fitly repay you for the injury done him . . .'

Without waiting to hear more, Sekinai leaped out, sword in hand, and slashed right and left, at the strangers. But the three men sprang to the wall of the adjoining building, and flitted up the wall like shadows, and . . .

*   *   *

* The shorter of the two swords carried by samurai. The longer sword was called *katana*.

Here the old narrative breaks off; the rest of the story existed only in some brain that has been dust for a century.

I am able to imagine several possible endings; but none of them would satisfy an Occidental imagination. I prefer to let the reader attempt to decide for himself the probable consequence of swallowing a Soul.

IKIRYŌ

Formerly, in the quarter of Reiganjima, in Yedo, there was a great porcelain shop called the Setomonodana, kept by a rich man named Kihei. Kihei had in his employ, for many years, a head clerk named Rokubei. Under Rokubei's care the business prospered; and at last it grew so large that Rokubei found himself unable to manage it without help. He therefore asked and obtained permission to hire an experienced assistant; and he then engaged one of his own nephews – a young man about twenty-two years old, who had learned the porcelain trade in Osaka.

The nephew proved a very capable assistant – shrewder in business than his experienced uncle. His enterprise extended the trade of the house, and Kihei was greatly pleased. But about seven months after his engagement, the young man became very ill, and seemed likely to die. The best physicians in Yedo were summoned to attend him; but none of them could understand the nature of his sickness. They prescribed no medicine, and expressed the opinion that such a sickness could only have been caused by some secret grief.

Rokubei imagined that it might be a case of lovesickness. He therefore said to his nephew:

'I have been thinking that, as you are still very young, you might have formed some secret attachment which is making you unhappy – perhaps even making you ill. If this be the truth, you certainly ought to tell me all about your troubles. Here I stand to you in the place of a father, as you are far away from your parents; and if you have any anxiety or sorrow, I am ready to do for you whatever a father should do. If money can help you, do not be ashamed to tell me, even though the amount be large. I think that I could assist you; and I am sure that Kihei would be glad to do anything to make you happy and well.'

The sick youth appeared to be embarrassed by these kindly assurances; and for some little time he remained silent. At last he answered:

'Never in this world can I forget those generous words. But I have no secret attachment – no longing for any woman. This sickness of mine is not a sickness that doctors can cure; and money could not help me in the least. The truth is, that I have been so persecuted in this house that I scarcely care to live. Everywhere – by day and by night, whether in the shop or in my room, whether alone or in company – I have been unceasingly followed and tormented by the Shadow of a woman. And it is long, long since I have been able to get even one night's rest. For so soon as I close my eyes, the Shadow of the woman takes me by the throat and strives to strangle me. So I cannot sleep . . .'

'And why did you not tell me this before?' asked Rokubei.

'Because I thought,' the nephew answered, 'that it would be of no use to tell you. The Shadow is not the ghost of a dead person. It is made by the hatred of a living person – a person whom you very well know.'

'What person?' questioned Rokubei, in great astonishment.'*

'The mistress of this house,' whispered the youth – 'the wife of Kihei Sama . . . She wishes to kill me.'

Rokubei was bewildered by this confession. He doubted nothing of what his nephew had said; but he could not imagine a reason for the haunting. An *Ikiryō*[1] might be caused by disappointed love, or by violent hate – without the knowledge of the person from whom it had emanated. To suppose any love in this case was impossible; the wife of Kihei was considerably more than fifty years of age. But, on the other hand, what could the young clerk have done to provoke hatred – a hatred capable of producing an *Ikiryō*? He had been irreproachably well conducted, unfailingly

* An *Ikiryō* is seen only by the person haunted. For another illustration of this curious belief, see the paper entitled 'The Stone Buddha' in my *Out of the East*, p. 171.

courteous, and earnestly devoted to his duties. The mystery troubled Rokubei; but, after careful reflection, he decided to tell everything to Kihei, and to request an investigation.

Kihei was astounded; but in the time of forty years he had never had the least reason to doubt the word of Rokubei. He therefore summoned his wife at once, and carefully questioned her, telling her, at the same time, what the sick clerk had said. At first she turned pale, and wept; but, after some hesitation, she answered frankly:

'I suppose that what the new clerk has said about the *Ikiryō* is true – though I really tried never to betray, by word or look, the dislike which I could not help feeling for him. You know that he is very skilful in commerce – very shrewd in everything that he does. And you have given him much authority in this house – power over the apprentices and the servants. But our only son, who should inherit this business, is very simple-hearted and easily deceived; and I have long been thinking that your clever new clerk might so delude our boy as to get possession of all this property. Indeed, I am certain that your clerk could at any time, without the least difficulty, and without the least risk to himself, ruin our business and ruin our son. And with this certainty in my mind, I cannot help fearing and hating the man. I have often and often wished that he were dead; I have even wished that it were in my own power to kill him . . . Yes, I know that it is wrong to hate any one in such a way; but I could not check the feeling. Night and day I have been wishing evil to that clerk. So I cannot doubt that he has really seen the thing of which he spoke to Rokubei.'

'How absurd of you,' exclaimed Kihei, 'to torment yourself thus! Up to the present time that clerk has done no single thing for which he could be blamed; and you have caused him to suffer cruelly . . . Now if I should send him away, with his uncle, to another town, to establish a branch business, could you not endeavour to think more kindly of him?'

'If I do not see his face or hear his voice,' the wife answered – 'if you will only send him away from this house – then I think that I shall be able to conquer my hatred of him.'

'Try to do so,' said Kihei; 'for, if you continue to hate him as you have been hating him, he will certainly die, and you will then be guilty of having caused the death of a man who has done us nothing but good. He has been, in every way, a most excellent servant.'

Then Kihei quickly made arrangements for the establishment of a branch house in another city; and he sent Rokubei there with the clerk, to take charge. And thereafter the *Ikiryō* ceased to torment the young man, who soon recovered his health.

THE STORY OF O-KAMÉ

O-Kamé, daughter of the rich Gonyémon of Nagoshi, in the province of Tosa, was very fond of her husband, Hachiyémon. She was twenty-two, and Hachiyémon twenty-five. She was so fond of him that people imagined her to be jealous. But he never gave her the least cause for jealousy; and it is certain that no single unkind word was ever spoken between them.

Unfortunately the health of O-Kamé was feeble. Within less than two years after her marriage she was attacked by a disease, then prevalent in Tosa, and the best doctors were not able to cure her. Persons seized by this malady could not eat or drink; they remained constantly drowsy and languid, and troubled by strange fancies. And, in spite of constant care, O-Kamé grew weaker and weaker, day by day, until it became evident, even to herself, that she was going to die.

Then she called her husband, and said to him:

'I cannot tell you how good you have been to me during this miserable sickness of mine. Surely no one could have been more kind. But that only makes it all the harder for me to leave you now . . . Think! I am not yet even twenty-five – and I have the best husband in all this world – and yet I must die! . . . Oh, no, no! It is useless to talk to me about hope; the best Chinese doctors could do nothing for me. I did think to live a few months longer; but when I saw my face this morning in the mirror, I knew that I must die to-day – yes, this very day. And there is something that I want to beg you to do for me – if you wish me to die quite happy.'

'Only tell me what it is,' Hachiyémon answered; 'and if it be in my power to do, I shall be more than glad to do it.'

'No, no – you will not be glad to do it,' she returned: 'you are still so young! It is difficult – very, very difficult – even to ask you to do such a thing; yet the wish for it is like a fire burning in my breast. I must speak it before I die ... My dear, you know that sooner or later, after I am dead, they will want you to take another wife. Will you promise me – can you promise me – not to marry again? ...'

'Only that!' Hachiyémon exclaimed. 'Why, if that be all that you wanted to ask for, your wish is very easily granted. With all my heart I promise you that no one shall ever take your place.'

'Aa! uréshiya!' cried O-Kamé,[1] half-rising from her couch; 'oh, how happy you have made me!'

And she fell back dead.

Now the health of Hachiyémon appeared to fail after the death of O-Kamé. At first the change in his aspect was attributed to natural grief, and the villagers only said, 'How fond of her he must have been!' But, as the months went by, he grew paler and weaker, until at last he became so thin and wan that he looked more like a ghost than a man. Then people began to suspect that sorrow alone could not explain this sudden decline of a man so young. The doctors said that Hachiyémon was not suffering from any known form of disease: they could not account for his condition; but they suggested that it might have been caused by some very unusual trouble of mind. Hachiyémon's parents questioned him in vain; he had no cause for sorrow, he said, other than what they already knew. They counselled him to remarry; but he protested that nothing could ever induce him to break his promise to the dead.

Thereafter Hachiyémon continued to grow visibly weaker, day by day; and his family despaired of his life. But one day his mother, who felt sure that he had been concealing something from her, adjured him so earnestly to tell her the real cause of his decline, and wept so bitterly before him, that he was not able to resist her entreaties.

'Mother,' he said, 'it is very difficult to speak about this matter, either to you or to any one; and, perhaps, when I have told you everything, you will not be able to believe me. But the truth is that O-Kamé can find no rest in the other world, and that the Buddhist services repeated for her have been said in vain. Perhaps she will never be able to rest unless I go with her on the long black journey. For every night she returns, and lies down by my side. Every night, since the day of her funeral, she has come back. And sometimes I doubt if she be really dead; for she looks and acts just as when she lived – except that she talks to me only in whispers. And she always bids me tell no one that she comes. It may be that she wants me to die; and I should not care to live for my own sake only. But it is true, as you have said, that my body really belongs to my parents, and that I owe to them the first duty. So now, mother, I tell you the whole truth . . . Yes: every night she comes, just as I am about to sleep; and she remains until dawn. As soon as she hears the temple-bell, she goes away.'

When the mother of Hachiyémon had heard these things, she was greatly alarmed; and, hastening at once to the parish-temple, she told the priest all that her son had confessed, and begged for ghostly help. The priest, who was a man of great age and experience, listened without surprise to the recital, and then said to her:
    'It is not the first time that I have known such a thing to happen; and I think that I shall be able to save your son. But he is really in great danger. I have seen the shadow of death upon his face; and, if O-Kamé return but once again, he will never behold another sunrise. Whatever can be done for him must be done quickly. Say nothing of the matter to your son; but assemble the members of both families as soon as possible, and tell them to come to the temple without delay. For your son's sake it will be necessary to open the grave of O-Kamé.'

So the relatives assembled at the temple; and when the priest had obtained their consent to the opening of the sepulchre, he led the way to the cemetery. Then, under his direction, the tombstone of O-Kamé was shifted, the grave opened, and the coffin raised. And when the coffin-lid had been removed, all present were startled; for O-Kamé sat before them with a smile upon her face, seeming as comely as before the time of her sickness; and there was not any sign of death upon her. But when the priest told his assistants

to lift the dead woman out of the coffin, the astonishment changed to fear; for the corpse was blood-warm to the touch, and still flexible as in life, notwithstanding the squatting posture in which it had remained so long.*

It was borne to the mortuary chapel; and there the priest, with a writing-brush, traced upon the brow and breast and limbs of the body the Sanscrit characters (*Bonji*) of certain holy talismanic words. And he performed a *Ségaki*-service for the spirit of O-Kamé, before suffering her corpse to be restored to the ground.

She never again visited her husband; and Hachiyémon gradually recovered his health and strength. But whether he always kept his promise, the Japanese story-teller does not say.

* The Japanese dead are placed in a sitting posture in the coffin, which is almost square in form.

THE STORY OF CHŪGORŌ

A long time ago there lived, in the Koishikawa quarter of Yedo, a
hatamoto[1] named Suzuki, whose *yashiki*[2] was situated on the
bank of the Yedogawa, not far from the bridge called Naka-
no-hashi. And among the retainers of this Suzuki there was an
ashigaru* named Chūgorō. Chūgorō was a handsome lad, very
amiable and clever, and much liked by his comrades.

For several years Chūgorō remained in the service of Suzuki,
conducting himself so well that no fault was found with him. But
at last the other *ashigaru* discovered that Chūgorō was in the habit
of leaving the *yashiki* every night, by way of the garden, and staying out until a little before dawn. At first they said nothing to
him about this strange behaviour; for his absences did not inter-
fere with any regular duty, and were supposed to be caused by
some love-affair. But after a time he began to look pale and weak;
and his comrades, suspecting some serious folly, decided to inter-
fere. Therefore, one evening, just as he was about to steal away
from the house, an elderly retainer called him aside, and said:

'Chūgorō, my lad, we know that you go out every night and
stay away until early morning; and we have observed that you are
looking unwell. We fear that you are keeping bad company, and
injuring your health. And unless you can give a good reason for
your conduct, we shall think that it is our duty to report this matter to the Chief Officer. In any case, since we are your comrades
and friends, it is but right that we should know why you go out at
night, contrary to the custom of this house.'

Chūgorō appeared to be very much embarrassed and alarmed

---

* The *ashigaru* were the lowest class of retainers in military service.

by these words. But after a short silence he passed into the garden, followed by his comrade. When the two found themselves well out of hearing of the rest, Chūgorō stopped, and said:

'I will now tell you everything; but I must entreat you to keep my secret. If you repeat what I tell you, some great misfortune may befall me.

'It was in the early part of last spring – about five months ago – that I first began to go out at night, on account of a love-affair. One evening, when I was returning to the *yashiki* after a visit to my parents, I saw a woman standing by the riverside, not far from the main gateway. She was dressed like a person of high rank; and I thought it strange that a woman so finely dressed should be standing there alone at such an hour. But I did not think that I had any right to question her; and I was about to pass her by, without speaking, when she stepped forward and pulled me by the sleeve. Then I saw that she was very young and handsome. "Will you not walk with me as far as the bridge?" she said; "I have something to tell you." Her voice was very soft and pleasant; and she smiled as she spoke; and her smile was hard to resist. So I walked with her toward the bridge; and on the way she told me that she had often seen me going in and out of the *yashiki*, and had taken a fancy to me. "I wish to have you for my husband," she said; "if you can like me, we shall be able to make each other very happy." I did not know how to answer her; but I thought her very charming. As we neared the bridge, she pulled my sleeve again, and led me down the bank to the very edge of the river. "Come in with me," she whispered, and pulled me toward the water. It is deep there, as you know; and I became all at once afraid of her, and tried to turn back. She smiled, and caught me by the wrist, and said, "Oh, you must never be afraid with me!" And, somehow, at the touch of her hand, I became more helpless than a child. I felt like a person in a dream who tries to run, and cannot move hand or foot. Into the deep water she stepped, and drew me with her; and I neither saw nor heard nor felt anything more until I found myself walking beside her through what seemed to be a great palace, full of light. I was neither wet nor cold: everything around me was dry and warm and beautiful. I could not understand where I was, nor how I had come there.

The woman led me by the hand: we passed through room after room – through ever so many rooms, all empty, but very fine – until we entered into a guest-room of a thousand mats. Before a great alcove, at the farther end, lights were burning, and cushions laid as for a feast; but I saw no guests. She led me to the place of honour, by the alcove, and seated herself in front of me, and said: "This is my home: do you think that you could be happy with me here?" As she asked the question she smiled; and I thought that her smile was more beautiful than anything else in the world; and out of my heart I answered, "Yes . . ." In the same moment I remembered the story of Urashima;[3] and I imagined that she might be the daughter of a god; but I feared to ask her any questions . . . Presently maid-servants came in, bearing rice-wine and many dishes, which they set before us. Then she who sat before me said: "To-night shall be our bridal night, because you like me; and this is our wedding-feast." We pledged ourselves to each other for the time of seven existences; and after the banquet we were conducted to a bridal chamber, which had been prepared for us.

'It was yet early in the morning when she awoke me, and said: "My dear one, you are now indeed my husband. But for reasons which I cannot tell you, and which you must not ask, it is necessary that our marriage remain secret. To keep you here until daybreak would cost both of us our lives. Therefore do not, I beg of you, feel displeased because I must now send you back to the house of your lord. You can come to me to-night again, and every night hereafter, at the same hour that we first met. Wait always for me by the bridge; and you will not have to wait long. But remember, above all things, that our marriage must be a secret, and that, if you talk about it, we shall probably be separated forever."

'I promised to obey her in all things – remembering the fate of Urashima – and she conducted me through many rooms, all empty and beautiful, to the entrance. There she again took me by the wrist, and everything suddenly became dark, and I knew nothing more until I found myself standing alone on the river bank, close to the Naka-no-hashi. When I got back to the *yashiki*, the temple bells had not yet begun to ring.

'In the evening I went again to the bridge, at the hour she had named, and I found her waiting for me. She took me with her, as before, into the deep water, and into the wonderful place where we had passed our bridal night. And every night, since then, I have met and parted from her in the same way. To-night she will certainly be waiting for me, and I would rather die than disappoint her: therefore I must go ... But let me again entreat you, my friend, never to speak to any one about what I have told you.'

The elder *ashigaru* was surprised and alarmed by this story. He felt that Chūgorō had told him the truth; and the truth suggested unpleasant possibilities. Probably the whole experience was an illusion, and an illusion produced by some evil power for a malevolent end. Nevertheless, if really bewitched, the lad was rather to be pitied than blamed; and any forcible interference would be likely to result in mischief. So the *ashigaru* answered kindly:

'I shall never speak of what you have told me – never, at least, while you remain alive and well. Go and meet the woman; but – beware of her! I fear that you are being deceived by some wicked spirit.'

Chūgorō only smiled at the old man's warning, and hastened away. Several hours later he re-entered the *yashiki*, with a strangely dejected look. 'Did you meet her?' whispered his comrade. 'No,' replied Chūgorō; 'she was not there. For the first time, she was not there. I think that she will never meet me again. I did wrong to tell you; I was very foolish to break my promise ...' The other vainly tried to console him. Chūgorō lay down, and spoke no word more. He was trembling from head to foot, as if he had caught a chill.

When the temple bells announced the hour of dawn, Chūgorō tried to get up, and fell back senseless. He was evidently sick – deathly sick. A Chinese physician was summoned.

'Why, the man has no blood!' exclaimed the doctor, after a careful examination; 'there is nothing but water in his veins! It will be very difficult to save him ... What maleficence is this?'

Everything was done that could be done to save Chūgorō's life – but in vain. He died as the sun went down. Then his comrade related the whole story.

'Ah! I might have suspected as much!' exclaimed the doctor . . . 'No power could have saved him. He was not the first whom she destroyed.'

'Who is she? – or what is she?' the *ashigaru* asked – 'a Fox-Woman?'

'No; she has been haunting this river from ancient time. She loves the blood of the young . . .'

'A Serpent-Woman? – A Dragon-Woman?'

'No, no! If you were to see her under that bridge by daylight, she would appear to you a very loathsome creature.'

'But what kind of a creature?'

'Simply a Frog – a great and ugly Frog!'

THE STORY OF
MIMI-NASHI-HŌÏCHI

More than seven hundred years ago, at Dan-no-ura, in the Straits of Shimonoséki, was fought the last battle of the long contest between the Heiké, or Taira clan, and the Genji, or Minamoto clan.[1] There the Heiké perished utterly, with their women and children, and their infant emperor likewise – now remembered as Antoku Tennō.[2] And that sea and shore have been haunted for seven hundred years ... Elsewhere I told you about the strange crabs found there, called Heiké crabs, which have human faces on their backs, and are said to be the spirits of the Heiké warriors.* But there are many strange things to be seen and heard along that coast. On dark nights thousands of ghostly fires hover about the beach, or flit above the waves – pale lights which the fishermen call *Oni-bi*, or demon-fires; and, whenever the winds are up, a sound of great shouting comes from that sea, like a clamor of battle.

In former years the Heiké were much more restless than they now are. They would rise about ships passing in the night, and try to sink them; and at all times they would watch for swimmers, to pull them down. It was in order to appease those dead that the Buddhist temple, Amidaji, was built at Akamagaséki.† A cemetery also was made close by, near the beach; and within it were set up monuments inscribed with the names of the drowned emperor and of his great vassals; and Buddhist services were regularly performed there, on behalf of the spirits of them. After the temple had been built, and the tombs erected, the Heiké gave less trouble

* See my *Kottō*, for a description of these curious crabs.
† Or, Simonoséki. The town is also known by the name of Bakkan.

than before; but they continued to do queer things at intervals – proving that they had not found the perfect peace.

Some centuries ago there lived at Akamagaséki a blind man named Hōïchi, who was famed for his skill in recitation and in playing upon the *biwa*.* From childhood he had been trained to recite and to play; and while yet a lad he had surpassed his teachers. As a professional *biwa-hōshi* he became famous chiefly by his recitations of the history of the Heiké and the Genji; and it is said that when he sang the song of the battle of Dan-no-ura 'even the goblins [*kijin*] could not refrain from tears'.

At the outset of his career, Hōïchi was very poor; but he found a good friend to help him. The priest of the Amidaji was fond of poetry and music; and he often invited Hōïchi to the temple, to play and recite. Afterwards, being much impressed by the wonderful skill of the lad, the priest proposed that Hōïchi should make the temple his home; and this offer was gratefully accepted. Hōïchi was given a room in the temple-building; and, in return for food and lodging, he was required only to gratify the priest with a musical performance on certain evenings, when otherwise disengaged.

One summer night the priest was called away, to perform a Buddhist service at the house of a dead parishioner; and he went there with his acolyte, leaving Hōïchi alone in the temple. It was a hot night; and the blind man sought to cool himself on the verandah before his sleeping-room. The verandah overlooked a small garden in the rear of the Amidaji. There Hōïchi waited for the priest's return, and tried to relieve his solitude by practicing upon his *biwa*. Midnight passed; and the priest did not appear. But the

---

* The *biwa*, a kind of four-stringed lute, is chiefly used in musical recitative. Formerly the professional minstrels who recited the *Heiké-Monogatari*,[3] and other tragical histories, were called *biwa-hōshi*, or 'lute-priests'. The origin of this appellation is not clear; but it is possible that it may have been suggested by the fact that 'lute-priests', as well as blind shampooers, had their heads shaven, like Buddhist priests. The *biwa* is played with a kind of plectrum, called *bachi*, usually made of horn.

atmosphere was still too warm for comfort within doors; and
Hōïchi remained outside. At last he heard steps approaching
from the back gate. Somebody crossed the garden, advanced to
the verandah, and halted directly in front of him – but it was not
the priest. A deep voice called the blind man's name – abruptly
and unceremoniously, in the manner of a samurai summoning
an inferior:

'Hōïchi!'

Hōïchi was too much startled, for the moment, to respond; and
the voice called again, in a tone of harsh command,

'Hōïchi!'

'*Hai!*'⁴ answered the blind man, frightened by the menace in
the voice – 'I am blind! – I cannot know who calls!'

'There is nothing to fear,' the stranger exclaimed, speaking
more gently. 'I am stopping near this temple, and have been sent
to you with a message. My present lord, a person of exceedingly
high rank, is now staying in Akamagaséki, with many noble
attendants. He wished to view the scene of the battle of Dan-no-
ura; and to-day he visited that place. Having heard of your skill in
reciting the story of the battle, he now desires to hear your performance: so you will take your *biwa* and come with me at once
to the house where the august assembly is waiting.'

In those times, the order of a samurai was not to be lightly dis-
obeyed. Hōïchi donned his sandals, took his *biwa*, and went away
with the stranger, who guided him deftly, but obliged him to walk
very fast. The hand that guided was iron; and the clank of the war-
rior's stride proved him fully armed – probably some palace-guard
on duty. Hōïchi's first alarm was over: he began to imagine himself in good luck; for, remembering the retainer's assurance about
a 'person of exceedingly high rank', he thought that the lord who
wished to hear the recitation could not be less than a *daimyō* of the
first class. Presently the samurai halted; and Hōïchi became aware
that they had arrived at a large gateway; and he wondered, for he
could not remember any large gate in that part of the town, except
the main gate of the Amidaji. '*Kaimon!*'* the samurai called – and

---

* A respectful term, signifying the opening of a gate. It was used by samurai
when calling to the guards on duty at a lord's gate for admission.

there was a sound of unbarring; and the twain passed on. They traversed a space of garden, and halted again before some entrance; and the retainer cried in a loud voice, 'Within there! I have brought Hōïchi.' Then came sounds of feet hurrying, and screens sliding, and rain-doors opening, and voices of women in converse. By the language of the women Hōïchi knew them to be domestics in some noble household; but he could not imagine to what place he had been conducted. Little time was allowed him for conjecture. After he had been helped to mount several stone steps, upon the last of which he was told to leave his sandals, a woman's hand guided him along interminable reaches of polished planking, and round pillared angles too many to remember, and over widths amazing of matted floor – into the middle of some vast apartment. There he thought that many great people were assembled: the sound of the rustling of silk was like the sound of leaves in a forest. He heard also a great humming of voices – talking in undertones; and the speech was the speech of courts. Hōïchi was told to put himself at ease, and he found a kneeling-cushion ready for him. After having taken his place upon it, and tuned his instrument, the voice of a woman – whom he divined to be the *Rōjo*, or matron in charge of the female service – addressed him, saying,

'It is now required that the history of the Heiké be recited, to the accompaniment of the *biwa*.'

Now the entire recital would have required a time of many nights: therefore Hōïchi ventured a question:

'As the whole of the story is not soon told, what portion is it augustly desired that I now recite?'

The woman's voice made answer:

'Recite the story of the battle at Dan-no-ura – for the pity of it is the most deep.'*

Then Hōïchi lifted up his voice, and chanted the chant of the fight on the bitter sea – wonderfully making his *biwa* to sound like the straining of oars and the rushing of ships, the whirr and the hissing of arrows, the shouting and trampling of men, the crashing of steel upon helmets, the plunging of slain in the flood.

---

* Or the phrase might be rendered, 'for the pity of that part is the deepest'. The Japanese word for pity in the original text is *awaré*.

And to left and right of him, in the pauses of his playing, he could hear voices murmuring praise: 'How marvelous an artist!' – 'Never in our own province was playing heard like this!' – 'Not in all the empire is there another singer like Hōïchi!' Then fresh courage came to him, and he played and sang yet better than before; and a hush of wonder deepened about him. But when at last he came to tell the fate of the fair and helpless – the piteous perishing of ·the women and children – and the death-leap of Nii-no-Ama, with the imperial infant in her arms[5] – then all the listeners uttered together one long, long shuddering cry of anguish; and thereafter they wept and wailed so loudly and so wildly that the blind man was frightened by the violence and grief that he had made. For much time the sobbing and the wailing continued. But gradually the sounds of lamentation died away; and again, in the great stillness that followed, Hōïchi heard the voice of the woman whom he supposed to be the *Rōjo*.

She said:

'Although we had been assured that you were a very skillful player upon the *biwa*, and without an equal in recitative, we did not know that any one could be so skillful as you have proved yourself to-night. Our lord has been pleased to say that he intends to bestow upon you a fitting reward. But he desires that you shall perform before him once every night for the next six nights – after which time he will probably make his august return-journey. To-morrow night, therefore, you are to come here at the same hour. The retainer who to-night conducted you will be sent for you . . . There is another matter about which I have been ordered to inform you. It is required that you shall speak to no one of your visits here, during the time of our lord's august sojourn at Akama-gaséki. As he is traveling incognito,* he commands that no mention of these things be made . . . You are now free to go back to your temple.'

After Hōïchi had duly expressed his thanks, a woman's hand conducted him to the entrance of the house, where the same retainer, who had before guided him, was waiting to take him

---

* 'Traveling incognito' is at least the meaning of the original phrase – 'making a disguised august-journey' (*shinobi no go-ryokō*).

home. The retainer led him to the verandah at the rear of the temple, and there bade him farewell.

It was almost dawn when Hōïchi returned; but his absence from the temple had not been observed – as the priest, coming back at a very late hour, had supposed him asleep. During the day Hōïchi was able to take some rest; and he said nothing about his strange adventure. In the middle of the following night the samurai again came for him, and led him to the august assembly, where he gave another recitation with the same success that had attended his previous performance. But during this second visit his absence from the temple was accidentally discovered; and after his return in the morning he was summoned to the presence of the priest, who said to him, in a tone of kindly reproach:

'We have been very anxious about you, friend Hōïchi. To go out, blind and alone, at so late an hour, is dangerous. Why did you go without telling us? I could have ordered a servant to accompany you. And where have you been?'

Hōïchi answered, evasively,

'Pardon me, kind friend! I had to attend to some private business; and I could not arrange the matter at any other hour.'

The priest was surprised, rather than pained, by Hōïchi's reticence: he felt it to be unnatural, and suspected something wrong. He feared that the blind lad had been bewitched or deluded by some evil spirits. He did not ask any more questions; but he privately instructed the men-servants of the temple to keep watch upon Hōïchi's movements, and to follow him in case that he should again leave the temple after dark.

On the very next night, Hōïchi was seen to leave the temple; and the servants immediately lighted their lanterns, and followed after him. But it was a rainy night, and very dark; and before the temple-folks could get to the roadway, Hōïchi had disappeared. Evidently he had walked very fast – a strange thing, considering his blindness; for the road was in a bad condition. The men hurried through the streets, making inquiries at every house which Hōïchi was accustomed to visit; but nobody could give them any news of him. At last, as they were returning to the temple by way of the shore, they were startled by the sound of a *biwa*, furiously played, in the cemetery of the Amidaji. Except for some ghostly fires – such as usually flitted there on dark nights – all was blackness in that direction. But the men at once hastened to the cemetery; and there, by the help of their lanterns, they discovered Hōïchi – sitting alone in the rain before the memorial tomb of Antoku Tennō, making his *biwa* resound, and loudly chanting the chant of the battle of Dan-no-ura. And behind him, and about him, and everywhere above the tombs, the fires of the dead were burning, like candles. Never before had so great a host of *Oni-bi* appeared in the sight of mortal man . . .

'Hōïchi San! – Hōïchi San!' the servants cried – 'you are bewitched! . . . Hōïchi San!'

But the blind man did not seem to hear. Strenuously he made his *biwa* to rattle and ring and clang; more and more wildly he chanted the chant of the battle of Dan-no-ura. They caught hold of him; they shouted into his ear,

'Hōïchi San! – Hōïchi San! – come home with us at once!'

Reprovingly he spoke to them:

'To interrupt me in such a manner, before this august assembly, will not be tolerated.'

Whereat, in spite of the weirdness of the thing, the servants could not help laughing. Sure that he had been bewitched, they now seized him, and pulled him up on his feet, and by main force hurried him back to the temple – where he was immediately relieved of his wet clothes, by order of the priest. Then the priest insisted upon a full explanation of his friend's astonishing behavior. Hōïchi long hesitated to speak. But at last, finding that his conduct had really alarmed and angered the good priest, he decided to abandon his reserve; and he related everything that had happened from the time of first visit of the samurai.

The priest said:

'Hōïchi, my poor friend, you are now in great danger! How unfortunate that you did not tell me all this before! Your wonderful skill in music has indeed brought you into strange trouble. By this time you must be aware that you have not been visiting any house whatever, but have been passing your nights in the cemetery, among the tombs of the Heiké; and it was before the memorial-tomb of Antoku Tennō that our people to-night found you, sitting in the rain. All that you have been imagining was illusion – except the calling of the dead. By once obeying them, you have put yourself in their power. If you obey them again, after what has already occurred, they will tear you in pieces. But they would have destroyed you, sooner or later, in any event . . . Now I shall not be able to remain with you to-night: I am called away to perform another service. But, before I go, it will be necessary to protect your body by writing holy texts upon it.'

Before sundown the priest and his acolyte stripped Hōïchi: then, with their writing-brushes, they traced upon his breast and back, head and face and neck, limbs and hands and feet – even upon the soles of his feet, and upon all parts of his body – the text of the holy sûtra called *Hannya-Shin-Kyo*.* When this had been done, the priest instructed Hōïchi, saying:

'To-night, as soon as I go away, you must seat yourself on the verandah, and wait. You will be called. But, whatever may happen, do not answer, and do not move. Say nothing and sit still – as if meditating. If you stir, or make any noise, you will be torn asunder. Do not get frightened; and do not think of calling for help – because no help could save you. If you do exactly as I tell you, the danger will pass, and you will have nothing more to fear.'

After dark the priest and the acolyte went away; and Hōïchi seated himself on the verandah, according to the instructions given

---

* The Smaller Pragña-Pâramitâ-Hridaya-Sûtra is thus called in Japanese. Both the smaller and larger sûtras called Pragña-Pâramitâ ('Transcendent Wisdom') have been translated by the late Professor Max Müller, and can be found in volume xlix of the *Sacred Books of the East* ('Buddhist Mahâyâna Sûtras').[6] Apropos of the magical use of the text, as described in this story, it is worth remarking that the subject of the sûtra is the Doctrine of the Emptiness of Forms – that is to say, of the unreal character of all phenomena or noumena . . . 'Form is emptiness; and emptiness is form. Emptiness is not different from form; form is not different from emptiness. What is form – that is emptiness. What is emptiness – that is form . . . Perception, name, concept, and knowledge, are also emptiness . . . There is no eye, ear, nose, tongue, body, and mind. But when the envelopment of consciousness has been annihilated, then he [*the seeker*] becomes free from all fear, and beyond the reach of change, enjoying final Nirvâna.'

him. He laid his *biwa* on the planking beside him, and, assuming the attitude of meditation, remained quite still – taking care not to cough, or to breathe audibly. For hours he stayed thus.

Then, from the roadway, he heard the steps coming. They passed the gate, crossed the garden, approached the verandah, stopped – directly in front of him.

'Hōïchi!' the deep voice called. But the blind man held his breath, and sat motionless. 'Hōïchi!' grimly called the voice a second time. Then a third time – savagely:

'Hōïchi!'

Hōïchi remained as still as a stone – and the voice grumbled:

'No answer! – that won't do! ... Must see where the fellow is.' ...

There was a noise of heavy feet mounting upon the verandah. The feet approached deliberately – halted beside him. Then, for long minutes – during which Hōïchi felt his whole body shake to the beating of his heart – there was dead silence.

At last the gruff voice muttered close to him:

'Here is the *biwa*; but of the biwa-player I see – only two ears! ... So that explains why he did not answer: he had no mouth to answer with – there is nothing left of him but his ears ... Now to my lord those ears I will take – in proof that the august commands have been obeyed, so far as was possible.' ...

At that instant Hōïchi felt his ears gripped by fingers of iron, and torn off! Great as the pain was, he gave no cry. The heavy footfalls receded along the verandah – descended into the garden – passed out to the roadway – ceased. From either side of his head, the blind man felt a thick warm trickling; but he dared not lift his hands ...

Before sunrise the priest came back. He hastened at once to the verandah in the rear, stepped and slipped upon something clammy, and uttered a cry of horror; for he saw, by the light of his lantern, that the clamminess was blood. But he perceived Hōïchi sitting there, in the attitude of meditation – with the blood still oozing from his wounds.

'My poor Hōïchi!' cried the startled priest – 'what is this? ... You have been hurt?'

At the sound of his friend's voice, the blind man felt safe. He burst out sobbing, and tearfully told his adventure of the night.

'Poor, poor Hōïchi!' the priest exclaimed – 'all my fault! – my very grievous fault! . . . Everywhere upon your body the holy texts had been written – except upon your ears! I trusted my acolyte to do that part of the work; and it was very, very wrong of me not to have made sure that he had done it! . . . Well, the matter cannot now be helped; we can only try to heal your hurts as soon as possible . . . Cheer up, friend! – the danger is now well over. You will never again be troubled by those visitors.'

With the aid of a good doctor, Hōïchi soon recovered from his injuries. The story of his strange adventure spread far and wide, and soon made him famous. Many noble persons went to Akama-gaséki to hear him recite; and large presents of money were given to him – so that he became a wealthy man . . . But from the time of his adventure, he was known only by the appellation of *Mimi-nashi-Hōïchi*: 'Hōïchi-the-Earless'.

JIKININKI

Once, when Musō Kokushi, a priest of the Zen sect, was journeying alone through the province of Mino, he lost his way in a mountain-district where there was nobody to direct him. For a long time he wandered about helplessly; and he was beginning to despair of finding shelter for the night, when he perceived, on the top of a hill lighted by the last rays of the sun, one of those little hermitages, called *anjitsu*, which are built for solitary priests. It seemed to be in ruinous condition; but he hastened to it eagerly, and found that it was inhabited by an aged priest, from whom he begged the favor of a night's lodging. This the old man harshly refused; but he directed Musō to a certain hamlet, in the valley adjoining where lodging and food could be obtained.

Musō found his way to the hamlet, which consisted of less than a dozen farm-cottages; and he was kindly received at the dwelling of the headman. Forty or fifty persons were assembled in the principal apartment, at the moment of Musō's arrival; but he was shown into a small separate room, where he was promptly supplied with food and bedding. Being very tired, he lay down to rest at an early hour; but a little before midnight he was roused from sleep by a sound of loud weeping in the next apartment. Presently the sliding-screens were gently pushed apart; and a young man, carrying a lighted lantern, entered the room, respectfully saluted him, and said:

'Reverend Sir, it is my painful duty to tell you that I am now the responsible head of this house. Yesterday I was only the eldest son. But when you came here, tired as you were, we did not wish that you should feel embarrassed in any way: therefore we did not tell you that father had died only a few hours before. The people whom you saw in the next room are the inhabitants of this village: they all assembled here to pay their last respects to the dead; and now they are going to another village, about three miles off – for by our custom, no one of us may remain in this village during the night after a death has taken place. We make the proper offerings and prayers; then we go away, leaving the corpse alone. Strange things always happen in the house where a corpse has thus been left: so we think that it will be better for you to come away with us. We can find you good lodging in the other village. But perhaps, as you are a priest, you have no fear of demons or evil spirits; and, if you are not afraid of being left alone with the body, you will be very welcome to the use of this poor house. However, I must tell you that nobody, except a priest, would dare to remain here to-night.'

Musō made answer:

'For your kind intention and your generous hospitality, I am deeply grateful. But I am sorry that you did not tell me of your father's death when I came; for, though I was a little tired, I certainly was not so tired that I should have found difficulty in doing my duty as a priest. Had you told me, I could have performed the service before your departure. As it is, I shall perform the service after you have gone away; and I shall stay by the body until morning. I do not know what you mean by your words about the danger of staying here alone; but I am not afraid of ghosts or demons: therefore please to feel no anxiety on my account.'

The young man appeared to be rejoiced by these assurances, and expressed his gratitude in fitting words. Then the other members of the family, and the folk assembled in the adjoining room, having been told of the priest's kind promises, came to thank him – after which the master of the house said:

'Now, reverend Sir, much as we regret to leave you alone, we must bid you farewell. By the rule of our village, none of us can stay here after midnight. We beg, kind Sir, that you will take every care of your honorable body, while we are unable to attend upon you. And if you happen to hear or see anything strange during our absence, please tell us of the matter when we return in the morning.'

*

All then left the house, except the priest, who went to the room where the dead body was lying. The usual offerings had been set before the corpse; and a small Buddhist lamp – *tōmyō* – was burning. The priest recited the service, and performed the funeral ceremonies – after which he entered into meditation. So meditating he remained through several silent hours; and there was no sound in the deserted village. But, when the hush of the night was at its deepest, there noiselessly entered a Shape, vague and vast; and in the same moment Musō found himself without power to move or speak. He saw that Shape lift the corpse, as with hands, devour it, more quickly than a cat devours a rat – beginning at the head, and eating everything: the hair and the bones and even the shroud. And the monstrous Thing, having thus consumed the body, turned to the offerings, and ate them also. Then it went away, as mysteriously as it had come.

When the villagers returned next morning, they found the priest awaiting them at the door of the headman's dwelling. All in turn saluted him; and when they had entered, and looked about the room, no one expressed any surprise at the disappearance of the dead body and the offerings. But the master of the house said to Musō:

'Reverend Sir, you have probably seen unpleasant things during the night: all of us were anxious about you. But now we are very happy to find you alive and unharmed. Gladly we would have stayed with you, if it had been possible. But the law of our village, as I told you last evening, obliges us to quit our houses after a death has taken place, and to leave the corpse alone. Whenever this law has been broken, heretofore, some great misfortune has followed. Whenever it is obeyed, we find that the corpse and the offerings disappear during our absence. Perhaps you have seen the cause.'

Then Musō told of the dim and awful Shape that had entered the death-chamber to devour the body and the offerings. No person seemed to be surprised by his narration; and the master of the house observed:

'What you have told us, reverend Sir, agrees with what has been said about this matter from ancient time.'

Musō then inquired:

'Does not the priest on the hill sometimes perform the funeral service for your dead?'

'What priest?' the young man asked.

'The priest who yesterday evening directed me to this village,' answered Musō. 'I called at his *anjitsu* on the hill yonder. He refused me lodging, but told me the way here.'

The listeners looked at each other, as in astonishment; and, after a moment of silence, the master of the house said:

'Reverend Sir, there is no priest and there is no *anjitsu* on the hill. For the time of many generations there has not been any resident-priest in this neighborhood.'

Musō said nothing more on the subject; for it was evident that his kind hosts supposed him to have been deluded by some goblin. But after having bidden them farewell, and obtained all necessary information as to his road, he determined to look again for the hermitage on the hill, and so to ascertain whether he had really been deceived. He found the *anjitsu* without any difficulty; and, this time, its aged occupant invited him to enter. When he had done so, the hermit humbly bowed down before him, exclaiming: 'Ah! I am ashamed! – I am very much ashamed! – I am exceedingly ashamed!'

'You need not be ashamed for having refused me shelter,' said Musō. 'You directed me to the village yonder, where I was very kindly treated; and I thank you for that favor.'

'I can give no man shelter,' the recluse made answer; 'and it is not for the refusal that I am ashamed. I am ashamed only that you should have seen me in my real shape – for it was I who devoured the corpse and the offerings last night before your eyes ... Know, reverend Sir, that I am a *jikininki**** – an eater of human flesh. Have pity upon me, and suffer me to confess the secret fault by which I became reduced to this condition.

---

* Literally, a man-eating goblin. The Japanese narrator gives also the Sanscrit term, 'Râkshasa'; but this word is quite as vague as *jikininki*, since there are many kinds of Râkshasas. Apparently the word *jikininki* signifies here one of the *Baramon-Rasetsu-Gaki* – forming the twenty-sixth class of pretas enumerated in the old Buddhist books.

'A long, long time ago, I was a priest in this desolate region. There was no other priest for many leagues around. So, in that time, the bodies of the mountain-folk who died used to be brought here – sometimes from great distances – in order that I might repeat over them the holy service. But I repeated the service and performed the rites only as a matter of business; I thought only of the food and the clothes that my sacred profession enabled me to gain. And because of this selfish impiety I was reborn, immediately after my death, into the state of a *jikininki*. Since then I have been obliged to feed upon the corpses of the people who die in this district: every one of them I must devour in the way that you saw last night ... Now, reverend Sir, let me beseech you to perform a *Ségaki*-service* for me: help me by your prayers, I entreat you, so that I may be soon able to escape from this horrible state of existence.' ...

No sooner had the hermit uttered this petition than he disappeared; and the hermitage also disappeared at the same instant. And Musō Kokushi found himself kneeling alone in the high grass, beside an ancient and moss-grown tomb of the form called *go-rin-ishi*,† which seemed to be the tomb of a priest.

---

* A *Ségaki*-service is a special Buddhist service performed on behalf of beings supposed to have entered into the condition of *gaki* (pretas), or hungry spirits. For a brief account of such a service, see my *Japanese Miscellany*.

† Literally, 'five-circle [or "five-zone"] stone'. A funeral monument consisting of five parts superimposed – each a different form – symbolizing the five mystic elements: Ether, Air, Fire, Water, Earth.

MUJINA

On the Akasaka Road, in Tōkyō, there is a slope called Kii-no-kuni-zaka – which means the Slope of the Province of Kii. I do not know why it is called the Slope of the Province of Kii. On one side of this slope you see an ancient moat, deep and very wide, with high green banks rising up to some place of gardens; and on the other side of the road extend the long and lofty walls of an imperial palace. Before the era of street-lamps and *jinrikishas*,[1] this neighborhood was very lonesome after dark; and belated pedestrians would go miles out of their way rather than mount the Kii-no-kuni-zaka, alone, after sunset.

All because of a Mujina that used to walk there.

The last man who saw the Mujina was an old merchant of the Kyōbashi quarter, who died about thirty years ago. This is the story, as he told it:

One night, at a late hour, he was hurrying up the Kii-no-kuni-zaka, when he perceived a woman crouching by the moat, all alone, and weeping bitterly. Fearing that she intended to drown herself, he stopped to offer her any assistance or consolation in his power. She appeared to be a slight and graceful person, handsomely dressed; and her hair was arranged like that of a young girl of good family. 'O-jochū,'* he exclaimed, approaching her – 'O-jochū, do not cry like that! . . . Tell me what the trouble is; and if there be any way to help you, I shall be glad to help you.' (He really meant what he said; for he was a very kind man.) But she

* O-jochū ('honourable damsel') – a polite form of address used in speaking to a young lady whom one does not know.

continued to weep – hiding her face from him with one of her long sleeves. 'O-jochū,' he said again, as gently as he could – 'please, please listen to me! . . . This is no place for a young lady at night! Do not cry, I implore you! – only tell me how I may be of some help to you!' Slowly she rose up, but turned her back to him, and continued to moan and sob behind her sleeve. He laid his hand lightly upon her shoulder, and pleaded: 'O-jochū! – O-jochū! – O-jochū! . . . Listen to me, just for one little moment! . . . O-jochū! – O-jochū!' . . . Then that O-jochū turned around, and dropped her sleeve, and stroked her face with her hand; and the man saw that she had no eyes or nose or mouth – and he screamed and ran away.

Up Kii-no-kuni-zaka he ran and ran; and all was black and empty before him. On and on he ran, never daring to look back; and at last he saw a lantern, so far away that it looked like the gleam of a firefly; and he made for it. It proved to be only the lantern of an itinerant *soba*-seller,* who had set down his stand by the road-side; but any light and any human companionship was good after that experience; and he flung himself down at the feet of the *soba*-seller, crying out, 'Ah! – aa!! – *aa!!!*' . . .

'*Koré! Koré!*' roughly exclaimed the *soba*-man. 'Here! what is the matter with you? Anybody hurt you?'

'No – nobody hurt me,' panted the other – 'only . . . Ah! – aa!' . . .

'– Only scared you?' queried the peddler, unsympathetically. 'Robbers?'

'Not robbers – not robbers,' gasped the terrified man . . . 'I saw . . . I saw a woman – by the moat; and she showed me . . . Ah! I cannot tell you what she showed me!' . . .

'*Hé!* Was it anything like THIS that she showed you?' cried the *soba*-man, stroking his own face – which therewith became like unto an Egg . . . And, simultaneously, the light went out.

---

* *Soba* is a preparation of buckwheat, somewhat resembling vermicelli.

ROKURO-KUBI

Nearly five hundred years ago there was a samurai, named Isogai Héïdazaëmon Takétsura, in the service of the Lord Kikuji, of Kyūshū.[1] This Isogai had inherited, from many warlike ancestors, a natural aptitude for military exercises, and extraordinary strength. While yet a boy he had surpassed his teachers in the art of swordsmanship, in archery, and in the use of the spear, and had displayed all the capacities of a daring and skillful soldier. Afterwards, in the time of the Eikyō* war, he so distinguished himself that high honors were bestowed upon him. But when the house of Kikuji came to ruin, Isogai found himself without a master. He might then easily have obtained service under another *daimyō*; but as he had never sought distinction for his own sake alone, and as his heart remained true to his former lord, he preferred to give up the world. So he cut off his hair, and became a traveling priest – taking the Buddhist name of Kwairyō.

But always, under the *koromo*† of the priest, Kwairyō kept warm within him the heart of the samurai. As in other years he had laughed at peril, so now also he scorned danger; and in all weathers and all seasons he journeyed to preach the good Law in places where no other priest would have dared to go. For that age was an age of violence and disorder; and upon the highways there was no security for the solitary traveler, even if he happened to be a priest.

In the course of his first long journey, Kwairyō had occasion to visit the province of Kai. One evening, as he was traveling through

---

* The period of Eikyō lasted from 1429 to 1441.
† The upper robe of a Buddhist priest is thus called.

the mountains of that province, darkness overcame him in a very lonesome district, leagues away from any village. So he resigned himself to pass the night under the stars; and having found a suitable grassy spot, by the roadside, he lay down there, and prepared to sleep. He had always welcomed discomfort; and even a bare rock was for him a good bed, when nothing better could be found, and the root of a pine-tree an excellent pillow. His body was iron; and he never troubled himself about dews or rain or frost or snow.

Scarcely had he lain down when a man came along the road, carrying an axe and a great bundle of chopped wood. This wood-cutter halted on seeing Kwairyō lying down, and, after a moment of silent observation, said to him in a tone of great surprise:

'What kind of a man can you be, good Sir, that you dare to lie down alone in such a place as this? . . . There are haunters about here – many of them. Are you not afraid of Hairy Things?'

'My friend,' cheerfully answered Kwairyō, 'I am only a wandering priest – a "Cloud-and-Water-Guest", as folks call it: *Unsui-no-ryokaku*. And I am not in the least afraid of Hairy Things – if you mean goblin-foxes, or goblin-badgers, or any creatures of that kind. As for lonesome places, I like them: they are suitable for meditation. I am accustomed to sleeping in the open air: and I have learned never to be anxious about my life.'

'You must be indeed a brave man, Sir Priest,' the peasant responded, 'to lie down here! This place has a bad name – a very bad name. But, as the proverb has it, *Kunshi ayayuki ni chikayor-azu* ['The superior man does not needlessly expose himself to peril']; and I must assure you, Sir, that it is very dangerous to sleep here. Therefore, although my house is only a wretched thatched hut, let me beg of you to come home with me at once. In the way of food, I have nothing to offer you; but there is a roof at least, and you can sleep under it without risk.'

He spoke earnestly; and Kwairyō, liking the kindly tone of the man, accepted this modest offer. The woodcutter guided him along a narrow path, leading up from the main road through mountain-forest. It was a rough and dangerous path – sometimes skirting precipices – sometimes offering nothing but a network of slippery roots for the foot to rest upon – sometimes winding over or between masses of jagged rock. But at last Kwairyō found himself upon a cleared space at the top of a hill, with a full moon shining overhead; and he saw before him a small thatched cottage, cheerfully lighted from within. The woodcutter led him to a shed at the back of the house, whither water had been conducted, through bamboo-pipes, from some neighboring stream; and the two men washed their feet. Beyond the shed was a vegetable garden, and a grove of cedars and bamboos; and beyond the trees appeared the glimmer of a cascade, pouring from some loftier height, and swaying in the moonshine like a long white robe.

As Kwairyō entered the cottage with his guide, he perceived four persons – men and women – warming their hands at a little fire kindled in the *ro** of the principal apartment. They bowed low to the priest, and greeted him in the most respectful manner. Kwairyō wondered that persons so poor, and dwelling in such a solitude, should be aware of the polite forms of greeting. 'These are good people,' he thought to himself; 'and they must have been taught by some one well acquainted with the rules of propriety.' Then turning to his host – the *aruji*, or house-master, as the others called him – Kwairyō said:

'From the kindness of your speech, and from the very polite welcome given me by your household, I imagine that you have not always been a woodcutter. Perhaps you formerly belonged to one of the upper classes?'

Smiling, the woodcutter answered:

'Sir, you are not mistaken. Though now living as you find me, I was once a person of some distinction. My story is the story of a ruined life – ruined by my own fault. I used to be in the service of a *daimyō*; and my rank in that service was not inconsiderable. But I loved women and wine too well; and under the influence of passion I acted wickedly. My selfishness brought about the ruin of our house, and caused the death of many persons. Retribution followed me; and I long remained a fugitive in the land. Now I often pray that I may be able to make some atonement for the evil

---

* A sort of little fireplace, contrived in the floor of a room, is thus described. The *ro* is usually a square shallow cavity, lined with metal and half-filled with ashes, in which charcoal is lighted.

which I did, and to reestablish the ancestral home. But I fear that I shall never find any way of so doing. Nevertheless, I try to overcome the karma of my errors by sincere repentance, and by helping as afar as I can, those who are unfortunate.'

Kwairyō was pleased by this announcement of good resolve; and he said to the *aruji*:

'My friend, I have had occasion to observe that man, prone to folly in their youth, may in after years become very earnest in right living. In the holy sûtras it is written that those strongest in wrong-doing can become, by power of good resolve, the strongest in right-doing. I do not doubt that you have a good heart; and I hope that better fortune will come to you. To-night I shall recite the sûtras for your sake, and pray that you may obtain the force to overcome the karma of any past errors.'

With these assurances, Kwairyō bade the *aruji* good-night; and his host showed him to a very small side-room, where a bed had been made ready. Then all went to sleep except the priest, who began to read the sûtras by the light of a paper lantern. Until a late hour he continued to read and pray: then he opened a little window in his little sleeping-room, to take a last look at the landscape before lying down. The night was beautiful: there was no cloud in the sky: there was no wind; and the strong moonlight threw down sharp black shadows of foliage, and glittered on the dews of the garden. Shrillings of crickets and bell-insects[2] made a musical tumult; and the sound of the neighboring cascade deepened with the night. Kwairyō felt thirsty as he listened to the noise of the water; and, remembering the bamboo aqueduct at the rear of the house, he thought that he could go there and get a drink without disturbing the sleeping household. Very gently he pushed apart the sliding-screens that separated his room from the main apartment; and he saw, by the light of the lantern, five recumbent bodies – without heads!

For one instant he stood bewildered – imagining a crime. But in another moment he perceived that there was no blood, and that the headless necks did not look as if they had been cut. Then he thought to himself: 'Either this is an illusion made by goblins, or I have been lured into the dwelling of a Rokuro-Kubi[3] ... In the book *Sōshinki* it is written that if one find the body of a Rokuro-Kubi without its head, and remove the body to another place, the head will never be able to join itself again to the neck. And the book further says that when the head comes back and finds that its body has been moved, it will strike itself upon the floor three times – bounding like a ball – and will pant as in great fear, and presently die. Now, if these be Rokuro-Kubi, they mean me no good; so I shall be justified in following the instructions of the book.' . . .

He seized the body of the *aruji* by the feet, pulled it to the window, and pushed it out. Then he went to the back-door, which he found barred; and he surmised that the heads had made their exit through the smoke-hole in the roof, which had been left open. Gently unbarring the door, he made his way to the garden, and proceeded with all possible caution to the grove beyond it. He heard voices talking in the grove; and he went in the direction of the voices – stealing from shadow to shadow, until he reached a good hiding-place. Then, from behind a trunk, he caught sight of the heads – all five of them – flitting about, and chatting as they flitted. They were eating worms and insects which they found on the ground or among the trees. Presently the head of the *aruji* stopped eating and said:

'Ah, that traveling priest who came to-night! – how fat all his body is! When we shall have eaten him, our bellies will be well filled . . . I was foolish to talk to him as I did; it only set him to reciting the sûtras on behalf of my soul! To go near him while he is reciting would be difficult; and we cannot touch him so long as he is praying. But as it is now nearly morning, perhaps he has gone to sleep . . . Some one of you go to the house and see what the fellow is doing.'

Another head – the head of a young woman – immediately rose up and flitted to the house, lightly as a bat. After a few minutes it came back, and cried out huskily, in a tone of great alarm: 'That traveling priest is not in the house; he is gone! But that is not the worst of the matter. He has taken the body of our *aruji*; and I do not know where he has put it.'

At this announcement the head of the *aruji* – distinctly visible in the moonlight – assumed a frightful aspect: its eyes opened monstrously; its hair stood up bristling; and its teeth gnashed. Then a cry burst from its lips; and – weeping tears of rage – it exclaimed:

'Since my body has been moved, to rejoin it is not possible! Then I must die! ... And all through the work of that priest! Before I die I will get at that priest! – I will tear him! – I will devour him! ... *And there he is* – behind that tree! – hiding behind that tree! See him! – the fat coward!' ... In the same moment the head of the *aruji*, followed by the other four heads, sprang at Kwairyō. But the strong priest had already armed himself by plucking up a young tree; and with that tree he struck the heads as they came – knocking them from him with tremendous blows. Four of them fled away. But the head of the *aruji*, though battered again and again, desperately continued to bound at the priest, and at last caught him by the left sleeve of his robe. Kwairyō, however, as quickly gripped the head by its topknot, and repeatedly struck it. It did not release its hold; but it uttered a long moan, and thereafter ceased to struggle. It was dead. But its teeth still held the sleeve; and, for all his great strength, Kwairyō could not force open the jaws.

With the head still hanging to his sleeve he went back to the house, and there caught sight of the other four Rokuro-Kubi squatting together, with their bruised and bleeding heads reunited to their bodies. But when they perceived him at the back-door all screamed, 'The priest! the priest!' – and fled, through the other doorway, out into the woods.

Eastward the sky was brightening; day was about to dawn; and Kwairyō knew that the power of the goblins was limited to the hours of darkness. He looked at the head clinging to his sleeve – its face all fouled with blood and foam and clay; and he laughed aloud as he thought to himself: 'What a *miyagé*!* – the head of a goblin!' After which he gathered together his few belongings, and leisurely descended the mountain to continue his journey.

Right on he journeyed, until he came to Suwa in Shinano; and into the main street of Suwa he solemnly strode, with the head dangling at his elbow. Then woman fainted, and children screamed and ran away; and there was a great crowding and clamoring until

---

* A present made to friends or to the household on returning from a journey is thus called. Ordinarily, of course, the *miyagé* consists of something produced in the locality to which the journey has been made: this is the point of Kwairyō's jest.

the *torité* (as the police in those days were called) seized the priest, and took him to jail. For they supposed the head to be the head of a murdered man who, in the moment of being killed, had caught the murderer's sleeve in his teeth. As for the Kwairyō, he only smiled and said nothing when they questioned him. So, after having passed a night in prison, he was brought before the magistrates of the district. Then he was ordered to explain how he, a priest, had been found with the head of a man fastened to his sleeve, and why he had dared thus shamelessly to parade his crime in the sight of people.

Kwairyō laughed long and loudly at these questions; and then he said:

'Sirs, I did not fasten the head to my sleeve: it fastened itself there – much against my will. And I have not committed any crime. For this is not the head of a man; it is the head of a goblin; and, if I caused the death of the goblin, I did not do so by any shedding of blood, but simply by taking the precautions necessary to assure my own safety.' . . . And he proceeded to relate the whole of the adventure – bursting into another hearty laugh as he told of his encounter with the five heads. But the magistrates did not laugh. They judged him to be a hardened criminal, and his story an insult to their intelligence. Therefore, without further questioning, they decided to order his immediate execution – all of them except one, a very old man. This aged officer had made no remark during the trial; but, after having heard the opinion of his colleagues, he rose up, and said: 'Let us first examine the head carefully; for this, I think, has not yet been done. If the priest has spoken truth, the head itself should bear witness for him . . . Bring the head here!'

So the head, still holding in its teeth the *koromo* that had been stripped from Kwairyō's shoulders, was put before the judges. The old man turned it round and round, carefully examined it, and discovered, on the nape of its neck, several strange red characters. He called the attention of his colleagues to these, and also bade them observe that the edges of the neck nowhere presented the appearance of having been cut by any weapon. On the contrary, the line of leverance was smooth as the line at which a falling leaf detaches itself from the stem . . . Then said the elder:

'I am quite sure that the priest told us nothing but the truth. This is the head of a Rokuro-Kubi. In the book *Nan-hō-ï-butsu-shi* it is written that certain red characters can always be found upon the nape of the neck of a real Rokuro-Kubi. There are the characters: you can see for yourselves that they have not been painted. Moreover, it is well known that such goblins have been dwelling in the mountains of the province of Kai from very ancient time . . . But you, Sir,' he exclaimed, turning to Kwairyō – 'what sort of sturdy priest may you be? Certainly you have given proof of a courage that few priests possess; and you have the air of a soldier rather than a priest. Perhaps you once belonged to the samurai-class?'

'You have guessed rightly, Sir,' Kwairyō responded. 'Before becoming a priest, I long followed the profession of arms; and in those days I never feared man or devil. My name then was Isogai Héïdazaëmon Takétsura of Kyūshū: there may be some among you who remember it.'

At the mention of that name, a murmur of admiration filled the court-room; for there were many present who remembered it. And Kwairyō immediately found himself among friends instead of judges – friends anxious to prove their admiration by fraternal kindness. With honor they escorted him to the residence of the *daimyō*, who welcomed him, and feasted him, and made him a handsome present before allowing him to depart. When Kwairyō left Suwa, he was as happy as any priest is permitted to be in this transitory world. As for the head, he took it with him – jocosely insisting that he intended it for a *miyagé*.

And now it only remains to tell what became of the head.

A day or two after leaving Suwa, Kwairyō met with a robber, who stopped him in a lonesome place, and bade him strip. Kwairyō at once removed his *koromo*, and offered it to the robber, who then first perceived what was hanging to the sleeve. Though brave, the highwayman was startled: he dropped the garment, and sprang back. Then he cried out: 'You! – what kind of a priest are you? Why, you are a worse man than I am! It is true that I have killed people; but I never walked about with anybody's head fastened to my sleeve . . . Well, Sir priest, I suppose we are of the same calling; and I must say that I admire you! . . . Now that head would be of use to me: I could frighten people with it. Will you sell it? You can have my robe in exchange for your *koromo*; and I will give you five *ryō* for the head.'

Kwairyō answered:

'I shall let you have the head and the robe if you insist; but I must tell you that this is not the head of a man. It is a goblin's head. So, if you buy it, and have any trouble in consequence, please to remember that you were not deceived by me.'

'What a nice priest you are!' exclaimed the robber. 'You kill men, and jest about it! . . . But I am really in earnest. Here is my robe; and here is the money; and let me have the head . . . What is the use of joking?'

'Take the thing,' said Kwairyō. 'I was not joking. The only joke – if there be any joke at all – is that you are fool enough to pay good money for a goblin's head.' And Kwairyō, loudly laughing, went upon his way.

Thus the robber got the head and the *koromo*; and for some time he played goblin-priest upon the highways. But, reaching the neighborhood of Suwa, he there learned the true story of the head; and he then became afraid that the spirit of the Rokuro-Kubi might give him trouble. So he made up his mind to take back the head to the place from which it had come, and to bury it with its body. He found his way to the lonely cottage in the mountains of Kai; but nobody was there, and he could not discover the body. Therefore he buried the head by itself, in the grove behind the cottage; and he had a tombstone set up over the grave; and he caused a *Ségaki*-service to be performed on behalf of the spirit of the Rokuro-Kubi. And that tombstone – known as the Tombstone of the Rokuro-Kubi – may be seen (at least so the Japanese story-teller declares) even unto this day.

YUKI-ONNA

In a village of Musashi Province, there lived two woodcutters: Mosaku and Minokichi. At the time of which I am speaking, Mosaku was an old man; and Minokichi, his apprentice, was a lad of eighteen years. Every day they went together to a forest situated about five miles from their village. On the way to that forest there is a wide river to cross; and there is a ferry-boat. Several times a bridge was built where the ferry is; but the bridge was each time carried away by a flood. No common bridge can resist the current there when the river rises.

Mosaku and Minokichi were on their way home, one very cold evening, when a great snowstorm overtook them. They reached the ferry; and they found that the boatman had gone away, leaving his boat on the other side of the river. It was no day for swimming; and the woodcutters took shelter in the ferryman's hut – thinking themselves lucky to find any shelter at all. There was no brazier in the hut, nor any place in which to make a fire: it was only a two-mat* hut, with a single door, but no window. Mosaku and Minokichi fastened the door, and lay down to rest, with their straw rain-coats over them. At first they did not feel very cold; and they thought that the storm would soon be over.

The old man almost immediately fell asleep; but the boy, Minokichi, lay awake a long time, listening to the awful wind, and the continual slashing of the snow against the door. The river was roaring; and the hut swayed and creaked like a junk at sea. It was a terrible storm; and the air was every moment becoming colder;

* That is to say, with a floor-surface of about six feet square.

and Minokichi shivered under his rain-coat. But at last, in spite of
the cold, he too fell asleep.

He was awakened by a showering of snow in his face. The door
of the hut had been forced open; and, by the snow-light (*yuki-
akari*), he saw a woman in the room – a woman all in white. She
was bending above Mosaku, and blowing her breath upon him;
and her breath was like a bright white smoke. Almost in the same
moment she turned to Minokichi, and stooped over him. He
tried to cry out, but found that he could not utter any sound. The
white woman bent down over him, lower and lower, until her
face almost touched him; and he saw that she was very beautiful – though her eyes made him afraid. For a little time she
continued to look at him; then she smiled, and she whispered: 'I
intended to treat you like the other man. But I cannot help feeling some pity for you – because you are so young … You are a
pretty boy, Minokichi; and I will not hurt you now. But, if you
ever tell anybody – even your own mother – about what you have
seen this night, I shall know it; and then I will kill you …
Remember what I say!'

With these words, she turned from him, and passed through the
doorway. Then he found himself able to move; and he sprang up,
and looked out. But the woman was nowhere to be seen; and the
snow was driving furiously into the hut. Minokichi closed the door,
and secured it by fixing several billets of wood against it. He wondered if the wind had blown it open; he thought that he might have
been only dreaming, and might have mistaken the gleam of the
snow-light in the doorway for the figure of a white woman: but he
could not be sure. He called to Mosaku, and was frightened because
the old man did not answer. He put out his hand in the dark, and
touched Mosaku's face, and found that it was ice! Mosaku was stark
and dead …

By dawn the storm was over; and when the ferryman returned to
his station, a little after sunrise, he found Minokichi lying senseless beside the frozen body of Mosaku. Minokichi was promptly
cared for, and soon came to himself; but he remained a long
time ill from the effects of the cold of that terrible night. He had
been greatly frightened also by the old man's death; but he said

nothing about the vision of the woman in white. As soon as he got well again, he returned to his calling – going alone every morning to the forest, and coming back at nightfall with his bundles of wood, which his mother helped him to sell.

One evening, in the winter of the following year, as he was on his way home, he overtook a girl who happened to be traveling by the same road. She was a tall, slim girl, very good-looking; and she answered Minokichi's greeting in a voice as pleasant to the ear as the voice of a song-bird. Then he walked beside her; and they began to talk. The girl said that her name was O-Yuki;* that she had lately lost both of her parents; and that she was going to Yedo, where she happened to have some poor relations, who might help her to find a situation as a servant. Minokichi soon felt charmed by this strange girl; and the more that he looked at her, the handsomer she appeared to be. He asked her whether she was yet betrothed; and she answered, laughingly, that she was free. Then, in her turn, she asked Minokichi whether he was married, or pledged to marry; and he told her that, although he had only a widowed mother to support, the question of an 'honorable daughter-in-law' had not yet been considered, as he was very young . . . After these confidences, they walked on for a long while without speaking; but, as the proverb declares, *Ki ga aréba, mé mo kuchi hodo ni mono wo iu*: 'When the wish is there, the eyes can say as much as the mouth.' By the time they reached the village, they had become very much pleased with each other; and then Minokichi asked O-Yuki to rest awhile at his house. After some shy hesitation, she went there with him; and his mother made her welcome, and prepared a warm meal for her. O-Yuki behaved so nicely that Minokichi's mother took a sudden fancy to her, and persuaded her to delay her journey to Yedo. And the natural end of the matter was that Yuki never went to Yedo at all. She remained in the house, as an 'honorable daughter-in-law'.

O-Yuki proved a very good daughter-in-law. When Minokichi's mother came to die – some five years later – her last words were

* This name, signifying 'Snow', is not uncommon. On the subject of Japanese female names, see my paper in the volume entitled *Shadowings*.

words of affection and praise for the wife of her son. And O-Yuki bore Minokichi ten children, boys and girls – handsome children all of them, and very fair of skin.

The country-folk thought O-Yuki a wonderful person, by nature different from themselves. Most of the peasant-women age early; but O-Yuki, even after having become the mother of ten children, looked as young and fresh as on the day when she had first come to the village.

One night, after the children had gone to sleep, O-Yuki was sewing by the light of a paper lamp; and Minokichi, watching her, said:

'To see you sewing there, with the light on your face, makes me think of a strange thing that happened when I was a lad of eighteen. I then saw somebody as beautiful and white as you are now – indeed, she was very like you.' . . .

Without lifting her eyes from her work, O-Yuki responded: 'Tell me about her . . . Where did you see her?'

Then Minokichi told her about the terrible night in the ferryman's hut – and about the White Woman that had stooped above him, smiling and whispering – and about the silent death of old Mosaku. And he said:

'Asleep or awake, that was the only time that I saw a being as beautiful as you. Of course, she was not a human being; and I was afraid of her – very much afraid – but she was so white! . . . Indeed, I have never been sure whether it was a dream that I saw, or the Woman of the Snow.' . . .

O-Yuki flung down her sewing, and arose, and bowed above Minokichi where he sat, and shrieked into his face: 'It was I – I – I! Yuki it was! And I told you then that I would kill you if you ever said one word about it! . . . But for those children asleep there, I would kill you this moment! And now you had better take very, very good care of them; for if ever they have reason to complain of you, I will treat you as you deserve!' . . .

Even as she screamed, her voice became thin, like a crying of wind; then she melted into a bright white mist that spired to the roof-beams, and shuddered away through the smoke-hole . . . Never again was she seen.

THE STORY OF AOYAGI

In the era of Bummei [1469–1486] there was a young samurai called Tomotada in the service of Hatakéyama Yoshimuné, the Lord of Noto. Tomotada was a native of Echizen; but at an early age he had been taken, as page, into the palace of the *daimyō* of Noto, and had been educated, under the supervision of that prince, for the profession of arms. As he grew up, he proved himself both a good scholar and a good soldier, and continued to enjoy the favor of his prince. Being gifted with an amiable character, a winning address, and a very handsome person, he was admired and much liked by his samurai-comrades.

When Tomotada was about twenty years old, he was sent upon a private mission to Hosokawa Masamoto, the great *daimyō* of Kyōto, a kinsman of Hatakéyama Yoshimuné. Having been ordered to journey through Echizen, the youth requested and obtained permission to pay a visit, on the way, to his widowed mother.

It was the coldest period of the year when he started; and, though mounted upon a powerful horse, he found himself obliged to proceed slowly. The road which he followed passed through a mountain-district where the settlements were few and far between; and on the second day of his journey, after a weary ride of hours, he was dismayed to find that he could not reach his intended halting-place until late in the night. He had reason to be anxious; for a heavy snowstorm came on, with an intensely cold wind; and the horse showed signs of exhaustion. But in that trying moment, Tomotada unexpectedly perceived the thatched roof of a cottage on the summit of a near hill, where willow-trees were growing. With difficulty he urged his tired animal to the dwelling; and he loudly knocked upon the storm-doors, which had been closed against the wind. An old woman opened them, and cried out compassionately at the sight of the handsome stranger: 'Ah, how pitiful! – a young gentleman traveling alone in such weather! . . . Deign, young master, to enter.'

Tomotada dismounted, and after leading his horse to a shed in the rear, entered the cottage, where he saw an old man and a girl warming themselves by a fire of bamboo splints. They respectfully invited him to approach the fire; and the old folks then proceeded to warm some rice-wine, and to prepare food for the traveler, whom they ventured to question in regard to his journey. Meanwhile the young girl disappeared behind a screen. Tomotada had observed, with astonishment, that she was extremely beautiful – though her attire was of the most wretched kind, and her long, loose hair in disorder. He wondered that so handsome a girl should be living in such a miserable and lonesome place.

The old man said to him:

'Honored Sir, the next village is far; and the snow is falling thickly. The wind is piercing; and the road is very bad. Therefore, to proceed further this night would probably be dangerous. Although this hovel is unworthy of your presence, and although we have not any comfort to offer, perhaps it were safer to remain to-night under this miserable roof . . . We would take good care of your horse.'

Tomotada accepted this humble proposal – secretly glad of the chance thus afforded him to see more of the young girl. Presently a coarse but ample meal was set before him; and the girl came from behind the screen, to serve the wine. She was now reclad, in a rough but cleanly robe of homespun; and her long, loose hair had been neatly combed and smoothed. As she bent forward to fill his cup, Tomotada was amazed to perceive that she was incomparably more beautiful than any woman whom he had ever before seen; and there was a grace about her every motion that astonished him. But the elders began to apologize for her, saying: 'Sir, our daughter, Aoyagi,* has been brought up here in the mountains, almost alone; and she knows nothing of gentle service. We

---

* The name signifies 'Green Willow'; though rarely met with, it is still in use.

pray that you will pardon her stupidity and her ignorance.' Tomotada protested that he deemed himself lucky to be waited upon by so comely a maiden. He could not turn his eyes away from her – though he saw that his admiring gaze made her blush; and he left the wine and food untasted before him. The mother said: 'Kind Sir, we very much hope that you will try to eat and to drink a little – though our peasant-fare is of the worst – as you must have been chilled by that piercing wind.' Then, to please the old folks, Tomotada ate and drank as he could; but the charm of the blushing girl still grew upon him. He talked with her, and found that her speech was sweet as her face. Brought up in the mountains as she might have been; but, in that case, her parents must at some time have been persons of high degree; for she spoke and moved like a damsel of rank. Suddenly he addressed her with a poem – which was also a question – inspired by the delight in his heart:

> 'Tadzunétsuru,
> Hana ka toté koso,
> Hi wo kurasé,
> Akénu ni otoru
> Akané sasuran?'

['Being on my way to pay a visit, I found that which I took to be a flower: therefore here I spend the day ... Why, in the time before dawn, the dawn-blush tint should glow – that, indeed, I know not.']*

Without a moment's hesitation, she answered him in these verses:

> 'Izuru hi no
> Honoméku iro wo
> Waga sodé ni

* The poem may be read in two ways; several of the phrases having a double meaning. But the art of its construction would need considerable space to explain, and could scarcely interest the Western reader. The meaning which Tomotada desired to convey might be thus expressed: 'While journeying to visit my mother, I met with a being lovely as a flower; and for the sake of that lovely person, I am passing the day here ... Fair one, wherefore that dawnlike blush before the hour of dawn? – can it mean that you love me?'

Tsutsumaba asu mo
Kimiya tomaran.'

['*If with my sleeve I hid the faint fair color of the dawning sun – then, perhaps, in the morning my lord will remain.*']*

Then Tomotada knew that she accepted his admiration; and he was scarcely less surprised by the art with which she had uttered her feelings in verse, than delighted by the assurance which the verses conveyed. He was now certain that in all this world he could not hope to meet, much less to win, a girl more beautiful and witty than this rustic maid before him; and a voice in his heart seemed to cry out urgently, 'Take the luck that the gods have put in your way!' In short he was bewitched – bewitched to such a degree that, without further preliminary, he asked the old people to give him their daughter in marriage – telling them, at the same time, his name and lineage, and his rank in the train of the Lord of Noto.

They bowed down before him, with many exclamations of grateful astonishment. But, after some moments of apparent hesitation, the father replied:

'Honored master, you are a person of high position, and likely to rise to still higher things. Too great is the favor that you deign to offer us; indeed, the depth of our gratitude therefore is not to be spoken or measured. But this girl of ours, being a stupid country-girl of vulgar birth, with no training or teaching of any sort, it would be improper to let her become the wife of a noble samurai. Even to speak of such a matter is not right . . . But, since you find the girl to your liking, and have condescended to pardon her peasant-manners and to overlook her great rudeness, we do gladly present her to you, for a humble handmaid. Deign, therefore, to act hereafter in her regard according to your august pleasure.'

Ere morning the storm had passed; and day broke through a cloudless east. Even if the sleeve of Aoyagi hid from her lover's eyes the rose-blush of that dawn, he could no longer tarry. But

---

* Another reading is possible; but this one gives the significance of the *answer* intended.

neither could he resign himself to part with the girl; and, when everything had been prepared for his journey, he thus addressed her parents:

'Though it may seem thankless to ask for more than I have already received, I must again beg you to give me your daughter for wife. It would be difficult for me to separate from her now; and as she is willing to accompany me, if you permit, I can take her with me as she is. If you will give her to me, I shall ever cherish you as parents . . . And, in the meantime, please to accept this poor acknowledgment of your kindest hospitality.'

So saying, he placed before his humble host a purse of gold *ryō*. But the old man, after many prostrations, gently pushed back the gift, and said:

'Kind master, the gold would be of no use to us; and you will probably have need of it during your long, cold journey. Here we buy nothing; and we could not spend so much money upon ourselves, even if we wished . . . As for the girl, we have already bestowed her as a free gift; she belongs to you: therefore it is not necessary to ask our leave to take her away. Already she has told us that she hopes to accompany you, and to remain your servant for as long as you may be willing to endure her presence. We are only too happy to know that you deign to accept her; and we pray that you will not trouble yourself on our account. In this place we could not provide her with proper clothing – much less with a dowry. Moreover, being old, we should in any event have to separate from her before long. Therefore it is very fortunate that you should be willing to take her with you now.'

It was in vain that Tomotada tried to persuade the old people to accept a present: he found that they cared nothing for money. But he saw that they were really anxious to trust their daughter's fate to his hands; and he therefore decided to take her with him. So he placed her upon his horse, and bade the old folks farewell for the time being, with many sincere expressions of gratitude. 'Honored Sir,' the father made answer, 'it is we, and not you, who have reason for gratitude. We are sure that you will be kind to our girl; and we have no fears for her sake.' . . .

*

[*Here, in the Japanese original, there is a queer break in the natural course of the narration, which therefrom remains curiously inconsistent. Nothing further is said about the mother of Tomotada, or about the parents of Aoyagi, or about the* daimyō *of Noto. Evidently the writer wearied of his work at this point, and hurried the story, very carelessly, to its startling end. I am not able to supply his omissions, or to repair his faults of construction; but I must venture to put in a few explanatory details, without which the rest of the tale would not hold together . . . It appears that Tomotada rashly took Aoyagi with him to Kyōto, and so got into trouble; but we are not informed as to where the couple lived afterwards.*]

. . . Now a samurai was not allowed to marry without the consent of his lord; and Tomotada could not expect to obtain this sanction before his mission had been accomplished. He had reason, under such circumstances, to fear that the beauty of Aoyagi might attract dangerous attention, and that means might be devised of taking her away from him. In Kyōto he therefore tried to keep her hidden from curious eyes. But a retainer of Lord Hosokawa one day caught sight of Aoyagi, discovered her relation to Tomotada, and reported the matter to the *daimyō*. Thereupon the *daimyō* – a young prince, and fond of pretty faces – gave orders that the girl should be brought to the palace; and she was taken thither at once, without ceremony.

Tomotada sorrowed unspeakably; but he knew himself powerless. He was only an humble messenger in the service of a far-off *daimyō*; and for the time being he was at the mercy of a much more powerful *daimyō*, whose wishes were not to be questioned. Moreover Tomotada knew that he had acted foolishly – that he had brought about his own misfortune, by entering into a clandestine relation which the code of the military class condemned. There was now but one hope for him – a desperate hope: that Aoyagi might be able and willing to escape and to flee with him. After long reflection, he resolved to try to send her a letter. The attempt would be dangerous, of course: any writing sent to her might find its way to the hands of the *daimyō*; and to send a love-letter to any inmate of the palace was an unpardonable offense.

But he resolved to dare the risk; and, in the form of a Chinese poem, he composed a letter which he endeavored to have conveyed to her. The poem was written with only twenty-eight characters. But with those twenty-eight characters he was about to express all the depth of his passion, and to suggest all the pain of his loss:*

> *Kōshi ō-son gojin wo ou;*
> *Ryokuju namida wo tarété rakin wo hitataru;*
> *Komon hitotabi irité fukaki koto umi no gotoshi;*
> *Koré yori shorō koré rojin*

[*Closely, closely the youthful prince now follows after the gem-bright maid;*
   The tears of the fair one, falling, have moistened all her robes.
   But the august lord, having once become enamored of her – the depth of his longing is like the depth of the sea.
   Therefore it is only I that am left forlorn – only I that am left to wander along.]

On the evening of the day after this poem had been sent, Tomotada was summoned to appear before the Lord Hosokawa. The youth at once suspected that his confidence had been betrayed; and he could not hope, if his letter had been seen by the *daimyō*, to escape the severest penalty. 'Now he will order my death,' thought Tomotada; 'but I do not care to live unless Aoyagi be restored to me. Besides, if the death-sentence be passed, I can at least try to kill Hosokawa.' He slipped his swords into his girdle, and hastened to the palace.

On entering the presence-room he saw the Lord Hosokawa seated upon the dais, surrounded by samurai of high rank, in caps and robes of ceremony. All were silent as statues; and while Tomotada advanced to make obeisance, the hush seemed to him sinister and heavy, like the stillness before a storm. But Hosokawa

---

* So the Japanese story-teller would have us believe – although the verses seem commonplace in translation. I have tried to give only their general meaning: an effective literal translation would require some scholarship.

suddenly descended from the dais, and, while taking the youth by the arm, began to repeat the words of the poem: *'Kōshi ō-son gojin wo ou.'* . . . And Tomotada, looking up, saw kindly tears in the prince's eyes.

Then said Hosokawa:

'Because you love each other so much, I have taken it upon myself to authorize your marriage, in lieu of my kinsman, the Lord of Noto; and your wedding shall now be celebrated before me. The guests are assembled; the gifts are ready.'

At a signal from the lord, the sliding-screens concealing a further apartment were pushed open; and Tomotada saw there many dignitaries of the court, assembled for the ceremony, and Aoyagi awaiting him in bride's apparel . . . Thus was she given back to him; and the wedding was joyous and splendid; and precious gifts were made to the young couple by the prince, and by the members of his household.

*   *   *

For five happy years, after that wedding, Tomotada and Aoyagi dwelt together. But one morning Aoyagi, while talking with her husband about some household matter, suddenly uttered a great cry of pain, and then became very white and still. After a few moments she said, in a feeble voice: 'Pardon me for thus rudely crying out – but the pain was so sudden! . . . My dear husband, our union must have been brought about through some karma-relation in a former state of existence; and that happy relation, I think, will bring us again together in more than one life to come. But for this present existence of ours, the relation is now ended; – we are about to be separated. Repeat for me, I beseech you, the *Nembutsu*-prayer – because I am dying.'

'Oh! what strange wild fancies!' cried the startled husband – 'you are only a little unwell, my dear one! . . . lie down for a while, and rest; and the sickness will pass.' . . .

'No, no!' she responded – 'I am dying! – I do not imagine it; I know! . . . And it were needless now, my dear husband, to hide the truth from you any longer: I am not a human being. The soul of a tree is my soul; the heart of a tree is my heart; the sap of the willow is my life. And some one, at this cruel moment, is cutting down my tree; that is why I must die! . . . Even to weep were now beyond my strength! – quickly, quickly repeat the *Nembutsu* for me . . . quickly! . . . Ah!' . . .

With another cry of pain she turned aside her beautiful head, and tried to hide her face behind her sleeve. But almost in the same moment her whole form appeared to collapse in the strangest way, and to sink down, down, down – level with the floor. Tomotada had spring to support her; but there was nothing to support! There lay on the matting only the empty robes of the fair creature and the ornaments that she had worn in her hair: the body had ceased to exist . . .

Tomotada shaved his head, took the Buddhist vows, and became an itinerant priest. He traveled through all the provinces of the empire; and, at holy places which he visited, he offered up prayers for the soul of Aoyagi. Reaching Echizen, in the course of his pilgrimage, he sought the home of the parents of his beloved. But when he arrived at the lonely place among the hills, where their dwelling had been, he found that the cottage had disappeared. There was nothing to mark even the spot where it had stood, except the stumps of three willows – two old trees and one young tree – that had been cut down long before his arrival.

Beside the stumps of those willow-trees he erected a memorial tomb, inscribed with divers holy texts; and he there performed many Buddhist services on behalf of the spirits of Aoyagi and of her parents.

THE DREAM OF AKINOSUKÉ

In the district called Toïchi of Yamato Province, there used to live a *gōshi* named Miyata Akinosuké ... [Here I must tell you that in Japanese feudal times there was a privileged class of soldier-farmers – free-holders – corresponding to the class of yeomen in England; and these were called *gōshi*.]

In Akinosuké's garden there was a great and ancient cedar-tree, under which he was wont to rest on sultry days. One very warm afternoon he was sitting under this tree with two of his friends, fellow-*gōshi*, chatting and drinking wine, when he felt all of a sudden very drowsy – so drowsy that he begged his friends to excuse him for taking a nap in their presence. Then he lay down at the foot of the tree, and dreamed this dream:

He thought that as he was lying there in his garden, he saw a procession, like the train of some great *daimyō* descending a hill near by, and that he got up to look at it. A very grand procession it proved to be – more imposing than anything of the kind which he had ever seen before; and it was advancing toward his dwelling. He observed in the van of it a number of young men richly appareled, who were drawing a great lacquered palace-carriage, or *gosho-guruma*, hung with bright blue silk. When the procession arrived within a short distance of the house it halted; and a richly dressed man – evidently a person of rank – advanced from it, approached Akinosuké, bowed to him profoundly, and then said:

'Honored Sir, you see before you a *kérai* [vassal] of the Kokuō of Tokoyo.* My master, the King, commands me to greet you in his

---

* This name 'Tokoyo' is indefinite. According to circumstances it may signify any unknown country – or that undiscovered country from whose bourn no

august name, and to place myself wholly at your disposal. He also bids me inform you that he augustly desires your presence at the palace. Be therefore pleased immediately to enter this honorable carriage, which he has sent for your conveyance.'

Upon hearing these words Akinosuké wanted to make some fitting reply; but he was too much astonished and embarrassed for speech; and in the same moment his will seemed to melt away from him, so that he could only do as the *kérai* bade him. He entered the carriage; the *kérai* took a place beside him, and made a signal; the drawers, seizing the silken ropes, turned the great vehicle southward; and the journey began.

In a very short time, to Akinosuké's amazement, the carriage stopped in front of a huge two-storied gateway (*rōmon*), of a Chinese style, which he had never before seen. Here the *kérai* dismounted, saying, 'I go to announce the honorable arrival' – and he disappeared. After some little waiting, Akinosuké saw two noble-looking men, wearing robes of purple silk and high caps of the form indicating lofty rank, come from the gateway. These, after having respectfully saluted him, helped him to descend from the carriage, and led him through the great gate and across a vast garden, to the entrance of a palace whose front appeared to extend, west and east, to a distance of miles. Akinosuké was then shown into a reception-room of wonderful size and splendor. His guides conducted him to the place of honor, and respectfully seated themselves apart; while serving-maids, in costume of ceremony, brought refreshments. When Akinosuké had partaken of the refreshments, the two purple-robed attendants bowed low before him, and addressed him in the following words – each speaking alternately, according to the etiquette of courts:

'It is now our honorable duty to inform you . . . as to the reason of your having been summoned hither . . . Our master, the King, augustly desires that you become his son-in-law . . . and it is his

---

traveller returns – or that Fairyland of far-eastern fable, the Realm of Hōrai. The term 'Kokuō' means the ruler of a country – therefore a king. The original phrase, *Tokoyo no Kokuō*, might be rendered here as 'the Ruler of the Hōrai', or 'the King of Fairyland'.

wish and command that you shall wed this very day ... the August Princess, his maiden-daughter ... We shall soon conduct you to the presence-chamber ... where His Augustness even now is waiting to receive you ... But it will be necessary that we first invest you ... with the appropriate garments of ceremony.'*

Having thus spoken, the attendants rose together, and proceeded to an alcove containing a great chest of gold lacquer. They opened the chest, and took from it various robes and girdles of rich material, and a *kamuri*, or regal headdress. With these they attired Akinosuké as befitted a princely bridegroom; and he was then conducted to the presence-room, where he saw the Kokuō of Tokoyo seated upon the *daiza*,† wearing a high black cap of state, and robed in robes of yellow silk. Before the *daiza*, to left and right, a multitude of dignitaries sat in rank, motionless and splendid as images in a temple; and Akinosuké, advancing into their midst, saluted the king with the triple prostration of usage. The king greeted him with gracious words, and then said:

'You have already been informed as to the reason of your having been summoned to Our presence. We have decided that you shall become the adopted husband of Our only daughter; and the wedding ceremony shall now be performed.'

As the king finished speaking, a sound of joyful music was heard; and a long train of beautiful court ladies advanced from behind a curtain to conduct Akinosuké to the room in which his bride awaited him.

The room was immense; but it could scarcely contain the multitude of guests assembled to witness the wedding ceremony. All bowed down before Akinosuké as he took his place, facing the King's daughter, on the kneeling-cushion prepared for him. As a maiden of heaven the bride appeared to be; and her robes were beautiful as a summer sky. And the marriage was performed amid great rejoicing.

---

* The last phrase, according to old custom, had to be uttered by both attendants at the same time. All these ceremonial observances can still be studied on the Japanese stage.

† This was the name given to the estrade, or dais, upon which a feudal prince or ruler sat in state. The term literally signifies 'great seat'.

Afterwards the pair were conducted to a suite of apartments that had been prepared for them in another portion of the palace; and there they received the congratulations of many noble persons, and wedding gifts beyond counting.

Some days later Akinosuké was again summoned to the throne-room. On this occasion he was received even more graciously than before; and the King said to him:

'In the southwestern part of Our dominion there is an island called Raishū. We have now appointed you Governor of that island. You will find the people loyal and docile; but their laws have not yet been brought into proper accord with the laws of Tokoyo; and their customs have not been properly regulated. We entrust you with the duty of improving their social condition as far as may be possible; and We desire that you shall rule them with kindness and wisdom. All preparations necessary for your journey to Raishū have already been made.'

So Akinosuké and his bride departed from the palace of Tokoyo, accompanied to the shore by a great escort of nobles and officials; and they embarked upon a ship of state provided by the king. And with favoring winds they safety sailed to Raishū, and found the good people of that island assembled upon the beach to welcome them.

Akinosuké entered at once upon his new duties; and they did not prove to be hard. During the first three years of his governorship he was occupied chiefly with the framing and the enactment of laws; but he had wise counselors to help him, and he never found the work unpleasant. When it was all finished, he had no active duties to perform, beyond attending the rites and ceremonies ordained by ancient custom. The country was so healthy and so fertile that sickness and want were unknown; and the people were so good that no laws were ever broken. And Akinosuké dwelt and ruled in Raishū for twenty years more – making in all twenty-three years of sojourn, during which no shadow of sorrow traversed his life.

But in the twenty-fourth year of his governorship, a great

misfortune came upon him; for his wife, who had borne him seven children – five boys and two girls – fell sick and died. She was buried, with high pomp, on the summit of a beautiful hill in the district of Hanryoko; and a monument, exceedingly splendid, was placed upon her grave. But Akinosuké felt such grief at her death that he no longer cared to live.

Now when the legal period of mourning was over, there came to Raishū, from the Tokoyo palace, a *shisha*, or royal messenger. The *shisha* delivered to Akinosuké a message of condolence, and then said to him:

'These are the words which our august master, the King of Tokoyo, commands that I repeat to you: "We will now send you back to your own people and country. As for the seven children, they are the grandsons and granddaughters of the King, and shall be fitly cared for. Do not, therefore, allow your mind to be troubled concerning them."'

On receiving this mandate, Akinosuké submissively prepared for his departure. When all his affairs had been settled, and the ceremony of bidding farewell to his counselors and trusted officials had been concluded, he was escorted with much honor to the port. There he embarked upon the ship sent for him; and the ship sailed out into the blue sea, under the blue sky; and the shape of the island of Raishū itself turned blue, and then turned grey, and then vanished forever . . . And Akinosuké suddenly awoke – under the cedar-tree in his own garden!

For a moment he was stupefied and dazed. But he perceived his two friends still seated near him – drinking and chatting merrily. He stared at them in a bewildered way, and cried aloud,

'How strange!'

'Akinosuké must have been dreaming,' one of them exclaimed, with a laugh. 'What did you see, Akinosuké, that was strange?'

Then Akinosuké told his dream – that dream of three-and-twenty years' sojourn in the realm of Tokoyo, in the island of Raishū; and they were astonished, because he had really slept for no more than a few minutes.

One *gōshi* said:

'Indeed, you saw strange things. We also saw something strange while you were napping. A little yellow butterfly was fluttering over your face for a moment or two; and we watched it. Then it alighted on the ground beside you, close to the tree; and almost as soon as it alighted there, a big, big ant came out of a hole and seized it and pulled it down into the hole. Just before you woke up, we saw that very butterfly come out of the hole again, and flutter over your face as before. And then it suddenly disappeared: we do not know where it went.'

'Perhaps it was Akinosuké's soul,' the other *gōshi* said; 'certainly I thought I saw it fly into his mouth . . . But, even if that butterfly was Akinosuké's soul, the fact would not explain his dream.'

'The ants might explain it,' returned the first speaker. 'Ants are queer beings – possibly goblins . . . Anyhow, there is a big ant's nest under that cedar-tree.' . . .

'Let us look!' cried Akinosuké, greatly moved by this suggestion. And he went for a spade.

The ground about and beneath the cedar-tree proved to have been excavated, in a most surprising way, by a prodigious colony of ants. The ants had furthermore built inside their excavations; and their tiny constructions of straw, clay, and stems bore an odd resemblance to miniature towns. In the middle of a structure considerably larger than the rest there was a marvelous swarming of small ants around the body of one very big ant, which had yellowish wings and a long black head.

'Why, there is the King of my dream!' cried Akinosuké; 'and there is the palace of Tokoyo! . . . How extraordinary! . . . Raishū ought to lie somewhere southwest of it – to the left of that big root . . . Yes! – here it is! . . . How very strange! Now I am sure that I can find the mountain of Hanryoko, and the grave of the princess.' . . .

In the wreck of the nest he searched and searched, and at last discovered a tiny mound, on the top of which was fixed a water-worn pebble, in shape resembling a Buddhist monument. Underneath it he found – embedded in clay – the dead body of a female ant.

RIKI-BAKA

His name was Riki, signifying Strength; but the people called him Riki-the-Simple, or Riki-the-Fool – 'Riki-Baka' – because he had been born into perpetual childhood. For the same reason they were kind to him – even when he set a house on fire by putting a lighted match to a mosquito-curtain, and clapped his hands for joy to see the blaze. At sixteen years he was a tall, strong lad; but in mind he remained always at the happy age of two, and therefore continued to play with very small children. The bigger children of the neighborhood, from four to seven years old, did not care to play with him, because he could not learn their songs and games. His favorite toy was a broomstick, which he used as a hobby-horse; and for hours at a time he would ride on that broomstick, up and down the slope in front of my house, with amazing peals of laughter. But at last he became troublesome by reason of his noise; and I had to tell him that he must find another playground. He bowed submissively, and then went off – sorrowfully trailing his broomstick behind him. Gentle at all times, and perfectly harmless if allowed no chance to play with fire, he seldom gave anybody cause for complaint. His relation to the life of our street was scarcely more than that of a dog or a chicken; and when he finally disappeared, I did not miss him. Months and months passed by before anything happened to remind me of Riki.

'What has become of Riki?' I then asked the old woodcutter who supplies our neighborhood with fuel. I remembered that Riki had often helped him to carry his bundles.

'Riki-Baka?' answered the old man. 'Ah, Riki is dead – poor fellow! ... Yes, he died nearly a year ago, very suddenly; the doctors said that he had some disease of the brain. And there is a strange story now about that poor Riki.

'When Riki died, his mother wrote his name, "Riki-Baka", in the palm of his left hand – putting "Riki" in the Chinese character, and "Baka" in *kana*.[1] And she repeated many prayers for him – prayers that he might be reborn into some more happy condition.

'Now, about three months ago, in the honorable residence of Nanigashi-Sama, in Kōjimachi, a boy was born with characters on the palm of his left hand; and the characters were quite plain to read "*RIKI-BAKA*"!

'So the people of that house knew that the birth must have happened in answer to somebody's prayer; and they caused inquiry to be made everywhere. At least a vegetable-seller brought word to them that there used to be a simple lad, called Riki-Baka, living in the Ushigome quarter, and that he had died during the last autumn; and they sent two menservants to look for the mother of Riki.

'Those servants found the mother of Riki, and told her what had happened; and she was glad exceedingly – for that Nanigashi house is a very rich and famous house. But the servants said that the family of Nanigashi-Sama were very angry about the word "Baka" on the child's hand. "And where is your Riki buried?" the servants asked. "He is buried in the cemetery of Zendōji," she told them. "Please to give us some of the clay of his grave," they requested.

'So she went with them to the temple Zendōji, and showed them Riki's grave; and they took some of the grave-clay away with them, wrapped up in a *furoshiki** . . . They gave Riki's mother some money – ten yen.' . . .

'But what did they want with that clay?' I inquired.

'Well,' the old man answered, 'you know that it would not do to let the child grow up with that name on his hand. And there is no other means of removing characters that come in that way upon the body of a child: *you must rub the skin with clay taken from the grave of the body of the former birth*.' . . .

---

* A square piece of cotton-goods, or other woven material, used as a wrapper in which to carry small packages.

THE MIRROR MAIDEN

In the period of the Ashikaga Shōgunate[1] the shrine of Ogawachi-Myōjin, at Minami-Isé, fell into decay; and the *daimyō* of the district, the Lord Kitahataké, found himself unable, by reason of war and other circumstances, to provide for the reparation of the building. Then the Shintō priest in charge, Matsumura Hyōgo, sought help at Kyōto from the great *daimyō* Hosokawa, who was known to have influence with the Shōgun. The Lord Hosokawa received the priest kindly, and promised to speak to the Shōgun about the condition of Ogawachi-Myōjin. But he said that, in any event, a grant for the restoration of the temple could not be made without due investigation and considerable delay; and he advised Matsumura to remain in the capital while the matter was being arranged. Matsumura therefore brought his family to Kyōto, and rented a house in the old Kyōgoku quarter.

This house, although handsome and spacious, had been long unoccupied. It was said to be an unlucky house. On the northeast side of it there was a well; and several former tenants had drowned themselves in that well, without any known cause. But Matsumura, being a Shintō priest, had no fear of evil spirits; and he soon made himself very comfortable in his new home.

In the summer of that year there was a great drought. For months no rain had fallen in the Five Home-Provinces; the river-beds dried up, the wells failed; and even in the capital there was a dearth of water. But the well in Matsumura's garden remained nearly full; and the water – which was very cold and clear, with a faint bluish tinge – seemed to be supplied by a spring. During the hot season many people came from all parts of the city to beg for water; and Matsumura allowed them to draw as much as they pleased. Nevertheless the supply did not appear to be diminished.

But one morning the dead body of a young servant, who had been sent from a neighboring residence to fetch water, was found floating in the well. No cause for a suicide could be imagined; and Matsumura, remembering many unpleasant stories about the well, began to suspect some invisible malevolence. He went to examine the well, with the intention of having a fence built around it; and while standing there alone he was startled by a sudden motion in the water, as of something alive. The motion soon ceased; and then he perceived, clearly reflected in the still surface, the figure of a young woman, apparently about nineteen or twenty years of age. She seemed to be occupied with her toilet: he distinctly saw her touching her lips with *béni*.* At first her face was visible in profile only; but presently she turned towards him and smiled. Immediately he felt a strange shock at his heart, and a dizziness came upon him like the dizziness of wine, and everything became dark, except that smiling face – white and beautiful as moonlight, and always seeming to grow more beautiful, and to be drawing him down – down – down into the darkness. But with a desperate effort he recovered his will and closed his eyes. When he opened them again, the face was gone, and the light had returned; and he found himself leaning down over the curb of the well. A moment more of that dizziness – a moment more of that dazzling lure – and he would never again have looked upon the sun . . .

Returning to the house, he gave orders to his people not to approach the well under any circumstances, or allow any person to draw water from it. And the next day he had a strong fence built round the well.

About a week after the fence had been built, the long drought was broken by a great rain-storm, accompanied by wind and lightning and thunder – thunder so tremendous that the whole city shook to the rolling of it, as if shaken by an earthquake. For three days and three nights the downpour and the lightnings and

* A kind of rouge, now used only to color the lips.

the thunder continued; and the Kamogawa rose as it had never risen before, carrying away many bridges. During the third night of the storm, at the Hour of the Ox, there was heard a knocking at the door of the priest's dwelling, and the voice of a woman pleading for admittance. But Matsumura, warned by his experience at the well, forbade his servants to answer the appeal. He went himself to the entrance, and asked,

'Who calls?'

A feminine voice responded: 'Pardon! it is I – Yayoi!* . . . I have something to say to Matsumura Sama – something of great moment. Please open!' . . .

Matsumura half opened the door, very cautiously; and he saw the same beautiful face that had smiled upon him from the well. But it was not smiling now: it had a very sad look.

'Into my house you shall not come,' the priest exclaimed. 'You are not a human being, but a Well-Person . . . Why do you thus wickedly try to delude and destroy people?'

The Well-Person made answer in a voice musical as a tinkling of jewels (*tama-wo-korogasu-koé*):

'It is of that very matter that I want to speak . . . I have never wished to injure human beings. But from ancient time a Poison-Dragon dwelt in that well. He was the Master of the Well; and because of him the well was always full. Long ago I fell into the water there, and so became subject to him; and he had power to make me lure people to death, in order that he might drink their blood. But now the Heavenly Ruler has commanded the Dragon to dwell hereafter in the lake called Torii-no-Iké, in the Province of Shinshū; and the gods have decided that he shall never be allowed to return to this city. So to-night, after he had gone away, I was able to come out, to beg for your kindly help. There is now very little water in the well, because of the Dragon's departure; and if you will order search to be made, my body will be found there. I pray you to save my body from the well without delay; and I shall certainly return your benevolence.' . . .

So saying, she vanished into the night.

*

* This name, though uncommon, is still in use.

Before dawn the tempest had passed; and when the sun arose there was no trace of cloud in the pure blue sky. Matsumura sent at an early hour for well-cleaners to search the well. Then, to everybody's surprise, the well proved to be almost dry. It was easily cleaned; and at the bottom of it were found some hair-ornaments of a very ancient fashion, and a metal mirror of curious form – but no trace of any body, animal or human.

Matusmura imagined, however, that the mirror might yield some explanation of the mystery; for every such mirror is a weird thing, having a soul of its own – and the soul of a mirror is feminine. This mirror, which seemed to be very old, was deeply crusted with scurf. But when it had been carefully cleaned, by the priest's order, it proved to be of rare and costly workmanship; and there were wonderful designs upon the back of it – also several characters. Some of the characters had become indistinguishable; but there could still be discerned part of a date, and ideographs signifying, 'third month, the third day'. Now the third month used to be termed Yayoi (meaning, the Month of Increase); and the third day of the third month, which is a festival day, is still called Yayoi-no-sekku. Remembering that the Well-Person called herself 'Yayoi', Matsumura felt almost sure that his ghostly visitant had been none other than the Soul of the Mirror.

He therefore resolved to treat the mirror with all the consideration due to a Spirit. After having caused it to be carefully repolished and resilvered, he had a case of precious wood made for it, and a particular room in the house prepared to receive it. On the evening of the same day that it had been respectfully deposited in that room, Yayoi herself unexpectedly appeared before the priest as he sat alone in his study. She looked even more lovely than before; but the light of her beauty was now soft as the light of a summer moon shining through pure white clouds. After having humbly saluted Matsumura, she said in her sweetly tinkling voice:

'Now that you have saved me from solitude and sorrow, I have come to thank you . . . I am indeed, as you supposed, the Spirit of the Mirror. It was in the time of the Emperor Saimei that I was first brought here from Kudara; and I dwelt in the august residence until the time of the Emperor Saga, when I was augustly bestowed upon the Lady Kamo, Naishinnō of the Imperial Court.* Thereafter I became an heirloom in the House of Fujiwara, and so remained until the period of Hōgen, when I was dropped into the well. There I was left and forgotten during the years of the great war.† The Master of the Well‡ was a venomous Dragon, who used to live in a lake that once covered a great part of this district. After the lake had been filled in, by government order, in order that houses might be built upon the place of it, the Dragon took possession of the well; and when I fell into the well I became subject to him; and he compelled me to lure many people to their deaths. But the gods have banished him forever . . . Now I have one more favor to beseech: I entreat that you will cause me to be offered up to the Shōgun, the Lord Yoshimasa, who by descent is related to my former possessors. Do me but this last great kindness, and it will bring you good-fortune . . . But I have also to warn you of a danger. In this house, after to-morrow, you must not stay, because it will be destroyed.' . . . And with these words of warning Yayoi disappeared.

Matsumura was able to profit by this premonition. He removed his people and his belongings to another district the next day; and almost immediately afterwards another storm arose, even more violent than the first, causing a flood which swept away the house in which he had been residing.

Some time later, by favor of the Lord Hosokawa, Matsumura

---

* The Emperor Saimei reigned from 655 to 662 (A. D.); the Emperor Saga from 810 to 842. Kudara was an ancient kingdom in southwestern Korea, frequently mentioned in early Japanese history. A *Naishinnō* was of Imperial blood. In the ancient court hierarchy there were twenty-five ranks or grades of noble ladies; that of Naishinnō was seventh in order of precedence.

† For centuries the wives of the emperors and the ladies of the Imperial Court were chosen from the Fujiwara clan. The period called Hōgen lasted from 1156 to 1159: the war referred to is the famous war between the Taira and Minamoto clans.

‡ In old-time belief every lake or spring had its invisible guardian, supposed to sometimes take the form of a serpent or dragon. The spirit of a lake or pond was commonly spoken of as *Iké-no-Mushi*, the Master of the Lake. Here we find the title 'Master' given to a dragon living in a well; but the guardian of wells is really the god Suijin.[2]

菊女ヶ妾
きくゆぎれい

三ヶ月上人
みかづきしやうにん

was enabled to obtain an audience of the Shōgun Yoshimasa, to whom he presented the mirror, together with a written account of its wonderful history. Then the prediction of the Spirit of the Mirror was fulfilled; for the Shōgun, greatly pleased with this strange gift, not only bestowed costly presents upon Matsumura, but also made an ample grant of money for the rebuilding of the Temple of Ogawachi-Myōjin.

THE STORY OF ITŌ
NORISUKÉ

In the town of Uji, in the province of Yamashiro, there lived, about six hundred years ago, a young samurai named Itō Tatéwaki Norisuké, whose ancestors were of the Heiké clan. Itō was of handsome person and amiable character, a good scholar and apt at arms. But his family were poor; and he had no patron among the military nobility – so that his prospects were small. He lived in a very quiet way, devoting himself to the study of literature, and having (says the Japanese story-teller) 'only the Moon and the Wind for friends'.

One autumn evening, as he was taking a solitary walk in the neighborhood of the hill called Kotobikiyama, he happened to overtake a young girl who was following the same path. She was richly dressed, and seemed to be about eleven or twelve years old. Itō greeted her, and said, 'The sun will soon be setting, damsel, and this is rather a lonesome place. May I ask if you have lost your way?' She looked up at him with a bright smile, and answered deprecatingly: 'Nay! I am a *miya-dzukai*,* serving in this neighborhood; and I have only a little way to go.'

By her use of the term *miya-dzukai*, Itō knew that the girl must be in the service of persons of rank; and her statement surprised him, because he had never heard of any family of distinction residing in that vicinity. But he only said: 'I am returning to Uji, where my home is. Perhaps you will allow me to accompany you on the way, as this is a very lonesome place.' She thanked him gracefully, seeming pleased by his offer; and they walked on together, chatting as they went. She talked about the weather, the flowers, the

* August-residence servant.

butterflies, and the birds; about a visit that she had once made to Uji, about the famous sights of the capital, where she had been born; and the moments passed pleasantly for Itō, as he listened to her fresh prattle. Presently, at a turn in the road, they entered a hamlet, densely shadowed by a grove of young trees.

[Here I must interrupt the story to tell you that, without having actually seen them, you cannot imagine how dark some Japanese country villages remain even in the brightest and hottest weather. In the neighborhood of Tōkyō itself there are many villages of this kind. At a short distance from such a settlement you see no houses: nothing is visible but a dense grove of evergreen trees. The grove, which is usually composed of young cedars and bamboos, serves to shelter the village from storms, and also to supply timber for various purposes. So closely are the trees planted that there is no room to pass between the trunks of them: they stand straight as masts, and mingle their crests so as to form a roof that excludes the sun. Each thatched cottage occupies a clear space in the plantation, the trees forming a fence about it, double the height of the building. Under the trees it is always twilight, even at high noon; and the houses, morning or evening, are half in shadow. What makes the first impression of such a village almost disquieting is, not the transparent gloom, which has a certain weird charm of its own, but the stillness. There may be fifty or a hundred dwellings; but you see nobody; and you hear no sound but the twitter of invisible birds, the occasional crowing of cocks, and the shrilling of cicadæ. Even the cicadæ, however, find these groves too dim, and sing faintly; being sun-lovers, they prefer the trees outside the village. I forgot to say that you may sometimes hear a viewless shuttle – *chaka-ton, chaka-ton*; but that familiar sound, in the great green silence, seems an elfish happening. The reason of the hush is simply that the people are not at home. All the adults, excepting some feeble elders, have gone to the neighboring fields, the women carrying their babies on their backs; and most of the children have gone to the nearest school, perhaps not less than a mile away. Verily, in these dim hushed villages, one seems to behold the mysterious perpetuation of conditions recorded in the texts of Kwang-Tze:

'*The ancients who had the nourishment of the world wished for nothing, and the world had enough: they did nothing, and all things were transformed: their stillness was abysmal, and the people were all composed.*']

. . . The village was very dark when Itō reached it; for the sun had set, and the after-glow made no twilight in the shadowing of the trees. 'Now, kind sir,' the child said, pointing to a narrow lane opening upon the main road, 'I have to go this way.' 'Permit me, then, to see you home,' Itō responded; and he turned into the lane with her, feeling rather than seeing his way. But the girl soon stopped before a small gate, dimly visible in the gloom – a gate of trelliswork, beyond which the lights of a dwelling could be seen. 'Here,' she said, 'is the honorable residence in which I serve. As you have come thus far out of your way, kind sir, will you not deign to enter and to rest a while?' Itō assented. He was pleased by the informal invitation; and he wished to learn what persons of superior condition had chosen to reside in so lonesome a village. He knew that sometimes a family of rank would retire in this manner from public life, by reason of government displeasure or political trouble; and he imagined that such might be the history of the occupants of the dwelling before him. Passing the gate, which his young guide opened for him, he found himself in a large quaint garden. A miniature landscape, traversed by a winding stream, was faintly distinguishable. 'Deign for one little moment to wait,' the child said; 'I go to announce the honorable coming;' and hurried toward the house. It was a spacious house, but seemed very old, and built in the fashion of another time. The sliding doors were not closed; but the lighted interior was concealed by a beautiful bamboo curtain extending along the gallery front. Behind it shadows were moving – shadows of women; and suddenly the music of a *koto*[1] rippled into the night. So light and sweet was the playing that Itō could scarcely believe the evidence of his senses. A slumbrous feeling of delight stole over him as he listened – a delight strangely mingled with sadness. He wondered how any woman could have learned to play thus – wondered whether the player could be a woman – wondered even whether he was hearing earthly music; for enchantment seemed to have entered into his blood with the sound of it.

The soft music ceased; and almost at the same moment Itō found the little *miya-dzukai* beside him. 'Sir,' she said, 'it is requested that you will honorably enter.' She conducted him to the entrance, where he removed his sandals; and an aged woman, whom he thought to be the *Rōjo*, or matron of the household, came to welcome him at the threshold. The old woman then led him through many apartments to a large and well-lighted room in the rear of the house, and with many respectful salutations requested him to take the place of honor accorded to guests of distinction. He was surprised by the stateliness of the chamber, and the curious beauty of its decorations. Presently some maid-servants brought refreshments; and he noticed that the cups and other vessels set before him were of rare and costly workmanship, and ornamented with a design indicating the high rank of the possessor. More and more he wondered what noble person had chosen this lonely retreat, and what happening could have inspired the wish for such solitude. But the aged attendant suddenly interrupted his reflections with the question:

'Am I wrong in supposing that you are Itō Sama, of Uji, Itō Tatéwaki Norisuké?'

Itō bowed in assent. He had not told his name to the little *miya-dzukai*, and the manner of the inquiry startled him.

'Please do not think my question rude,' continued the attendant. 'An old woman like myself may ask questions without improper curiosity. When you came to the house, I thought that I knew your face; and I asked your name only to clear away all doubt, before speaking of other matters. I have some thing of moment to tell you. You often pass through this village, and our young Himégimi-Sama* happened one morning to see you going by; and ever since that moment she has been thinking about you, day and night. Indeed, she thought so much that she became ill; and we have been very uneasy about her. For that reason I took

* A scarcely translatable honorific title compounded of the word *himé* (princess) and *kimi* (sovereign, master or mistress, lord or lady, etc.).

means to find out your name and residence; and I was on the point of sending you a letter when – so unexpectedly! – you came to our gate with the little attendant. Now, to say how happy I am to see you is not possible; it seems almost too fortunate a happening to be true! Really I think that this meeting must have been brought about by the favor of Enmusubi-no-Kami – that great God of Izumo who ties the knots of fortunate union. And now that so lucky a destiny has led you hither, perhaps you will not refuse – if there be no obstacle in the way of such a union – to make happy the heart of our Himégimi-Sama?'

For the moment Itō did not know how to reply. If the old woman had spoken the truth, an extraordinary chance was being offered to him. Only a great passion could impel the daughter of a noble house to seek, of her own will, the affection of an obscure and masterless samurai, possessing neither wealth nor any sort of prospects. On the other hand, it was not in the honorable nature of the man to further his own interests by taking advantage of a feminine weakness. Moreover, the circumstances were disquietingly mysterious. Yet how to decline the proposal, so unexpectedly made, troubled him not a little. After a short silence, he replied:

'There would be no obstacle, as I have no wife, and no betrothed, and no relation with any woman. Until now I have lived with my parents; and the matter of my marriage was never discussed by them. You must know that I am a poor samurai, without any patron among persons of rank; and I did not wish to marry until I could find some chance to improve my condition. As to the proposal which you have done me the very great honor to make, I can only say that I know myself yet unworthy of the notice of any noble maiden.'

The old woman smiled as if pleased by these words, and responded:

'Until you have seen our Himégimi-Sama, it were better that you make no decision. Perhaps you will feel no hesitation after you have seen her. Deign now to come with me, that I may present you to her.'

She conducted him to another larger guest-room, where preparations for a feast had been made, and having shown him the place of honor, left him for a moment alone. She returned accompanied by the Himégimi-Sama; and, at the first sight of the young mistress, Itō felt again the strange thrill of wonder and delight that had come to him in the garden, as he listened to the music of the *koto*. Never had he dreamed of so beautiful a being. Light seemed to radiate from her presence, and to shine through her garments, as the light of the moon through flossy clouds; her loosely flowing hair swayed about her as she moved, like the boughs of the drooping willow bestirred by the breezes of spring; her lips were like flowers of the peach besprinkled with morning dew. Itō was bewildered by the vision. He asked himself whether he was not looking upon the person of Amano-kawara-no-Ori-Himé herself, – the Weaving-Maiden who dwells by the shining River of Heaven.[2]

Smiling, the aged woman turned to the fair one, who remained speechless, with downcast eyes and flushing cheeks, and said to her:

'See, my child! – at the moment when we could least have hoped for such a thing, the very person whom you wished to meet has come of his own accord. So fortunate a happening could have been brought about only by the will of the high gods. To think of it makes me weep for joy.' And she sobbed aloud. 'But now,' she continued, wiping away her tears with her sleeve, 'it only remains for you both – unless either prove unwilling, which I doubt – to pledge yourselves to each other, and to partake of your wedding feast.'

Itō answered by no word: the incomparable vision before him had numbed his will and tied his tongue. Maid-servants entered, bearing dishes and wine: the wedding feast was spread before the pair; and the pledges were given. Itō nevertheless remained as in a trance: the marvel of the adventure, and the wonder of the beauty of the bride, still bewildered him. A gladness, beyond aught that he had ever known before, filled his heart – like a great silence. But gradually he recovered his wonted calm; and thereafter he found himself able to converse without embarrassment. Of the wine he partook freely; and he ventured to speak, in a self-depreciating but merry way, about the doubts and fears that had oppressed him. Meanwhile the bride remained still as moonlight, never lifting her eyes, and replying only by a blush or a smile when he addressed her.

Itō said to the aged attendant:

'Many times, in my solitary walks, I have passed through this village without knowing of the existence of this honorable dwelling. And ever since entering here, I have been wondering why this noble household should have chosen so lonesome a place of sojourn … Now that your Himégimi-Sama and I have become pledged to each other, it seems to me a strange thing that I do not yet know the name of her august family.'

At this utterance, a shadow passed over the kindly face of the old woman; and the bride, who had yet hardly spoken, turned pale, and appeared to become painfully anxious. After some moments of silence, the aged woman responded:

'To keep our secret from you much longer would be difficult; and I think that, under any circumstances, you should be made aware of the facts, now that you are one of us. Know then, Sir Itō, that your bride is the daughter of Shigéhira-Kyō, the great and unfortunate San-mi Chüjō.'

At those words – 'Shigéhira-Kyō, San-mi Chüjō' – the young samurai felt a chill, as of ice, strike through all his veins. Shigéhira-Kyō, the great Heiké general[3] and statesman, had been dust for centuries. And Itō suddenly understood that everything around him – the chamber and the lights and the banquet – was a dream of the past; that the forms before him were not people, but shadows of people dead.

But in another instant the icy chill had passed; and the charm returned, and seemed to deepen about him; and he felt no fear. Though his bride had come to him out of Yomi – out of the place of the Yellow Springs of Death – his heart had been wholly won. Who weds a ghost must become a ghost; yet he knew himself ready to die, not once, but many times, rather than betray by word or look one thought that might bring a shadow of pain to the brow of the beautiful illusion before him. Of the affection proffered he had no misgiving: the truth had been told him when any unloving purpose might better have been served by deception. But these thoughts and emotions passed in a flash, leaving him resolved to accept the strange situation as it had presented itself, and to act just as he would have done if chosen, in the years of Jū-ei,[4] by Shigéhira's daughter.

'Ah, the pity of it!' he exclaimed; 'I have heard of the cruel fate of the august Lord Shigéhira.'

'Ay,' responded the aged woman, sobbing as she spoke; 'it was indeed a cruel fate. His horse, you know, was killed by an arrow, and fell upon him; and when he called for help, those who had lived upon his bounty deserted him in his need. Then he was taken prisoner, and sent to Kamakura, where they treated him shamefully, and at last put him to death.* His wife and child – this dear maid here – were then in hiding; for everywhere the Heiké were being sought out and killed. When the news of the Lord Shigéhira's death reached us, the pain proved too great for the mother to bear, so the child was left with no one to care for her but me – since her kindred had all perished or disappeared. She was only five years old. I had been her milk-nurse, and I did what I could for her. Year after year we wandered from place to place, traveling in pilgrim-garb . . . But these tales of grief are ill-timed,' exclaimed the nurse, wiping away her tears; 'pardon the foolish heart of an old woman who cannot forget the past. See! the little maid whom I fostered has now become a Himégimi-Sama indeed! – were we living in the good days of the Emperor Takakura, what a destiny might be reserved for her! However, she has obtained the husband whom she desired; that is the greatest happiness . . . But the hour is late. The bridal-chamber has been prepared; and I must now leave you to care for each other until morning.'

She rose, and sliding back the screens parting the guest-room from the adjoining chamber, ushered them to their sleeping

---

* Shigéhira, after a brave fight in defense of the capital – then held by the Taïra (or Heiké) party – was surprised and routed by Yoshitsuné, leader of the Minamoto forces. A soldier named Iyénaga, who was a skilled archer, shot down Shigéhira's horse; and Shigéhira fell under the struggling animal. He cried to an attendant to bring another horse; but the man fled. Shigéhira was then captured by Iyénaga, and eventually given up to Yoritomo, head of the Minamoto clan, who caused him to be sent in a cage to Kamakura. There, after sundry humiliations, he was treated for a time with consideration – having been able, by a Chinese poem, to touch even the cruel heart of Yoritomo. But in the following year he was executed by request of the Buddhist priests of Nanto, against whom he had formerly waged war by order of Kiyomori.

apartment. Then, with many words of joy and congratulation, she withdrew; and Itō was left alone with his bride.

As they reposed together, Itō said:

'Tell me, my loved one, when was it that you first wished to have me for your husband.'

(For everything appeared so real that he had almost ceased to think of the illusion woven around him.)

She answered, in a voice like a dove's voice:

'My august lord and husband, it was at the temple of Ishiyama, where I went with my foster-mother, that I saw you for the first time. And because of seeing you, the world became changed to me from that hour and moment. But you do not remember, because our meeting was not in this, your present life: it was very, very long ago. Since that time you have passed through many deaths and births, and have had many comely bodies. But I have remained always that which you see me now: I could not obtain another body, nor enter into another state of existence, because of my great wish for you. My dear lord and husband, I have waited for you through many ages of men.'

And the bridegroom felt nowise afraid at hearing these strange words, but desired nothing more in life, or in all his lives to come, than to feel her arms about him, and to hear the caress of her voice.

But the pealing of a temple-bell proclaimed the coming of dawn. Birds began to twitter; a morning breeze set all the trees a-whispering. Suddenly the old nurse pushed apart the sliding screens of the bridal-chamber, and exclaimed:

'My children, it is time to separate! By daylight you must not be together, even for an instant: that were fatal! You must bid each other good-bye.'

Without a word, Itō made ready to depart. He vaguely understood the warning uttered, and resigned himself wholly to destiny. His will belonged to him no more; he desired only to please his shadowy bride.

She placed in his hands a little *suzuri*, or ink-stone, curiously carved, and said:

'My young lord and husband is a scholar; therefore this small gift will probably not be despised by him. It is of strange fashion because it is old, having been augustly bestowed upon my father by the favor of the Emperor Takakura. For that reason only, I thought it to be a precious thing.'

Itō, in return, besought her to accept for a remembrance the *kōgai** of his sword, which were decorated with inlaid work of silver and gold, representing plum-flowers and nightingales.

Then the little *miya-dzukai* came to guide him through the garden, and his bride with her foster-mother accompanied him to the threshold.

As he turned at the foot of the steps to make his parting salute, the old woman said:

'We shall meet again the next Year of the Boar, at the same hour of the same day of the same month that you came here. This being the Year of the Tiger, you will have to wait ten years. But, for reasons which I must not say, we shall not be able to meet again in this place; we are going to the neighborhood of Kyōto, where the good Emperor Takakura and our fathers and many of our people are dwelling. All the Heiké will be rejoiced by your coming. We shall send a *kago*† for you on the appointed day.'

Above the village the stars were burning as Itō passed the gate; but on reaching the open road he saw the dawn brightening beyond leagues of silent fields. In his bosom he carried the gift of his bride. The charm of her voice lingered in his ears – and nevertheless, had it not been for the memento which he touched with questioning fingers, he could have persuaded himself that the memories of the night were memories of sleep, and that his life still belonged to him.

But the certainty that he had doomed himself evoked no least regret: he was troubled only by the pain of separation, and the thought of the seasons that would have to pass before the illusion could be renewed for him. Ten years! – and every day of those years would seem how long! The mystery of the delay he could

---

* This was the name given to a pair of metal rods attached to a sword-sheath, and used like chop-sticks. They were sometimes exquisitely ornamented.

† A kind of palanquin.

not hope to solve; the secret ways of the dead are known to the gods alone.

Often and often, in his solitary walks, Itō revisited the village at Kotobikiyama, vaguely hoping to obtain another glimpse of the past. But never again, by night or by day, was he able to find the rustic gate in the shadowed lane; never again could he perceive the figure of the little *miya-dzukai*, walking alone in the sunset-glow.

The village people, whom he questioned carefully, thought him bewitched. No person of rank, they said, had ever dwelt in the settlement; and there had never been, in the neighborhood, any such garden as he described. But there had once been a great Buddhist temple near the place of which he spoke; and some gravestones of the temple-cemetery were still to be seen. Itō discovered the monuments in the middle of a dense thicket. They were of an ancient Chinese form, and were covered with moss and lichens. The characters that had been cut upon them could no longer be deciphered.

Of his adventure Itō spoke to no one. But friends and kindred soon perceived a great change in his appearance and manner. Day by day he seemed to become more pale and thin, though physicians declared that he had no bodily ailment; he looked like a ghost, and moved like a shadow. Thoughtful and solitary he had always been, but now he appeared indifferent to everything which had formerly given him pleasure – even to those literary studies by means of which he might have hoped to win distinction. To his mother – who thought that marriage might quicken his former ambition, and revive his interest in life – he said that he had made a vow to marry no living woman. And the months dragged by.

At last came the Year of the Boar, and the season of autumn; but Itō could no longer take the solitary walks that he loved. He could not even rise from his bed. His life was ebbing, though none could divine the cause; and he slept so deeply and so long that his sleep was often mistaken for death.

Out of such a sleep he was startled, one bright evening, by the voice of a child; and he saw at his bedside the little *miya-dzukai* who had guided him, ten years before, to the gate of the vanished garden. She saluted him, and smiled, and said: 'I am bidden to tell you that you will be received to-night at Ōhara, near Kyōto, where the new home is, and that a *kago* has been sent for you.' Then she disappeared.

Itō knew that he was being summoned away from the light of the sun; but the message so rejoiced him that he found strength to sit up and call his mother. To her he then for the first time related the story of his bridal, and he showed her the ink-stone which had been given him. He asked that it should be placed in his coffin – and then he died.

The ink-stone was buried with him. But before the funeral ceremonies it was examined by experts, who said that it had been made in the period of *Jō-an* (1169 A. D.),[5] and that it bore the seal-mark of an artist who had lived in the time of the Emperor Takakura.[6]

Appendix

NIGHTMARE-TOUCH

I

What *is* the fear of ghosts among those who believe in ghosts?

All fear is the result of experience – experience of the individual or of the race – experience either of the present life or of lives forgotten. Even the fear of the unknown can have no other origin. And the fear of ghosts must be a product of past pain.

Probably the fear of ghosts, as well as the belief in them, had its beginning in dreams. It is a peculiar fear. No other fear is so intense; yet none is so vague. Feelings thus voluminous and dim are super-individual mostly – feelings inherited – feelings made within us by the experience of the dead.

What experience?

Nowhere do I remember reading a plain statement of the reason why ghosts are feared. Ask any ten intelligent persons of your acquaintance, who remember having once been afraid of ghosts, to tell you exactly why they were afraid – to define the fancy behind the fear; and I doubt whether even one will be able to answer the question. The literature of folk-lore – oral and written – throws no clear light upon the subject. We find, indeed, various legends of men torn asunder by phantoms; but such gross imaginings could not explain the peculiar quality of ghostly fear. It is not a fear of bodily violence. It is not even a reasoning fear – not a fear that can readily explain itself – which would not be the case if it were founded upon definite ideas of physical danger. Furthermore, although primitive ghosts may have been imagined as capable of tearing and devouring, the common idea of a ghost is certainly that of a being intangible and imponderable.*

Now I venture to state boldly that the common fear of ghosts is *the fear of being touched by ghosts* – or, in other words, that the imagined Supernatural is dreaded mainly because of its imagined power to touch. Only to *touch*, remember! – not to wound or to kill.

But this dread of the touch would itself be the result of experience – chiefly, I think, of prenatal experience stored up in the individual by inheritance, like the child's fear of darkness. And who can ever have had the sensation of being touched by ghosts? The answer is simple: *Everybody who has been seized by phantoms in a dream.*

Elements of primeval fears – fears older than humanity – doubtless enter into the child-terror of darkness. But the more definite fear of ghosts may very possibly be composed with inherited results of dream-pain – ancestral experience of nightmare. And the intuitive terror of supernatural touch can thus be evolutionally explained.

Let me now try to illustrate my theory by relating some typical experiences.

II

When about five years old I was condemned to sleep by myself in a certain isolated room, thereafter always called the Child's Room. (At that time I was scarcely ever mentioned by name, but only referred to as 'the Child'.) The room was narrow, but very high, and, in spite of one tall window, very gloomy. It contained a fire-place wherein no fire was ever kindled; and the Child suspected that the chimney was haunted.

* I may remark here that in many old Japanese legends and ballads, ghosts are represented as having power to pull off people's heads. But so far as the origin of the fear of ghosts is concerned, such stories explain nothing – since the experiences that evolved the fear must have been real, not imaginary, experiences.

A law was made that no light should be left in the Child's Room at night – simply because the Child was afraid of the dark. His fear of the dark was judged to be a mental disorder requiring severe treatment. But the treatment aggravated the disorder. Previously I had been accustomed to sleep in a well-lighted room, with a nurse to take care of me. I thought that I should die of fright when sentenced to lie alone in the dark, and – what seemed to me then abominably cruel – actually *locked* into my room, the most dismal room of the house. Night after night when I had been warmly tucked into bed, the lamp was removed; the key clicked in the lock; the protecting light and the footsteps of my guardian receded together. Then an agony of fear would come upon me. Something in the black air would seem to gather and grow – (I thought that I could even *hear* it grow) – till I had to scream. Screaming regularly brought punishment; but it also brought back the light, which more than consoled for the punishment. This fact being at last found out, orders were given to pay no further heed to the screams of the Child.

Why was I thus insanely afraid? Partly because the dark had always been peopled for me with shapes of terror. So far back as memory extended, I had suffered from ugly dreams; and when aroused from them I could always see the forms dreamed of, lurking in the shadows of the room. They would soon fade out; but for several moments they would appear like tangible realities. And they were always the same figures ... Sometimes, without any preface of dreams, I used to see them at twilight-time – following me about from room to room, or reaching long dim hands after me, from story to story, up through the interspaces of the deep stairways.

I had complained of these haunters only to be told that I must never speak of them, and that they did not exist. I had complained to everybody in the house; and everybody in the house had told me the very same thing. But there was the evidence of my eyes! The denial of that evidence I could explain only in two ways: Either the shapes were afraid of big people, and showed themselves to me alone, because I was little and weak; or else the entire household had agreed, for some ghastly reason, to say what was not true. This latter theory seemed to me the more probable one, because I had several times perceived the shapes when I was not unattended; and the consequent appearance of secrecy frightened me scarcely less than the visions did. Why was I forbidden to talk about what I saw, and even heard – on creaking stairways – behind wavering curtains?

'Nothing will hurt you' – this was the merciless answer to all my pleadings not to be left alone at night. But the haunters *did* hurt me. Only – they would wait until after I had fallen asleep, and so into their power – for they possessed occult means of preventing me from rising or moving or crying out.

Needless to comment upon the policy of locking me up alone with these fears in a black room. Unutterably was I tormented in that room – for years! Therefore I felt relatively happy when sent away at last to a children's boarding-school, where the haunters very seldom ventured to show themselves.

They were not like any people that I had ever known. They were shadowy dark-robed figures, capable of atrocious self-distortion – capable, for instance, of growing up to the ceiling, and then across it, and then lengthening themselves, head-downwards, along the opposite wall. Only their faces were distinct; and I tried not to look at their faces. I tried also in my dreams – or thought that I tried – to awaken myself from the sight of them by pulling at my eyelids with my fingers; but the eyelids would remain closed, as if sealed . . . Many years afterwards, the frightful plates in Orfila's *Traité des Exhumés*,[1] beheld for the first time, recalled to me with a sickening start the dream-terrors of childhood. But to understand the Child's experience, you must imagine Orfila's drawings intensely alive, and continually elongating or distorting, as in some monstrous anamorphosis.

Nevertheless the mere sight of those nightmare-faces was not the worst of the experiences in the Child's Room. The dreams always began with a suspicion, or sensation of something heavy in the air – slowly quenching will – slowly numbing my power to move. At such times I usually found myself alone in a large unlighted apartment; and, almost simultaneously with the first sensation of fear, the atmosphere of the room would become suffused, half-way to the ceiling, with a somber yellowish glow, making objects dimly visible – though the ceiling itself remained pitch-black. This was not a true appearance of light: rather it seemed as if the black air were changing color from beneath ... Certain terrible aspects of sunset, on the eve of storm, offer like effects of sinister color ... Forthwith I would try to escape – (feeling at every step a sensation *as of wading*) – and would sometimes succeed in struggling half-way across the room; but there I would always find myself brought to a standstill – paralyzed by some innominable opposition. Happy voices I could hear in the next room; I could see light through the transom over the door that I had vainly endeavored to reach; I knew that one loud cry would save me. But not even by the most frantic effort could I raise my voice above a whisper ... And all this signified only that the Nameless was coming – was nearing – was mounting the stairs. I could hear the step – booming like the sound of a muffled drum – and I wondered why nobody else heard it. A long, long time the haunter would take to come – malevolently pausing after each ghastly footfall. Then, without a creak, the bolted door would open – slowly, slowly – and the thing would enter, gibbering soundlessly – and put out hands – and clutch me – and toss me to the black ceiling – and catch me descending to toss me up again, and again, and again ... In those moments the feeling was not fear: fear itself had been torpified by the first seizure. It was a sensation that has no name in the language of the living. For every touch brought a shock of something infinitely worse than pain – something that thrilled into the innermost secret being of me – a sort of abominable electricity, discovering unimagined capacities of suffering in totally unfamiliar regions of sentiency ... This was commonly the work of a single tormentor; but I can also remember having been caught by a group, and tossed from one to another – seemingly for a time of many minutes.

III

Whence the fancy of those shapes? I do not know. Possibly from some impression of fear in earliest infancy; possibly from some experience of fear in other lives than mine. That mystery is forever insoluble. But the mystery of the shock of the touch admits of a definite hypothesis.

First, allow me to observe that the experience of the sensation itself cannot be dismissed as 'mere imagination'. Imagination means cerebral activity: its pains and its pleasures are alike inseparable from nervous operation, and their physical importance is sufficiently proved by their physiological effects. Dream-fear may kill as well as other fear; and no emotion thus powerful can be reasonably deemed undeserving of study.

One remarkable fact in the problem to be considered is that the sensation of seizure in dreams differs totally from all sensations familiar to ordinary waking life. Why this differentiation? How to interpret the extraordinary massiveness and depth of the thrill?

I have already suggested that the dreamer's fear is most probably not a reflection of relative experience, but represents the incalculable total of ancestral experience of dream-fear. If the sum of the experience of active life be transmitted by inheritance, so must likewise be transmitted the summed experience of the life of sleep. And in normal heredity either class of transmissions would probably remain distinct.

Now, granting this hypothesis, the sensation of dream-seizure would have had its beginnings in the earliest phases of dream-consciousness – long prior to the apparition of man. The first creatures capable of thought and fear must often have dreamed of being caught by their natural enemies. There could not have been much imagining of pain in these primal dreams. But higher nervous development in later forms of being would have been accompanied with larger susceptibility to dream-pain. Still later, with the growth of reasoning-power, ideas of the supernatural would have changed and intensified the character of dream-fear. Furthermore, through all the course of evolution, heredity would have been accumulating the experience of such feeling. Under those forms of imaginative pain evolved through reaction of religious beliefs, there would persist some dim survival of savage primitive fears, and again, under this, a dimmer but incomparably deeper substratum of ancient animal-terrors. In the dreams of the modern child all these latencies might quicken – one below another – unfathomably – with the coming and the growing of nightmare.

It may be doubted whether the phantasms of any particular nightmare have a history older than the brain in which they move. But the shock of the touch would seem to indicate *some point of dream-contact with the total race-experience of shadowy seizure*. It may be that profundities of Self – abysses never reached by any ray from the life of sun – are strangely stirred in slumber, and that out of their blackness immediately responds a shuddering of memory, measureless even by millions of years.

Notes

Editorial notes have been provided here to give commentary where possible on aspects of the text not already annotated by Hearn himself. The editor wishes to record his profound thanks to the distinguished scholar Mrs Yoshiko Ushioda, former curator of the Japanese Art Collection at the Chester Beatty Library, Dublin, for her assistance with some of the more obscure elements in the notes.

OF GHOSTS AND GOBLINS

From *Glimpses of Unfamiliar Japan* (Boston: Houghton Mifflin Company, 1894), vol. 2, pp. 648–55.

1. *OF GHOSTS AND GOBLINS* : The text here is an extract from a longer version of the story in Hearn's *Glimpses of Unfamiliar Japan*, in which he recalls watching a fantastical magic-lantern show at a night festival with his gardener Kinjurō, which inspires Kinjurō to tell the tale that follows, starting from the second paragraph of section VI of the original text.
2. *kwan*: A coffin.
3. *'Then the girl . . . you are a man!''* [. . .]: The following section is headed 'VII' in the original text.
4. *daimyō*: The *daimyō* were the feudal lords of Japan, exercising great influence from the tenth to the mid nineteenth century, when the caste was abolished in 1871, following the Meiji Restoration in 1868.
5. *ihai*: A mortuary tablet.
6. *'Anata!'*: 'You!'

THE DREAM OF A SUMMER DAY

From *'Out of the East': Reveries and Studies in New Japan* (Boston: Houghton Mifflin Company, 1895), pp. 1–27.

1. *yukata*: A lightweight kimono, worn in the summer and traditionally made of indigo-dyed cotton.
2. *kuruma*: A type of vehicle or cart. In Hearn's day it was the equivalent of a rickshaw or *jinrikisha* (see note 1 for 'Mujina' below).
3. *'Manyefushifu'*: The title is translated as 'Collection of a Myriad Leaves' by Basil Hall Chamberlain in *The Classical Poetry of the Japanese* (London: Trübner & Co., 1880), p. 9. Chamberlain dates the first bringing together of the twenty volumes that make up the original collection of poetry to the eighth century (p. 10). Translations of a selection of poems from the original work form the bulk of his volume, including a translation in verse of the ballad 'The Fisher Boy Urashima' (pp. 33–5), Chamberlain noting that Urashima's tomb and various objects associated with him were still on display at a temple near Yokohama (p. 36). The story was also translated by diplomat and scholar, William George Aston.
4. *Aston*: William George Aston (1841–1911), born near Derry in what is now Northern Ireland, was a British diplomat and a scholar of the language and culture of both Japan and Korea. He served as a diplomat in both countries, retiring from the diplomatic service on the grounds of ill-health in 1889. He also translated 'The Legend of Urashima' in his *A Grammar of the Japanese Written Language* (London/Yokohama: Trübner & Company/Lane, Crawford & Company, 1877), pp. xvi–xx.
5. *Chamberlain*: See the Introduction, note 14, and note 3 above.
6. *Mikado Yuriaku*: Yūryaku (r. AD 457–79) was the twenty-first emperor of Japan.
7. *in the second year of Tenchiyō, in the reign of the Mikado Go-Junwa*: Tenchō was a Japanese era lasting from 824 to 834 and incorporating the reign of the emperor Junna (824–33). Japanese eras generally reflect the reign of emperors and years are counted by reference to an emperor's years on the throne, hence the year in question here would be 825.
8. *kurumaya*: The runner who pulled the *kuruma* (see note 2 above).
9. *sen*: A Japanese coin worth one-hundredth of a yen, the basic currency unit.

10. *The Classical Poetry of the Japanese . . . in Trübner's Oriental Series*:
     See note 3 above.

11. *Doyō, or the Period of Greatest Heat, in the twenty-sixth year of Meiji*: In
     the Japanese lunar calendar, the *doyō* is an eighteen-day time period
     prior to a change of seasons. Hearn is referring to the period around
     late July/early August when heat and humidity are at their highest
     in Japan. The twentieth-sixth year of the Meiji era (1868–1912) was
     1894.

12. *Miō-jin*: In William George Aston's *Shintō (The Way of the Gods)*
     (London: Longmans, Green, 1905), a *Miōjin-oroshi* is defined as a
     Shintōist medium (p. 356).

13. *Romaji*: Romaji or Romanji are the terms used in Latin script for
     the romanization of the Japanese written language.

IN CHOLERA-TIME

From *Kokoro: Hints and Echoes of Japanese Inner Life* (Boston: Houghton
Mifflin Company, 1896), pp. 257–65.

1.   *the late war*: A reference to the First Sino-Japanese War (1894–5).
2.   *'Chan-chan . . . hané!'*: 'Little boys can cut off a Chinese head!'
3.   *the legend of the Sai-no-Kawara*: In Japanese Buddhist mythology,
     the Sai no Kawara is a sandy beach where the souls of dead chil-
     dren do penance in the netherworld.
4.   *Manyemon*: Inagaki Manyemon, a veteran samurai, was the father
     of Inagaki Kinjūrō, who, with his wife, Tomi, adopted Hearn's
     wife, Setsu, as an infant and brought her up under the fosterage
     then still common in Japan. Setsu remained with the Inagaki
     household until she began living with Hearn (see Yoji Hasegawa
     (ed.), *A Walk in Kumamoto: The Life and Times of Setsu Koizumi,
     Lafcadio Hearn's Japanese Wife* (Folkestone: Global Oriental, 1997),
     pp. 50–51).
5.   *the twenty-eighth year of Meiji*: The twenty-eighth year of the Meiji
     era was 1896.
6.   *Bosatsu*: The Sanskrit *bodhisattva*, somebody who helps others to
     achieve enlightenment, is rendered *bosatsu* in Japanese.
7.   *amé syrup*: *Amé* is a contraction of *mizuamé*, a Japanese sweetener
     with a taste similar to honey and used in the making of sweets.

NINGYŌ-NO-HAKA

From *Gleanings in Buddha-Fields: Studies of Hand and Soul in the Far East* (Boston: Houghton Mifflin Company, 1897), pp. 124–31.

1. *kakémono*: A Japanese scroll painting or piece of calligraphy.
2. *'Aa fushigi . . . komatta ne?'*: A way of showing sympathy in response to being told about a distressing situation when one can't think of what else to say.

THE ETERNAL HAUNTER

From *Exotics and Retrospectives* (Boston: Little, Brown and Company, 1898), pp. 293–99.

1. *'Chikanobu'*: Toyohara ('Yōshū') Chikanobu (1838–1912) was one of the outstanding Japanese woodblock artists of the Meiji era.
2. *Psyche*: A reference to the classical Greek tale of the love between Psyche and Cupid, culminating, after various obstacles have been overcome, in their marriage. Psyche is also the Greek term for 'soul' or 'spirit'.
3. *the World-Tree, Yggdrasil*: Yggdrasil is the tree of life in Norse mythology, containing and connecting all the nine worlds of this belief system.
4. *Echo*: Echo in Greek mythology was a mountain nymph who incurred the jealousy of Zeus's wife, Hera, who restricted her speech to the last words spoken to her. Unable to tell Narcissus of her feelings for him, Echo had to watch him fall in love with his own reflection and waste away.

FRAGMENT

From *In Ghostly Japan* (Boston: Little, Brown and Company, 1899), pp. 3–7.

A PASSIONAL KARMA

From *In Ghostly Japan*, pp. 73–113.

1. *Kikugorō*: Onoe Kikugorō V (1844–1903) was a celebrated Kabuki actor of the Meiji era.
2. *the Botan-Dōrō, or 'Peony-Lantern'*: *Botan Dōrō*, translated as 'The Peony-Lantern', was a Japanese ghost story derived from a Chinese original. Hearn's story is based on a version performed in the Kabuki theatre in Tokyo by Kikugorō and his company in 1892.
3. *Enchō*: *Botan Dōrō* was adapted in 1884 by Enchō Sanyūtei (1839–1900) into a *raguko* (literally, 'fallen words'), an entertainment performed by a lone storyteller.
4. *O-Tsuyu*: 'O' is an honorific prefix that can be applied to Japanese nouns, adjectives and verbs.
5. *Sama*: A respectful honorific suffix attached to the end of a name.
6. *Kwannon*: The Japanese goddess of mercy.
7. *the Satsuma war*: The Anglo-Satsuma War of 1863 was an incident in which the Royal Navy bombarded the Japanese city of Kagoshima in retaliation for its ships being fired on by Japanese coastal batteries.
8. *Kern's translation of the Saddharma-Pundarika, ch. xxvi*: A reference to H. Kern (trans.), *The Saddharma-Pundarîka, or The Lotus of the True Law* (Oxford: Clarendon Press, 1884).
9. *ryō*: The currency unit used in Japan prior to the Meiji era.
10. *Fudō*: Fudō Myō-ō is a deity of esoteric Japanese Buddhism.
11. *Jizō*: The representation of the figure of the Buddha as a protector of children and travellers. There are many small statues to him throughout Japan.

INGWA-BANASHI

From *In Ghostly Japan*, pp. 205–12.

1. *Ingwa-Banashi*: 'Tales of Fate'.
2. *tenth . . . twelfth Bunsei*: A period of Japanese history, Bunsei (1818–30) is usually twinned with the earlier Bunka era to form the Bunka-Bunsei or Kasei period (1804–30).
3. *Kōkwa*: An era in Japanese history (1844–8).

STORY OF A TENGU

From *In Ghostly Japan*, pp. 215–21.

1. *Emperor Go-Reizei*: Go-Reizei (r. 1045–68) was the seventieth emperor of Japan.

2. *Tengu*: The *tengu* ('heavenly dog') is a demonic supernatural being in Japanese folklore that can also be a Shintō god (*kami*). It is often depicted as a cross between a bird of prey and a human.

3. *the holy mountain Gridhrakûta*: Also known as 'Vulture Peak Mountain', this was a site frequented by the Buddha where he preached a number of key sermons.

4. *Vulture Peak*: See previous note.

5. *Mandârava and Manjûshaka flowers*: These were among the Four Flowers of Heaven that, according to the Buddhist scriptures, rained down on the Buddha as he preached to a multitude of bodhisattvas – a sign of celestial approval. In Japan the mandarava flower is usually equated with the datura, but it is actually the Indian coral tree (*Erythrina variegata*), which produces clusters of bright red flowers.

THE RECONCILIATION

From *Shadowings* (Boston: Little, Brown and Company, 1900), pp. 5–11.

1. *for the time of seven existences*: For seven successive lifetimes; based on the Buddhist belief in repeated cycles of birth and death. See also Hearn's footnote on p. 45.

A LEGEND OF FUGEN-BOSATSU

From *Shadowings*, pp. 15–19.

THE CORPSE-RIDER

From *Shadowings*, pp. 33–8.

THE SYMPATHY OF BENTEN

From *Shadowings*, pp. 41–54.

1. *Emperor Seiwa*: Seiwa (r. 858–76) was the fifty-sixth emperor of Japan.

2.   *Genroku*: An era of Japanese history (1688–1704), regarded as the golden age of the Edo period (1603–1868).

3.   *Goddess Benten*: Benten is a contraction of 'Benzaiten', a Buddhist goddess of wisdom in Japan, derived from the Hindu goddess Saraswati. She is often depicted holding a *biwa*, the traditional Japanese lute that features in 'The Story of Mimi-Nashi-Hōïchi' in this volume.

4.   *Shirushi aréto . . . Chigiri narétomo*: 'When first love is over, it's like a broom, so well used that only the handle remains and is of no use.'

5.   *Sama*: A respectful honorific suffix attached to the end of a name.

THE GRATITUDE OF THE SAMÉBITO

From *Shadowings*, pp. 57–66.

OF A PROMISE KEPT

From *A Japanese Miscellany* (Boston: Little, Brown and Company, 1901), pp. 5–11.

1.   *the festival Chōyō*: *Chōyō no Sekku*, the 'Chrysanthemum Festival', is held on the ninth day of the ninth month, i.e. 9 September.

2.   *Ugétsu Monogatari*: A reference to *Ugetsu Monogatari* ('Tales of Moonlight and Rain'), a collection of nine supernatural tales by Ueda Akinari (1734–1809), first published in 1776. Hearn's story follows the outlines of one of the tales, 'Kikka no Chigiri' ('The Chrysanthemum Pledge'), based on a Chinese original featuring a man who, unable to keep a promise to visit a friend's house because he is imprisoned, commits suicide so that his ghost can fulfil his commitment.

3.   *harakiri*: More commonly known as *seppuku*, *harakiri* is a form of Japanese ritual suicide by means of disembowelment.

OF A PROMISE BROKEN

From *A Japanese Miscellany*, pp. 15–26.

1.   *kaimyō*: The name Japanese Buddhist monks and nuns are given when entering the religious life.

BEFORE THE SUPREME COURT

From *A Japanese Miscellany*, pp. 29–34.

1. *The great Buddhist priest ... says in his book Kyō-gyō Shin-shō*: The actual title of the text is *Ken Jōdo Shinjitsu Kyōgyōshō Monrui* ('A Collection of Passages Revealing the True Teaching, Practice and Realization of the Pure Land [Path]'), usually abbreviated to *Kyōgyōshinshō*, and it is the principal work of Shinran Shōnin (1173–1263), a Pure Land Buddhist. Written between 1217 and 1224, it sets out the fundamental principles of the True Sect of Pure Land Buddhism.

2. *Nihon-Rei-Iki*: Abbreviated from *Nihonkoku Genpō Zen'aku Ryōiki*, which translates as 'Ghostly Strange Records from Japan', it was written between between AD 787 and 824.

3. *Bukkyō-Hyakkwa-Zenshō*: A multi-volume encyclopedia of Buddhism included in the list of 'old Japanese books' from which Hearn in the introduction to his *Kwaidan* (Boston: Houghton Mifflin Company, 1904) states he had drawn many of his 'Weird Tales'.

THE STORY OF KWASHIN KOJI

From *A Japanese Miscellany*, pp. 37–51.

1. *kakémono*: A Japanese scroll painting.

2. *Yasō-Kidan*: Translated literally as 'Night-Window Demon Talk', *Yasō-Kidan* is a collection of horror stories edited by Ishikawa Kōsai (1833–1918), a Japanese writer and scholar of classical Chinese literature.

3. *Oda Nobunaga*: Oda Nobunaga (1534–82) was a leading statesman dedicated to unifying Japan.

4. *Kwannon*: The Japanese goddess of mercy.

5. *ryō*: The currency unit used in Japan prior to the Meiji era (1868–1912).

6. *Lord Nobunaga came to his death ... Akéchi Mitsuhidé*: Akechi Mitsuhide (1528–82) was a military commander under Oda Nobunaga whose rebellion against his master in 1582 led to Nobunaga's death.

THE STORY OF UMÉTSU CHŪBEI

From *A Japanese Miscellany*, pp. 55–61.

1. *Lord Tomura Jūdayū*: Tomura Jūdayū, also known as Tomura Yoshi-ari, was an elder (*karō*) of the Satake clan which participated in the civil war that followed the restoration of imperial rule in 1868, ending up on the emperor's side.
2. *tasuki-cords*: A *tasuki* is a sash used to hold up the sleeves of a kimono.

THE LEGEND OF, YUREI-DAKI

From *Kottō: Being Japanese Curios, With Sundry Cobwebs* (New York: Macmillan Company, 1902), pp. 3–7.

IN A CUP OF TEA

From *Kottō*, pp. 11–17.

1. *the third Tenwa*: The third year of the Tenwa or Tenna era (1681–4), or 1684.

IKIRYŌ

From *Kottō*, pp. 29–35.

1. *Ikiryō*: In Japanese folklore, the spirit of a living person who could haunt others.

THE STORY OF O-KAMÉ

From *Kottō*, pp. 47–54.

1. *'Aa! uréshiya!' cried O-Kamé*: O-Kamé's words may be translated as 'How wonderful!' or, more literally, 'How happy!', which is fitting as *O-Kame* is a happy female face, traditionally depicted as a mask or figurine.

THE STORY OF CHŪGORŌ

From *Kottō*, pp. 73–82.

1. *hatamoto*: A *hatamoto* (the literal meaning of which is 'at the base
    of the flag') was an upper-rank samurai employed directly by the
    shōguns of feudal Japan.
2. *yashiki*: The residence or estate of a noble.
3. *the story of Urashima*: See 'The Dream of a Summer Day' in this
    volume.

THE STORY OF MIMI-NASHI-HŌÏCHI

From *Kwaidan: Stories and Studies of Strange Things* (Boston: Houghton
Mifflin Company, 1904), pp. 3–20.

1. *at Dan-no-ura, in the Straits of Shimonoséki, was fought the last
    battle . . . Minamoto clan*: The battle of Dan-no-ura was an important
    naval engagement that took place off the southern tip of Honshū,
    Japan's main island, on 25 April 1185, in which the Minamoto
    (Genji) clan defeated the Taira (Heike) clan.
2. *Antoku Tennō*: The boy-emperor Antoku (r. 1180–85), the eighty-
    first emperor (*tennō*) of Japan, was among those who died in the
    battle.
3. *Heiké-Monogatari*: *Heike Monogatari* ('The Story of the Heike'),
    compiled before 1330, recounts the fight between the Heike
    (Taira) and Minamoto clans for control of Japan.
4. *'Hai!'*: 'Yes!'
5. *the death-leap of Nii-no-Ama, with the imperial infant in her arms*: An
    incident at the battle of Dan-no-ura in which Nii-no-Ama, possibly
    his grandmother, jumped into the sea with the young emperor,
    Antoku, in her arms, causing them both to drown rather than be
    captured by the enemy.
6. *Professor Max Müller . . . Sacred Books of the East*: A series of English
    translations of the major religious texts of Asia in fifty volumes,
    edited by Max Müller (1823–1900), published between 1879 and
    1910.

JIKININKI

From *Kwaidan*, pp. 65–73.

MUJINA

From *Kwaidan*, pp. 77–80.

1. *jinrikishas*: Translated literally from Japanese as 'man-powered vehicle', a *jinrikisha* is essentially a two-wheeled cart pulled by a man that usually functions as a small taxi.

ROKURO-KUBI

From *Kwaidan*, pp. 83–99.

1. *Lord Kikuji, of Kyūshū*: It is assumed that Hearn is referring here to the Kikuchi *daimyō* family of Kyūshū, famed for its devotion to the emperor of Japan, which played a prominent role in repulsing the Mongol invasions of Japan in the thirteenth century.
2. *bell-insects*: The bell insect or *suzumushi* (*Homoeogryllus japonicus*) is a Japanese tree cricket whose distinctive song is much appreciated in Japan.
3. *Rokuro-Kubi*: A Japanese ghoul that takes human form and can either stretch its neck or detach its head, which can then move about independently.

YUKI-ONNA

From *Kwaidan*, pp. 111–18.

THE STORY OF AOYAGI

From *Kwaidan*, pp. 121–36.

THE DREAM OF AKINOSUKÉ

From *Kwaidan*, pp. 145–55.

RIKI-BAKA

From *Kwaidan*, pp. 159–62.

1.   *kana*: *Kana* are Japanese scripts which, together with *Kanji*, Chinese characters, make up the Japanese writing system.

THE MIRROR MAIDEN

From *The Romance of the Milky Way* (Boston: Houghton Mifflin Company, 1905), pp. 127–37.

1.   *Shōgunate*: The system of government under which Japan was ruled by shōguns, effectively military dictators, with the emperor reduced to a largely symbolic role, from 1185 to 1868.
2.   *Suijin*: The Shintō god of water.

THE STORY OF ITŌ NORISUKÉ

From *The Romance of the Milky Way*, pp. 141–65.

1.   *koto*: A Japanese stringed instrument.
2.   *Amano-kawara-no-Ori-Himé . . . River of Heaven*: One of Japan's most famous weaving myths concerns Orihime – the daughter of a divine emperor, Tentei, ruler of the heavens – who was sad because she had been too busy to fall in love. Her father arranged for her to marry Kengyuu but then separated them as Orihime was neglecting her weaving, with each now living on different sides of the river of the Milky Way. They were allowed to meet only on one night of the year, that of the seventh day of the seventh month.
3.   *the great Heiké general:* Hearn is referring here to the epic twelfth-century struggle between the Heike or Taira clan and the

Minamoto clan which was the subject of 'The Story of Mimi-Nashi-Hōïchi' (see p. 139).

4. *the years of Jü-ei*: The Juei era in Japan spanned the years from 1182 to 1184. The reigning emperors were the Taira ruler Antoku (r. 1180–85) and the Minamoto ruler Go-Toba (r. 1183–98), proclaimed emperor while Antoku was still alive.

5. *the period of Jō-an (1169 A. D.)*: The Jōan era spanned the years from 1171 to 1175, so Hearn's date of AD 1169 is slightly inaccurate.

6. *Emperor Takakura*: Takakura (r. 1168–80) was the eightieth emperor of Japan.

APPENDIX: NIGHTMARE-TOUCH

From *Shadowings*, pp. 235–46.

1. *Orfila's Traité des Exhumés*: Mathieu Joseph Bonaventure Orfila (1787–1853) was an important figure in the development of forensic medicine. His studies included the decomposition of bodies, on which topic he published *Traité des exhumations juridiques: et considérations sur les changemens physiques que les cadavres éprouvent en se pourrissant dans la terre, dans l'eau, dans les fosses d'aisance et dans le fumier* ('Treatise on legal exhumations and an investigation into the physical changes undergone by cadavers decomposing in soil, water, cesspits and manure') in Paris in 1831.